THE DITCH

This Large Print Book carries the
Seal of Approval of N.A.V.H.

THE DITCH

HERMAN KOCH

*Translated from the Dutch
by Sam Garrett*

THORNDIKE PRESS
A part of Gale, a Cengage Company

A Cengage Company

Farmington Hills, Mich • San Francisco • New York • Waterville, Maine
Meriden, Conn • Mason, Ohio • Chicago

Originally published in Dutch in the Netherlands as *De Greppel* by Ambo Anthos, Amsterdam, in 2016.

Copyright © 2016 by Herman Koch.

Translation copyright © 2019 by Sam Garrett.

Thorndike Press, a part of Gale, a Cengage Company.

Thorndike Press® Large Print Core.

The text of this Large Print edition is unabridged.

Other aspects of the book may vary from the original edition.

Set in 16 pt. Plantin.

LIBRARY OF CONGRESS CIP DATA ON FILE.
CATALOGUING IN PUBLICATION FOR THIS BOOK
IS AVAILABLE FROM THE LIBRARY OF CONGRESS

ISBN-13: 978-1-4328-6497-2 (hardcover alk. paper)

Published in 2019 by arrangement with Hogarth, an imprint of Random House, a division of Penguin Random House LLC

Printed in Mexico
1 2 3 4 5 6 7 23 22 21 20 19

THE DITCH

■ ■ ■ ■

Part I

■ ■ ■ ■

1

Let me call her Sylvia. That's not her real name — her real name would only confuse things. People make all kinds of assumptions when it comes to names, especially when a name isn't from around here, when they don't have a clue about how to pronounce it, let alone spell it. So let's just say that it's not a Dutch name. My wife is not from Holland. Where she *is* from is something I'd rather leave up in the air for the time being. Those in our immediate surroundings, of course, know where she's from. And people who read the newspaper and watch the news with any regularity can't really have missed it either. But most people have bad memories. They may have heard it once, then forgotten.

Robert Walter? His wife's foreign, right?

Yes, that's right, she's from . . . from . . . Come on, help me out here . . . People associate all kinds of things with countries of origin. To each country its own prejudices. It starts as soon as you get to Belgium. Do I need to repeat here the kinds of prejudices we Dutch people have when it comes to Belgians? When it comes to the Germans, the French, the Italians? Go a bit farther east and a bit farther south and the people gradually change color. At first it's only their hair: it gets darker, and finally it turns black altogether. After that, the same process repeats itself, but now with their skin. To the east it turns yellower, to the south it gets blacker and blacker.

And it gets hotter. South of Paris, the temperature starts to rise. When the weather's hot, it becomes a lot harder to work. One feels more like sitting in the shade of yonder palm. Even farther south, one stops working altogether. Mostly, one just takes a breather.

When our daughter was born, the name "Sylvia" was the second on our list of names. The second on a list of three, the name we would have given her if we hadn't named her Diana. Or to put it differently: if we'd had three daughters instead of only one, they would have been named Diana, Sylvia, and Julia. We also had three names ready for any boys who came along, but I won't list them here. We don't have boys.

We also don't have daughters. We have only Diana.

It's probably clear to you by now that Diana isn't our daughter's real name either. First of all, for reasons of privacy — she has to be able to live a life of her own, which is hard enough already when a girl has a father like me. But it's no coincidence that all three of those names have three syllables and that they all end in an *a*. When it came time to choose our daughter's name (her real name), I made a concession. I felt that my wife had a tough enough time of it as it was, in a country not her own. That I shouldn't go burdening her on top of all that with a daughter with a Dutch name. It would be a name from her country. A girl's name she could say out loud each day, a familiar name, a warm sound in the midst of all that harsh gargling and bleak hawking we call the Dutch language.

The same goes for my wife's name. In addition to her person, I also fell in love right away with her name. I say it as often as I can — long ago, too, in the middle of the night, all on my lonesome, in the boarding house where I had to spend the night because there was no room for me at her parents'. It's something in the sound of it: somewhere between melting chocolate and

11

a wood fire, in terms of the taste and the aroma. When I don't call her by her first name, I call her "sweetheart" — not in Dutch, no, in Dutch I'd have a hard time getting the word out of my mouth, only ironically at best, as in: *But sweetheart, you should have thought about that beforehand.*

"Sweetheart" in my wife's language, though, sounds precisely the way "sweetheart" should sound. Like the name of a dessert, or more like a hot, sticky beverage that leaves a warm, tingling trail behind as it goes down your throat, but also like the warmth of a blanket someone lays over your shoulders: *Come to me now, sweetheart.*

My wife — Sylvia! Her new name is starting to grow on me — is from a country that shall remain unnamed for the time being. A country about which a lot of preconceived notions exist. Notions both favorable and unfavorable. From "passionate" and "temperamental," it's only a small step to "hot-tempered." A *crime passionel* (the term says it already) is a crime we tend to situate more readily in the south and east than in northern climes. In some countries, they just happen to lose their tempers more quickly than we do; at first it's only voices shouting in the night, but then suddenly there is the glint of moonlight on a drawn blade. The standard of living is lower there, the discrepancies between rich and poor are immense, stealing is viewed with more sympathy than in our country, but the culprits are viewed with less — they consider themselves lucky if the police get to them before the injured party arrives to settle accounts.

I myself am absolutely not free of preconceived notions.

In light of my official capacity, though, I'm supposed to be — and I just happen to make a good show of it. In the last few years I've had a cup of tea (or a beer, or something stronger) with every minority group our city has on offer. I've swung along with music not my own, raised a slice of some vague meat dish to my lips — but that doesn't make me free of prejudices. I've always cherished my preconceived notions as something bound up inextricably with my own person. Or, to put it more precisely: without those prejudices, I would have been a different person. That, in the first instance, is how I look at the foreigner: with the naturally suspicious eye of the farmer who sees a stranger entering his yard. Is the stranger coming in peace, or shall I turn the dogs on him?

But now something has happened that has thrown everything for a loop, something with my wife. Something that perhaps has more to do with her country of origin, her place of birth, than I care to admit — with her cultural background, I venture cautiously, in order to say nothing of that dubious concept of "national character." At least, not for the time being.

I ask myself to what extent I can hold her responsible, and to what extent it might be the fault of her native country.

I wonder whether I'm capable of telling the two apart — whether I ever will be capable of that. Whether I would have reacted differently if Sylvia had been just another Dutchwoman. Sometimes a prejudice can serve as a mitigating circumstance, sometimes as a damning one. *That's just the way those people are, it's in their blood.* What it is precisely that is in their blood, well, everyone can fill that in for themselves: the thievery, the knife fighting, the lying, the wife-beating, the bashing of other population groups that don't belong in their backward village, the cruel games with animals, the religious customs involving the shedding of blood, the intentional mutilation of one's own body, the overabundance of gold teeth, the arranged marriages of sons and daughters; but on the other hand also the food that tastes so much better than it

14

does here, the parties that go on all night, the sense of "we only live once, tomorrow we may die," the music that seems much more stirring, more melancholy, closer to the heart, the men who let their eye fall on a woman and can never be discouraged, the women who want one specific man, only that one, you can see it in their gaze, in the fire in their eyes — but when they catch their husband with another woman they jam a knife between his ribs or cut off his balls while he's asleep.

And that's as it should be too, I think to myself, I who try to remain free of prejudices but am not — and never have been either. And what if those prejudices suddenly turn against you? How do you react then? As the Dutchman who wants to be seen as tolerant of other peoples and cultures? Or as something a little more in line with the country of origin, with the national character, of the other?

Until now, the two have always been good bedfellows. Night after night I've shared my bed with those preconceived notions. But what if you wake up early one morning to find the sheets beside you cold and unused? It is still dark, through the curtains a crack of light from a streetlamp shines on the turned-back feather bed. What time is it, for

God's sake? She should have been home ages ago.

You prick up your ears, you hear bare feet padding down the hallway, but it's your daughter, who's now knocking on the bedroom door.

"Where's Mama?" she asks.

"I don't know," you answer truthfully.

2

It happened at the New Year's reception, on Thursday, January 16. Why does it have to be so late in the month? I asked the first time after my appointment, and at least once more after that. Why so far along into the new year, just when we're breathing a sigh of relief because the New Year's receptions are — at least for another year — over at last? I've forgotten what the exact answer was. Something about tradition. "That's the way we've always done it," I recall the city manager replying vaguely (the former city manager, that is; one of our first tasks in the new year was to find a suitable replacement for him). He shrugged as he said it, but in his eyes I saw something else. *Because! That's why!* is what his look said, as though speaking to a child who wants to know why it can't go outside and play for five minutes before dinner.

Everyone was there. Of the "triad" —

which is what they call the three-man team of police commissioner, district attorney, and myself — I caught sight only of the DA. He was standing beside the table full of hors d'oeuvres, sliding a handful of salt peanuts or cocktail snacks into his mouth. On the table were wooden serving trays with cheese cubes, and platters with pieces of raw herring that had little cocktail sticks with red, white, and blue Dutch flags stuck into them.

As far as I could tell at a glance, all the aldermen were already there, and most of the council members too. For the rest, a few representatives of trade and industry, people from the art world, the club president of Ajax. Without a doubt, at some point he was going to start in about the national championship celebration. About last year's celebration, to be more precise. Which, for the third year in a row, had been held in an open lot beside the Amsterdam ArenA, jammed in between the Heineken Music Hall and the office tower of Deutsche Bank. ArenA Boulevard sucks in air like a wind tunnel; the tower and the stadium do the rest. On calm days it's the ideal playground for wind funnels and mini-tornadoes. Sand, newspapers, empty French-fry and hamburger containers are drawn into the air. There they hang, orbiting around, until the wind gets bored and smacks them down a few hundred meters farther — often enough, right on the heads of the shoppers headed for Mediamarkt, Decathlon, and Perry Sport.

Catcalls had been my due. And rightly so. I realized that it had been a hopeless error of judgment on my part, that I had given in too quickly to the arguments advanced by the other two members of the triad. The city. Downtown. The safety risks. Of course, a team that has just won the national championship should have its victory celebration downtown. At Leidseplein, on the balcony of the municipal theater, players and trainer holding aloft the champion's cup for the cheering supporters to admire. But in preceding years those celebrations had all ended in disturbances. Smashed bus shelters, concrete planters thrown through shopwindows. Looting. Groups of drunken and high hooligans climbing the light towers. And then, as the crowning touch — like in a Western, when the cavalry arrives at the fort beleaguered by Indians — the charges carried out by the mounted police. "Potentially fatal" situations had arisen, that was how the next day's papers quoted the police commissioner. Things could have spun even further out of control. Serious injuries.

Perhaps even a fatality.

Hence the vacant lot with whirlwinds. Not much to vandalize there. ArenA Boulevard, with its tempting array of plate-glass windows, could easily be blocked off by a few platoons of riot police. That was a lot harder in downtown Amsterdam, with its tangle of narrow streets and alleyways. But despite the red flares and the smoke, the celebration really did look horribly dismal, with the beats of Bob Marley's "Three Little Birds" drifting away feebly amid the office towers. That's how it seemed to me, especially when I played back the news footage that evening, footage that would travel all around the world: Ajax may no longer have been the superpower it was in the 1970s and mid-1990s, but it was still very much a legendary club, one whose name was spoken with respect. The whole world would see that Holland's best soccer club was celebrating its championship on a dismal concrete lot.

My wife always goes with me to the New Year's reception. Even though she detests them — in fact, she detests all occasions that smack of officialdom. Sylvia has never wanted to be "the wife of," the woman in the shadows; she prefers to live her own life, and we try to keep her public appearances to a minimum. But the New Year's reception is an exception. She knows how bored I get at things like that. It's inevitable. The glass in the hand. The dish of salted nuts. The babbling on about nothing — and I know that other people can see it miles away too, my desire to get out of there as quickly as possible shines right through me. "Just tell me if you want me to go along," she always says. "If you really want me to be there, then I will. For you."

That's how we've divided up our roles. That's our agreement. As soon as I put on my most pitiful expression and look at her with the hammy, imploring look that I save for special occasions, Sylvia knows how things stand. I never have to say anything more. "Okay, don't start crying," she says. "I'll go along. What should I wear?"

Foreign heads of state I can deal with on my own, the opening of a new subway station, the farewell party for a museum director, a symphony conductor's seventieth birthday. The heads of state tend to walk around looking a little forlorn; by the time they get here they've already spent half the day in The Hague, in the company of our prime minister. But after that half a day, the visiting head of state and our prime minister clearly have nothing more to say to each other. The boredom hangs in the air like an odorless but deadly gas. I feel sorry for them, for the heads of state. I too have spent the occasional half-day with the prime minister. No, not half a day, a couple of hours at most; during a dinner, a boat tour of the canals, a film premiere. You toss a coin in his slot and something always rolls out — but rarely anything useful. You've got people like that: you talk to them and they answer you right away, a little too readily perhaps, they don't take time to think about it. Maybe they're afraid of silence, I don't know, even half a second of silence seems to feel like an eternity to them. In any case, I'm not the only one; after a few hours in the company of our prime minister, the foreign heads of state go looking for someone else too — for a breath of fresh air.

Now it's time for me to tell you something about myself. Something which, lacking proper explanation, might sound like pure vanity, but which definitely isn't that. I'll try to stick to the facts. Fact is, for example, that you won't feel bored any too quickly when I'm around. I see the way the heads of state cast about. They may be standing beside the prime minister and the minister of foreign affairs, but they're dying to get out of there, they've stopped listening already, mostly they wear this glassy-eyed stare. Maybe what they really feel like doing is taking a little nap, but — that being out of the question — they'll settle for a double vodka or a cigarette out on the balcony. All I have to do is wait until that restless, glassy-eyed look settles on me, you can set your watch by it. I radiate it, I don't have to put any effort into it at all, it's written all over my face: that I've had enough of this too, that I'm just as fed up as they are. They step away from the circle of blowhards and come over to me.

"Mr. Mayor . . . ," they start in, they've forgotten my name of course, but I don't hold that against them. "Robert, call me Robert," I say and nod toward the balcony doors at the far end of the room. "Want to pop out for a smoke?" I quit smoking twenty years ago, but I always have a pack and a lighter on me, for emergencies.

On our way to the balcony, I catch the eye of one of the waiters walking around with trays of red or white wine, water and fresh-squeezed orange juice.

"Maybe you'd like something else?" I say to the head of state. "Vodka, whiskey? Maybe a little brandy? I'll have a double vodka," I tell the waiter, just to help the head of state along a little. "From the freezer, if you've got it. Otherwise on the rocks. We'll be out there, on the balcony."

No, when it comes to visits from presidents, premiers, lord mayors, and royal families from abroad, I can get along without my wife's company. Sometimes I give in, though, when she makes it clear that she would actually love to go along. When Barack Obama came to town, for example. "If Obama comes, you have to promise me to take me along," she said. "And why should I?" I asked, purely for form's sake, because I knew the answer already. "He just happens to be a good-looking man, darling," she said. "Women all think he's good-looking." "Like George Clooney?" I asked. "Like George Clooney," my wife said, "although I can't really feature Barack Obama doing a Nespresso commercial."

In any case, when members of the royal family come to Amsterdam, I always want to have Sylvia at my side. I don't know what it is, but I literally dummy up whenever I'm around that white-wine-slurping, beer-guzzling, and chain-smoking family. I start breathing audibly. I start developing itches in places it would be incommodious to scratch. Like having a mosquito bite under a plaster cast. I start sweating, the rings of perspiration form on my shirt, and that realization makes me sweat only harder. I go to the toilet, unbutton my shirt, and, using a few papers towels, do my best to wipe down my chest, armpits, and stomach. I try to stay away as long as possible, I lock myself up in a cubicle and read the news on my iPhone without a single item actually getting through to me. *God,* I whisper to myself, *let this day pass from me,* or words to that effect.

It's the same thing that happens with movies sometimes; after ten minutes you know it's not going anywhere, you need to get out of there, but you stay in your seat anyway. Maybe it will get better later on, you tell yourself, while every fiber of your being has already tensed for the impending escape. With Sylvia at my side, though, it's bearable. She's an easy talker. All her countrymen are easy talkers; it comes as naturally to them as breathing. She asks the princess, who is the queen these days, where she bought her shoes. With the prince, currently our king, she has a good long talk about pheasant hunting. It helps that people in her native culture view hunting differently than we do here. More liberally. In my wife's country, the fact that the meat on our plates comes from living animals is in sharper focus than it is with us. Probably, I sometimes allow myself to think, because it was less long ago that people there had to hunt in order to eat.

So here's what happened at the New Year's reception: I did indeed find myself locked in conversation with the president of Ajax. My wife announced that she was going for a quick look at the hors d'oeuvres. "Can I bring you two something?" she asked before she left, but we both shook our heads.

Less than a minute later — I had just assured the president that any celebration this year would take place downtown, no matter what, regardless of any objections from the other two members of the triad — I looked around and saw her, not close to the table of hors d'oeuvres, but more to the back of the room, close to the door that led to the central corridor of city hall and the toilet blocks. The person she was talking to had his back half-turned to me; a man, I saw, but I couldn't tell right away who it was. But when Sylvia raised her bottle of beer and clinked it against his, and when the man then turned and glanced around the room, I saw that it was Alderman Maarten van Hoogstraten.

"We, as a club, would of course be delighted if it could all take place downtown

26

again," I heard the soccer club president saying close to my ear. "And we'll do all we can to make sure everything proceeds in an orderly fashion. Rioting, of course, is not good advertising for the Ajax brand."

"The city is what I'm aiming for too," I said. "Of course we'll have to wait and see, but this would make it the fifth championship in a row. Special attention will be paid to that. Here, but also abroad. So we don't want to see footage of a dismal concrete lot, we want to see canals, the Rijksmuseum, the concert hall, the City Theater."

I counted to three, then took another look at the spot close to the door at the back of the room. At that very moment my wife tossed back her head and laughed; the alderman had his hand on her elbow and was whispering something in her ear.

"Well, now that you mention it," the president said, "we've been talking, because it would indeed be the fifth time, about doing something special. A boat procession through the canals, for instance." Now Sylvia looked around, her gaze sweeping the crowd. Was she looking for me? Or was she only making sure that no one was watching her and the alderman? For a full half-second I was sure that our gazes crossed, but the

27

next moment Sylvia was already looking away.

"I won't say that I'd already thought of that," I said. "But a boat parade is exactly what I had in mind. Thousands of people along the quays. The television viewer in France, Italy, China, and America gets a glorious view of Amsterdam. We want helicopters to fly over and film the city too. But if you'll excuse me, we can talk more about this later on, right now I really have to —" I pointed to an imaginary someone who wanted to talk to me, somewhere in the vicinity of the hors d'oeuvres, someone who had supposedly caught my eye.

"Of course. Go right ahead. You have other things to see to. I'm already very pleased to hear this. Can I discuss it with the board, or would that be premature?"

"Hold off on that a bit. I want to run it past the triad first, for form's sake. But I'll let you know as soon as I can."

I took a few steps to one side, toward the snack table, then I cut left. Keeping my head down, so that no one would detain me, I edged my way through the crowd.

"Maarten," I said.

"Robert . . ."

I had approached my wife and the alderman from an angle; with my last step

28

forward, I placed myself in their field of vision.

"Getting bored?" my wife asked.

I took a good look at her face. I searched for signs of anything you might consider out of the ordinary: a slight blush, a batting of the lashes, or even only an undisguisable irritation at the fact that I had come to interrupt their cozy little tête-à-tête.

"Yes, I'm bored," I said. "I feel like going home pretty soon."

"But we just got here!"

Maarten van Hoogstraten looked at me. I was expecting him to look at Sylvia too — but he didn't.

"I was just leaving . . . ," the alderman said. "I still have to . . . I was actually out to get a drink for Lodewijk. I should have gone back to him a long time ago."

He raised his hand to my wife's elbow, touched her briefly.

"Sylvia," he said.

Then he clinked his beer bottle against mine. "Robert."

And then he was gone. "We're going," I said.

"But you can't just do that, can you?"

"Oh, yes, I can. If you go to the restroom first, then I'll come five minutes later. Behind the toilet blocks is the service

29

staircase; we go down two flights, and we're outside."

"Is something wrong, Robert? Aren't you feeling well?"

"I feel fine. But I'm fed up. It just isn't my day. And we've done it before, Sylvia. Remember Bernhard and Christine's wedding?"

"Yes. And the coronation."

During the reception, after the wedding of my best friend and his third wife, we had first gone to hide in one of the side rooms. Then, five minutes apart, we had snuck out to the street on the canal side. And during Willem-Alexander's coronation we had found a side door. We ran the first part of the way, then ducked down an alleyway into a café.

The trick was to not say goodbye to anyone. To disappear at one go. The other people in the room simply assumed you were still there. Maybe you were back in the kitchen, or up on the top floor, where the music was playing so loudly.

"See you in five minutes?" I asked my wife.

"Sure," she said.

3

That night in bed — my wife was still in the bathroom — I played the scene back about ten times in my mind. First from start to finish, then from finish to start. In slow motion. Frame by frame. I tried to stop the action at the moment when my wife looked from me to the alderman. I corrected myself: *avoided* looking at the alderman.

"Sylvia." With his free hand, Maarten van Hoogstraten had touched her elbow briefly by way of farewell. Touched it *again,* I couldn't help thinking. For the second time already. In his other hand he was holding his bottle of beer. A bottle. Not a glass. So he could use his hands freely, it had occurred to me in a flash. And now, in bed, with my eyes closed, it occurred to me again. To have at least one hand free for touching the ladies. The mayor's wife. The mayor's lawfully wedded wife, I thought for just a moment, but pushed the thought

31

away as quickly as it had come.

"Robert." Now Van Hoogstraten was looking at me; he raised his bottle, clinked the bottom of it against mine.

He was just leaving, he announced. I had barely come up to them, and he already had to leave. With some flimsy excuse that he also laid on a little too thick. Something about a drink he had to fetch for someone. Nothing that couldn't wait a few minutes.

Something didn't feel right, but I couldn't put my finger on it straightaway.

After we left city hall through the front entrance, we had walked up in the direction of Rembrandtplein.

"You think they've missed you yet?" my wife asked as we were crossing the Blauwbrug. A completely normal question — too normal, perhaps. We already knew full well; we both knew that we weren't being missed anywhere. *Where were you?* People asked sometimes, the day after a party. *I didn't see you around anymore.* The best thing was to turn the question back on them. *So where were* you? *I looked for you. On the balcony. In the kitchen. I hung around talking for a while in that little room, where all the coats were. With . . . oh, what's her name again . . . the one with the overbite . . .*

"I don't think so," I answered as blandly

32

as I could. "Only people who overestimate their own importance think that everyone is going to miss them."

A late tour boat motored by beneath the bridge, with candles lit on all the little tables — the passengers were probably being served cheap red wine and cheese cubes with mustard. It was so quiet on the bridge that I thought I could hear my heart pounding. The best thing, just to get it over with, would be to ask Sylvia right away: *How long have you two been seeing each other?* The more direct the question, the easier it would be for me to judge from my wife's reaction whether I was right or whether I was mistaken. I could also start in a bit more circumspectly. *You two were having an awfully good time together, you and Maarten. What were you talking about?* But I knew what I was afraid of. My wife would laugh right in my face. *Come on, Robert, grow up!* She would laugh so hard that her cheeks would turn all red, so that I couldn't see whether she was blushing or not.

But she might also react very differently. Offended. *You're not serious, I hope? Please, tell me you're kidding. Me, with Maarten van Hoogstraten? What kind of person do you think I am?* She might start crying. Only a bit: a couple of glistening tears would be enough. I wouldn't pursue it any further. I'd probably tell her that I was sorry for ever having entertained such a silly thought. She, with Maarten van Hoogstraten! It *was* a silly thought, and completely unfounded. My wife had had a conversation with one of my aldermen during the New Year's reception. She had clearly enjoyed herself. My wife had tossed back her head and laughed loudly at something the alderman said to her. Okay, it was hard to imagine, Maarten van Hoogstraten wasn't really known as a humorist, but theoretically speaking it was not entirely impossible. The alderman had gone out of his way to amuse my wife, and in going out of his way he had outdone himself. He had made an intelligent woman laugh. No mean feat. But what exactly had he said? I caught myself wanting to know. What the hell could have been funny enough to make my wife toss back her head and burst out laughing?

Crossing Rembrandtplein, we came past Café Schiller. As casually as possible, without slowing and without looking at her, I suggested that we pop in for a nightcap. The whole time, though, I was paying keen attention to her reaction. If she were having a secret affair with Alderman Van Hoogstraten, wouldn't she rather go home as

34

quickly as possible? To bed with a good book, or to catch the tail end of a talk show on TV — anything, as long as she didn't have to talk, as long as she didn't have to listen to questions she couldn't answer without blushing? Besides the possibility of having her laugh in my face or start crying when I asked her straight-out whether she was having an affair with the alderman, there was a very different reaction I feared: that she would admit to the affair without batting an eye. Maybe in the too-familiar words you normally hear only on soap operas and in movies, but — if all goes well — never in real life.

Yes, Robert. Maarten and I are involved. It's been going on for quite some time now. He hasn't told his wife yet, but he's going to leave her. And I am going to leave you. I never thought I would have to say this to you, but it's true: I love someone else. Maarten and I love each other.

After these sentences had been pronounced, my life would come to an end. My whole life, everything I had. I thought about our daughter, about Diana. She would be graduating from high school this year. I heard myself tell my wife: *Shall we wait to tell her until finals are over? She might get really confused.*

Yes, my life would end. Our life. Life as we had lived it till then, the three of us. My daughter would lock herself in her room and cry. Her mother might be the main culprit, but she would never look at me in the same way again either. We were her parents, we had made a mess of things together. That was true, wasn't it? If Sylvia had been happy with me, she never would have fallen in love with someone else, would she? Diana, too, had been happy with us throughout her growing-up years, our unconditional love had given her self-confidence. Our love for each other, and our shared love for her. She had both feet firmly on the ground, so firmly that even during puberty she had never rebelled against us. In the evening she would snuggle up between us on the couch, her head against my shoulder, her legs slung over her mother's legs. But something of all that would be destroyed for good, retroactively, if my wife were to leave us and move in with the alderman. Maybe Diana would choose sides with me, at first, but in a way no father would ever want: out of pity for the betrayed husband. *Poor Daddy.* Maybe she would cook for me the first few months, toss my underpants in the washing machine, iron my shirts. She would warn me about my

36

unshaven appearance, the quantity of hard liquor I would knock back in my rage and sorrow. *You should look at yourself in the mirror, Daddy. You should smell yourself. You don't want people to see you like this.* Ultimately she would lose respect for me, maybe not stop loving me, but it would be a pitying kind of love at best. The kind of love you might give a pet that's been run over, a cat with paralyzed hindquarters, an old person who can no longer go to the toilet on their own. After those first few months had passed, she would leave me too. In retrospective effect, she would come to see her entire safe life with her parents as a lie. That's the way those things went. Even though nothing had gone wrong right up until the end. So maybe, before that, it hadn't been as perfect as it seemed either. Who knows, maybe this wasn't the first time something like this had happened. Maybe she had been too young at the time, too naive, too loving to notice a thing. Her parents, her perfect parents, whom she had always bragged about to her friends, a father and a mother who outshone the fathers and mothers of those same boyfriends and girlfriends, fathers and mothers who had broken up long before or who were always arguing. In the end, her parents had proven just as depraved and despicable as the rest.

"Okay, one for the road," my wife said. "But really only one. I'm tired and I don't want to get to bed too late."

We found a table all the way at the back, in a section of the café where no one else was seated. Not a bad spot if someone started crying, I couldn't help thinking. If one of the two of us started screaming at the other. *Don't look right away, but that table over there in the corner, that's the mayor. And that woman is probably his wife. Looks like they're not having a lot of fun. If you ask me, she's crying.*

Sylvia asked for a glass of red wine; I ordered a beer.

"Oh, that was another terrible one," I said. "I'm really not up to this. During the preselection round, they probably should have asked me: 'Are you able to stomach receptions where people stand around with glasses in their hand and chitchat? No? Really not? Well then, you're probably not cut out to be mayor. You'd have to spend three-quarters of your time with a glass in your hand, talking about the weather.' "

The look my wife gave me then I can only describe as loving. I had decided to go on acting as normal as possible — or, rather, to apply every fiber of my being to acting precisely as I would have otherwise — but meanwhile, never to take my eye off the ball.

"What is it? What are you laughing about?" I asked.

"Nothing. It's because I could see it on your face a mile away. That you wanted to get out of there. And you're still wearing that same look. You just can't hide it. It's written all over your face. It's so funny."

I listened to my wife. I listened to each word. To each sentence. And to the extent that time allowed, I ran each word and each sentence back again in my mind. The first time I listened to her as though nothing was going on: as though we were just sitting there having a nightcap, the mayor and his wife, after running away from a deadly boring New Year's reception. So sweet, the way they sit there laughing at the memory of it, so pleased that they had actually dared to do it — so happy, the two of them, after so many years together.

The second time, though, I listened to the sentences as though they had a false bottom. As though my wife were only playacting and had to do her utmost to make normal-sounding sentences come out of her mouth. If she was acting, then she was doing a damned good job of it. But wasn't she laying it on just a little too thick, with that bit about being charmed by my visible boredom at the New Year's reception?

I could just blurt it out, of course, catch her off-balance when she has her guard down. But no, too soon for that, I decided half a second later. First a little more chitchat; wait until the next beer. I had to be particularly careful about my facial expression. It was true, she was absolutely right, my face reflected everything that went on in my mind. *What were you and Maarten van Hoogstraten talking about anyway? You two seemed to be enjoying yourselves.* If I adopted the wrong expression, I would ruin everything. The best thing would be to put on a smile first. Not a political smile. A real one. That was already tough enough. All politicians who have ever received media training have worked on their smiles. But you could tell right away when they weren't real, because their eyes never smiled along with the rest; the smiles were stuck to their faces like a sticker to a bargain-basement DVD.

I have never received media training. I'm what they call "a natural." You can't media-train a natural. *Cut the baloney,* that's my political message. When a journalist's question irritates me, you can see that irritation all over my face. When I can't help laughing about something, I laugh. Generally speaking, I don't like watching myself on TV, but of course it happens anyway. I see my face on the local news station or the eight o'clock news, and no matter how critically I view myself at such times, I see immediately that I got it right. The proper distance when questions are asked about offensive chanting during a football match; the deep, sincere sigh after the umpteenth liquidation in the month-long power struggle in the underworld; but most of all, perhaps, in the pitch-perfect tone of my short speech last Remembrance Day. Everyone could see that I meant it, because I did mean it — that's how simple such things can be. And before the speech and the two minutes of silence, perhaps the realest face of all, when I left the palace beside the king and queen, the short walk to the monument on Dam Square. I walked beside them, but you could tell from my face, no, from all my body language, that I was keeping my distance, that I didn't belong there. *I'm only walking beside them because that's what protocol demands,* said my face, said also the literal distance at which my body found itself from the royal couple. *If some evening I were to feel lonely or unhappy, these are the last people I would call.*

41

I had finished my beer a long time ago; my wife was still fussing with the wine at the bottom of her glass.

"Shall we go for another one?" I asked.

"You know, this Maarten van Hoogstraten," my wife said. "I always thought he had no sense of humor at all. You told me that too, once. But he told me a story back at the reception, I almost died laughing. No, really, I never would have expected that from him."

And while Sylvia started telling me the story and I gestured to the waitress for a second round of beer and red wine, I had to do my best not to laugh too heartily — not to betray my suspicions with a shit-eating grin from ear to ear.

For what else could it mean, the fact that my wife was now telling me in great detail the "funny story" she'd heard from Van Hoogstraten — something about how his children's pet rabbit had gnawed through the HDMI cable on the TV, but I was only half listening, at moments of great relief we only half listen — other than that I had been getting wound up about nothing at all?

"In the end, I couldn't tell what was funnier," she said when the story was finished. "Whether it was the rabbit or the combination of the rabbit and Maarten trying to catch it. I mean, he is sort of stiff. Well, not exactly stiff: more like a straight arrow. Someone who isn't completely at home in their own body. Anyway, I was trying to visualize it, him crawling under the couch, trying to grab that rabbit but missing every time, and I got the helpless giggles. I saw him looking at me, sort of like: *Well, it wasn't* that *funny.* It really *was* funny though, the way he told it, too, but part of it was unintentionally funny, of course. But now that I think about it: Do you suppose he realized that I wasn't just laughing at his story but also partly at him? That I was laughing at him?"

Despite myself, I was probably grinning then anyway, there was no stopping it. My wife and Alderman Van Hoogstraten! Where had I come up with that? Someday, maybe a year from now, I could tell her about it, as an anecdote. *You remember that time at the New Year's reception, when you were talking with Maarten van Hoogstraten? Do you know what crossed my mind for a moment?* No, I decided then and there in Café Schiller, I would never tell her about it. Never! She might take it as an insult.

"I wouldn't worry about it," I told her. "He is sort of rectilinear, like you say. People like that only take things at face value. I'll bet you he's still beaming with pride at having made you laugh like that."

A woman like you, I'd almost added. *A woman who sees straight through the rectilinear Dutch.*

4

As I said, that evening in bed I played the whole scene back in my mind — but in the reassuring knowledge by then that I had been all worked up about nothing. I started at the end, at the moment when we left Café Schiller and Sylvia took my arm as we walked down the street. That's how we walked those last few hundred meters to our front door, a normal couple of a certain age, walking arm-in-arm. Not to keep each other from falling, but out of love, out of fondness, because both husband and wife enjoy each other's company.

Had we said anything else? Hardly. The subject of Van Hoogstraten, in any case, had been put to bed earlier, in the café. My memory is one of my strong points; I remember a lot, sometimes more than strictly necessary. A little over twenty years ago we took a trip through the American West; the trip lasted six weeks and I still remember every town and whistle-stop where we spent the night, every motel, every restaurant. That was before Diana was born, we both still smoked, the dashboard of our Chevrolet Lumina rental was littered with used packs of Marlboros. What good is remembering all that, you might ask? But I like it, it calms me: the idea that it doesn't all just disappear. In bed at night, when I can't sleep, I take the trip all over again, from the moment we landed in Los Angeles, happy hour at the hotel, the five or six margaritas we drank there, the heat on the following day, the road to Las Vegas, the endless freight trains. A memory like a movie, but with no need of film. No, we weren't the kind to keep picture albums, no ordering of things, no chronologically pasted-in vacations, no exact dates, no quasi-cute captions; everything we have is kept in boxes and rarely taken out: maybe five times in the last twenty years, I'd figure.

That's what they call the "long-term memory," but at my age — I turned sixty last year — the short-term memory is another kettle of fish: Where did I put my reading glasses, my cell phone, the keys to my bike? I'm standing in the bathroom, I came here to get something, to do some-thing, I was probably looking for something.

But what?

That's the way I now reconstructed, step by step, from back to front, the moment when I unlocked the front door downstairs. The streetlights along the canal, the black branches of the trees, a duck between the parked cars who, startled by our approach and quacking loudly, flapped off into the water. *I think he's sort of nice.* That's what my wife said, yes, somewhere between Rembrandtplein and home we had started talking about our daughter's new boyfriend. *I think it's nice that he's not really Dutch.*

Maybe "new boyfriend" isn't quite the right term, "first real boyfriend" might be more like it. The boys came and went, they lined up to go out with our Diana; sometimes she would bring one of them home for dinner and he wouldn't speak a word, or at most "Thank you very much, ma'am." Or: "Maybe something like European Studies, sir." If they had been able to pant like a dog, with their tongues hanging out of their mouths, they would have. They couldn't believe that they were really here, at the same table with a girl like our Diana. But it rarely lasted longer than a couple of weeks; in any case, we never saw them at the dinner table again.

Two months, though, was a different

thing. During those two months, the new boy had come to dinner at least five times. And unlike the boys who languished, he simply joined in the conversation. He didn't say too much, or too little; he wasn't the kind of assertive blabbermouth who talks your ear off. He was polite, a tad bit shy perhaps; even after repeated urging to call me by my first name, he kept on saying "sir." Finally I let it go, I figured he was probably brought up that way and that it made things easier for him — but three days earlier, while we were sitting on the couch watching *Expedition Robinson,* he suddenly called my wife "Sylvia." "I think that swimming champ is sort of a loser too, Sylvia," he said about one of the female contestants. "They should send her home as soon as possible."

Like my wife, I also thought he was a nice boy. In my case, that's really saying something. I've imagined often enough how I would react if my daughter came home with a boy who wasn't very nice. I thought about my face. I wouldn't be able to hide it: I would shake the hand of the boy who wasn't very nice and adopt an expression like I was sniffing at a suspect carton of milk. *Way past expiration,* that's what everyone, but especially my daughter, would be able to read from my expression.

But I had nothing to fear when it came to the new boy, at least nothing to do with my own facial expressions. The first time we shook hands he looked at me openly and candidly and introduced himself — but I had already seen it. Only shy people can look so open and candid, I knew that from experience. I had seen that look often enough in the mirror, when I was practicing it. And indeed, after the initial greeting, the boy lowered his eyes right away, let go of my hand, then looked at me again and smiled. It was a real smile, not candid perhaps, but certainly disarming. He saw it too, then, he let me know with a smile. It's like the way motorcyclists or runners raise a hand in greeting when they pass each other. Shy people can hide their shyness from the outside world for a long, long time, but never from someone who is just as shy as they are.

It came as a surprise to me, during our short walk home from Café Schiller, when my wife said she liked the boy because he was "not really Dutch." That was probably understandable, considering that she wasn't really Dutch either; on the other hand, in her own culture, prejudices about other cultures were much more pronounced. Or let me put that differently: Where she came from, they held no prejudices against holding prejudices. Everything was in the service of preserving one's own kind. There, what a boy or girl brought home with them was weighed in a much finer balance. Foreign blood was viewed with definite suspicion. Things that came in from outside could weaken one's own kind.

"You know what Diana told me a while back?" she asked me last night, as we were climbing the last three steps to our front door. "That he always holds the door open for her. At a café. In a restaurant. He even helps her push the chair in closer to the table. And when he's parked somewhere he always hops out, walks around the car, and opens the door for her."

What, is he studying to become a cabdriver? The question was on the tip of my tongue, but I gulped it down before it could cross my lips — this was no moment for sarcasm. There, at the threshold of our home, our official residence, Maarten van Hoogstraten crossed my mind for a moment, by then as something that was disappearing farther and farther over the horizon, like after a visit to the dental hygienist: your gums are still tingling but in a pleasant way, rosy, as though they've just taken a long walk on the beach.

Maarten van Hoogstraten. They didn't make them any Dutcher than that. Dutcher than a head of endive brought in after a first night's frost, Dutcher than a pair of clogs with little windmills painted on the insteps, Dutcher than cheese and milk, bread for breakfast and lunch, Dutcher than a hole in the ice, than that one single cookie to go with your tea before the lid goes back on the tin.

I pushed against our front door, pushed it all the way open, then stepped inside quickly to hold it open for my wife.

"Ladies first," I said.

5

And then, in bed, as I heard Sylvia turn on her electric toothbrush in the bathroom, then all of a sudden I knew.

I knew what didn't add up.

Running again through the evening, I had arrived at Café Schiller, not the moment when we came back outside, but before that, when we paused on Rembrandtplein and I suggested we go in for a drink.

And she, after a slight hesitation, agreed.

So far, so good. If my wife had known that I suspected her of having an extramarital affair, that suspicion would only have deepened if she had refused a last drink at Café Schiller.

But during the half second or less that her hesitation lasted, she hadn't looked at me.

She had tilted her head and turned to look at the front door of the café.

Okay, sounds good. No, she'd said something else, something about being tired and not wanting to stay up late. *I'm tired and I don't want to get to bed too late.*

At the little table inside, of course, there was no way we could avoid eye contact. It was there, at that table, that she had dished me up the story about the alderman — about his intentional or unintentional funniness.

But once we were back outside, after taking my arm, she had — as far as I could remember — spent most of the time looking at the ground: at the street, the pavement.

That was all believable enough; it was dark out, in Amsterdam at night you often keep your eyes on the ground in order not to step in something or twist your ankle on a loose paving stone.

But even at home, when I made a gracious display of holding the door open for her, she hadn't looked at me. She had wiped her feet, she had stamped her boots a few times on the doormat, the way you do when you've been walking through the snow and don't want to track it into the house.

But it wasn't snowing. The streets were dry.

She had looked at her feet. Then she went upstairs ahead of me.

I rewound it all the way now, skipping a

few scenes, until we were back at the New Year's reception. At the moment when I came up to my wife and the alderman.

Maarten.

Robert . . .

The brief conversation that followed I could no longer remember word for word. The alderman had taken leave of us within thirty seconds, saying something about someone who was waiting for him to bring them a drink.

He had looked at me for a moment.

But Sylvia had not.

What didn't add up was this: This was the first time Maarten van Hoogstraten and I had seen each other since the Christmas recess. That made sense, that was entirely possible. The alderman had taken an extra week's vacation, and so missed the first plenary council meeting.

Ordinarily, after some standard comment about the weather, the quality of the wine or the nightly news, this was the moment when one asked about the children. About the Christmas vacation that was not even three weeks behind us ("Did you all get away at Christmas or New Year's?"). But none of that happened. My wife and the alderman didn't look at each other either, I realized, reconstructing as best I could. No, they were both looking at me. Because they didn't dare to look at each other. Because they were afraid their glances would give them away. That they would start blushing.

That's where I hit pause. I tried to take a step back. Because what if my imagination had been running away with me? What if I had been imagining everything? It could be. That was still possible. There was no evidence. No concrete proof. No one had actually started to stammer or blush. All I could do was listen to my senses. And my senses said that it was unusual, to put it mildly, that my wife and Alderman Van Hoogstraten had not spoken a word to each other from the moment I joined them — and then, when we parted, had not even looked at each other.

I could still hear the sound of the electric toothbrush coming from the bathroom. I squeezed my eyes shut even tighter, I concentrated on the sound, the image of my wife standing at the sink. In front of the mirror above the sink. Was she looking at herself at that moment? At her own face? *Her guilty face,* it occurred to me in a flash. Was she brushing her teeth differently than she did on other evenings? Was she staying in the bathroom longer than normal? To practice the neutral expression she would wear when she came back into the bedroom?

What expression does a woman wear when she's cheating on her husband? What expression, above all, must she take care *not* to wear?

I listened closely. Every thirty seconds the toothbrush paused for a moment. Left uppers, right uppers, lower left, lower right. Every evening I try to go on brushing for the full two minutes, but rarely get all the way. Somewhere halfway, but probably much sooner than that, my concentration flags. Toothpaste foam and water drip down over the brush, over my fingers, my hands, my chin. In the mirror, meanwhile, I look like a slobbering old man. I turn off the toothbrush. I've already forgotten how many thirty-second rounds I've done.

Was Sylvia brushing her teeth more absentmindedly than usual tonight? Or more dreamily? Because she was thinking about him? I moaned quietly. I listened. The toothbrush rattled on for a bit, then all was quiet in the bathroom. I rubbed my eyelids softly with my fingertips and tried to imagine my wife in there. Her reflection in the mirror — how she, in turn, looked at her own reflection.

Did she look at it guiltily? Or with a smile? Because she had succeeded so well in deceiving her husband with someone else? Without him having noticed anything yet? Or was it only a smile of infatuation? Was she in love? That was the first time the thought came up. *In love.* It was almost unbearable. Inadmissible, even. For about ten seconds I struggled to think about something else: about the president of Ajax, the moment when he had slipped a handful of salted nuts into his mouth, his Adam's apple bobbing up and down as he swallowed, but before the ten seconds were over the alderman's face loomed up again. *His silly face,* I thought right away, but no, I shouldn't think that way: I had to remain objective. I had to try to understand. To apply all the capacities at my disposal in figuring out why my wife would want to take that silly face in her hands, and then press her lips against the alderman's flabby, always a bit too moist, and unmanly lips.

I didn't hear Sylvia come into the room — and I hadn't seen her either: apparently I'd been lying there with my eyes closed, pondering. Before I knew what was happening, she had turned back the featherbed and crawled in beside me.

She placed her iPhone on the nightstand, then clicked off her reading light.

"Good night," I said.

"Oh, I thought you were asleep already."

I turned off my reading lamp too.

What I had to say now was better said in the dark.

"Sylvia?"

"Hmm?"

"I have to go to a funeral tomorrow. Hans van Wezel, you know, the city manager?"

It remained quiet for a moment.

"Oh, yes, that horrible business."

I took a deep breath — I tried not to inhale too loudly. "Normally speaking, I wouldn't ask you, but would you please go along with me?"

"Robert . . ."

"It's just that I suddenly realized that I would really like to have you with me. I have to speak at the funeral. A few words. I mean, it's bad enough as it is. If I . . . I'd really like to see your face. Everyone will be there. I'd really like to be able to look up at you every once in a while, while I'm giving my speech."

I heard my wife sigh.

"I've got something tomorrow afternoon. Diana and I agreed to go shopping for clothes. Is this really . . . It's such a nasty story, too, Robert. Do I really have to be there?"

I rolled onto my side, placed my hand

carefully on her stomach.

"I wasn't planning to ask you. It's because of tonight, all those faces at the reception . . . Please? Will you please go with me? For me?"

I had put on my begging tone — in my thoughts, I was down on my knees in front of her.

"What time does it start? I mean, maybe I can go into town with Diana when it's over. I don't have to hang around there for hours afterward, do I?"

I lay on my back with my eyes open and listened to my wife's measured breathing. Sometimes she snored a little, but it was a cute kind of snore: not the sawing-through-giant-redwoods kind of snoring that has destroyed so many marriages, no, more like a quiet whistle or creak — a rural sound, like a barn door or a shutter moving in the wind. But tonight there was only her breathing, her regular breathing: in and out, like the ticking of a clock. When I'm having a hard time getting to sleep, I sometimes pay attention to my own breathing. I'm rarely able to keep that up for more than thirty seconds, but I know that I've felt my eyelids droop any number of times while listening to my wife's breathing.

Tomorrow afternoon I would put an end to all the uncertainty. Everyone would be at the funeral: most of the council members, almost all the aldermen. A chance was sure to present itself at some point, when Sylvia and Alderman Van Hoogstraten were standing next to each other. Right at the start, maybe, when the family was welcoming the mourners; or later, in the procession to graveside — and otherwise at the kaffeeklatsch afterward.

This time I would look at them differently. I would look at them through the eyes of a husband who knows he is being deceived.

6

The former city manager is no longer with us. Hans van Wezel did not resign, and we did not fire him either. Or perhaps it would be more accurate to say: he didn't give us a chance. He could have, he could have resigned. He would not have received an honorable discharge, that was impossible, it would have leaked out sooner or later anyway, but at least we could have done it discreetly, we wouldn't have had to make a production out of it.

"Have you been taking more money out of the cashbox lately?" my secretary had asked me one day, shortly after the Christmas recess.

"No, not that I know of," I said. "Actually, never. I mean, I take some out every once in a while, but never more than ten or fifteen euros for a sandwich and a cup of coffee along the way."

The cashbox. I need to explain that. The

cashbox is a little, red metal box with a lock on it. It probably looks more like a breadbox than anything else, and it's in the bookcase in my office. In plain sight. Ready cash, that's what it's for. Even a mayor needs a little ready cash. My secretary puts a few hundred euros in it now and then, in small denominations: tens, twenties. When the money's almost gone, she fills it again.

I keep the key to the cashbox in the top drawer of my desk. A drawer that can be locked, too, but I almost never do. My office door has a lock on it, of course, but I never use that during the day, only when I go home at night.

To make a long story short, my secretary had noticed that, in the last three months, the cashbox needed filling all the time. Hence her asking me whether I was using it more than usual. But my spending patterns hadn't changed, I was 100 percent sure of that. I preferred not to use the cashbox. It was something instinctive: Why, with my salary, should I declare every single cup of coffee? I preferred to pay for my own coffee, toasted cheese and tartar sandwiches, out of my own pocket, and I never asked for a receipt. The fact of the matter was, I took a little money out of the cashbox every now and then, but only to please my secretary.

When I did that I would ask for a receipt and put it in the compartment in the right side of the box, along with the other receipts. The compartment on the left was for the tens and twenties.

My secretary, the city manager, and I were the only ones with a key to my office. The office I almost never locked during the day. In theory, anyone could have walked into my office, taken the key from my desk drawer, and pulled money out of the cashbox — but only in theory.

"How much is missing?" I asked my secretary.

"During the last three months, somewhere between six and eight hundred euros. That is, if you're sure you didn't take out more than thirty a month. For the months before that, I'd have to figure it out."

We thought the city manager would deny everything, but as soon as we confronted him he burst into tears. "I don't know," he whimpered when we asked him why he'd done it. "I really don't know."

For a moment, we were dumbstruck. I was just about to ask him what he had done with the money, whether he had gambled it away or just bought a new TV, when he said he would give it all back.

"All of it," Hans van Wezel blubbered.

"Not just the money. The laptops and cell phones too. I didn't sell any of it. It's all at my place, in the storage closet."

Later on, my secretary and I tried to reconstruct whether one of us, directly or indirectly, had asked about anything but the money from the cashbox, but we couldn't. Things were stolen all the time at city hall anyway, nothing was safe there: laptops, iPads, and phones even disappeared from the council chambers. We decided not to go to the police with it. We settled for firing him, effective the end of the month. A letter of recommendation was, of course, out of the question.

A few days after our decision was made, the city manager knocked on my office door.

"Couldn't you reconsider?" he asked, after closing the door behind him and sinking into the chair across from my desk. "I can really give it all back. The money too. I've still got it."

"That's not the point, Hans," I said. "But it might not be a bad idea to get help. To go into therapy, I mean."

His lower lip began to quake. I thought he was going to burst into tears again, but he took a few deep breaths and looked at me.

"There's no way I can do that," he said. "My wife would never understand. And my children. How am I supposed to explain this to my children?"

I vaguely recalled that the city manager had two children in their teens. A boy and a girl . . . No, two girls. I always made a point of remembering such things: the names of wives and children, birthdays and anniversaries. Not that I knew all that by heart, of course, my secretary did it for me. Mrs. Schreuder had a big fat notebook for that very purpose. A black, rectangular notebook. At around ten each morning, when she came in with my second cup of coffee of the day, she would have that notebook under her arm. "Alderman Hawinkels's son turns eighteen today," she would read aloud. "His name is Pieter. The wife of Theo, the doorkeeper — her name is Annie — will be released from the hospital tomorrow. But don't ask him any more than that. Finished with active treatment, I think they call it. But let him tell you about it himself, if he feels like it."

So when I ran into Alderman Hawinkels during the course of the day, in the hall or at the self-service buffet in the cafeteria, I would casually shake his hand. "Congratulations with Pieter. You think he's ready for his finals?" I would lean over the doorkeeper's counter and pull a packet of tissues out of my inside pocket. "I understand, Theo. I understand very well. You know, why don't you just take the day off tomorrow, the whole day? You're needed at home more than we need you here. We'll muddle along without you for a day."

The mayor with the human face, that's what they called me once in a four-page profile in *Het Parool*. That was the headline above the interview: "Robert Walter: The Mayor with the Human Face." It was sort of strange; I'd been in office for less than a year, it seemed to imply that my predecessor's face had been somehow less than human. Which wasn't all that far-fetched, in fact. Mayor Jan van Hiemstra–Henegouwen had had an aristocratic air about him, and that's putting it mildly. As though he felt he was too good for a city like Amsterdam. A man who shakes his head and actually pulls up his pant legs as he steps over a dog turd. On Queen's Day, at a stand selling hot dogs and hamburgers, he had asked for a knife and fork. And at one of the annual memorial services for the victims of the El Al jet that crashed into the flats in the Bijlmer, he had said: "They were also our people. No matter how you look at it, they were from Amsterdam too."

Maybe I *was* remote, strict, maybe I did

have a short fuse — all qualities that appeared more than once in the course of the interview — but I had my face going for me. It often looked grouchy, angry even, but when I suddenly laughed or told a joke, you could see the people relax.

Now, to my horror, or my amazement — it's hard to pinpoint the exact emotion anymore (and besides, aren't horror and amazement simply two branches off the same emotional trunk?) — I saw that the city manager was leaning down to get something out of his bag. His bag, which was leaning against one leg of his chair. No, I can't recall my exact emotion, but I do remember the details of what happened. The way the only thing you might remember about an accident is that hubcap, the windshield wipers that went on sweeping back and forth senselessly, even though it had stopped raining a long time ago. The radio that went on broadcasting live coverage of a football match.

The city manager's bag was one of those brown leather school satchels, with worn spots. The kind of satchel that stupid boys took to school with them long ago, boys who parted their hair on the side, who rooted for the Americans instead of the Vietcong. These days you saw satchels like that only in the hands of certain unworldly schoolteachers, civil servants, or bookkeepers, men over fifty who also tended to view the cell phone as a diabolical contraption.

Hans van Wezel leaned down and took a rope out of the satchel. When it comes to the rope, too, everything in my memory zooms in on the details. It was a fairly thick rope, the kind they use to hang swings on, a little less thick than the climbing ropes in a gym. It was brand-new, never been used, bought this morning or yesterday afternoon at a hardware store for the sole purpose of pulling it out of the worn brown leather satchel here, today, before my eyes.

"I'm desperate," the city manager said. "You better realize what you're doing to me. If you stick to your decision, I'll go out today and hang myself."

7

The funeral was at Nieuwe Ooster, my favorite cemetery. People who consider themselves important often sign up for the waiting list at Zorgvlied instead, even before they're dead. There's no denying that Zorgvlied is a lovely cemetery, too, but it's too crowded for my taste. I don't know how it works with cemeteries and waiting lists, but a day will have to come when there's just no room left for anyone else there. When they'll have to hang a sign out by the gate: NO VACANCY. A backlit sign, like the ones at motels and boardinghouses. At Nieuwe Ooster, though, they can go on socking them away for years. There's plenty of room and more between the thick, old trees. It's got light and shadow. It breathes. Zorgvlied is more like a country town, a village, a holiday park where they've built the bungalows close together to boost turnover.

I've been to these funerals often enough

before, funerals for suicides. Sometimes the act itself had been in the air for years, other times it came as a complete surprise. On the surface, everything is just the way it is at other funerals: the flowers, the ribbons, the carefully chosen clothing, the sunglasses when the weather's nice, the refreshment room afterward, the slices of cake, the flimsy sandwiches, the occasional guest — it's eleven o'clock in the morning — knocking back his first vino blanco of the day. But the speeches echo with incomprehension. With wondering why. *We respect your decision.* Okay, that's what they say in the death notices sometimes, it's the code that lets the outsider know that one is talking about a self-chosen death, words that come back in the funeral speeches.

But when you look at it in the cold, clear light of day, there's nothing to respect. We tie ourselves in knots trying to give the suicide a dignified send-off. To bring them to their final resting place, as they put it so nicely. But what about the others, the ones who have stayed behind? With their perplexity? With their anger?

How could you, you dirty, egotistical bastard! is what we actually feel like shouting at the coffin. *What made you think you could duck out and leave this mess behind? Just because*

His Highness "couldn't face it anymore"? "I saw no other way out," that's what your suicide note said. But what made you think that? Of course there was another way out. You were just too lazy, you didn't feel like listening to us, you always were a lousy listener. Chickenshit! Piss off to your grave, you!

That's the crux of it, after all; the best thing is to simply look it in the eye. Suicides, with the exception of the psychiatric cases — the patients with psychoses, the bipolar — rarely stand out by virtue of their exceptional backbone. That's hard to explain, hard to say out loud: at least if you want to spare the survivors. Although I sometimes have the feeling that the survivors are the ones who understand best. People who take their own lives aren't the smartest of the bunch. It took me years, half my life, to figure that out. It's the thread that connects all suicides. Average intelligence. Or a little less than average. No clever clogs, in any case. However, a pinhead with an IQ of zero is too stupid to even come up with the idea. Or too lazy. He'd rather loll around on the couch a little longer, rather than try to figure out how many sleeping pills you need in order never to wake up again.

For the sake of argument, see me as the

measure of an above-average intelligence. Would I ever take my own life? No. Never. No matter what. I have, however, toyed with the thought of suicide. Not so often these days, though. More when I was back in my twenties. But I think all intelligent people do that, toy with the thought. It's sort of like being up on top of a tall building and looking over the edge, the miniature cars far below, the people the size of ants, the sounds of fire engines and ambulance sirens in the distance. Then the fantasy of climbing over the balustrade, onto the roof: the last tumble you'll ever take has started, the ultimate free fall.

What suicides don't understand is that life has to be lived down to the butt-end, that's all. Maybe your family finds out that you're nothing but a common thief, but no amount of shame can offset life itself. Even through the bars of our cell we can see the sun come up, hear a bird sing. From the prison kitchen, the smell of food reaches our nostrils: not very nice food, sure, but when you're dead you can't smell anything at all. Why else would death row prisoners try to prolong their lives for as long as possible? Why are they grateful for every stay of execution? Because they'd rather be given life imprisonment. "Life imprisonment" —

the term says it all. For as long as your life goes on. Someone embezzles ten million euros and, rather than be unmasked, tosses himself from the tenth floor of an office building. Not very smart. In fact, just plain stupid. Someone loses the love of their life. *I can't live without him/her,* the widow or widower says. But that's not true. There is mourning, there is bereavement, there is pain — but mourning, bereavement, and pain actually give you back the sense of being alive. Maybe even more alive than you were before your loss. Without him/ her, life has no meaning, the survivors say; but if life has ever had any meaning, it's now. A man takes a little money out of a cashbox, he stuffs a wayward iPad into his brown book bag, in the cloakroom he may rummage through coat pockets to see if there's anything valuable in them. He gets caught, he gets fired. No charges are pressed against him. He is given the chance to lose gracefully. Dishonorably, but without disgrace. Then he makes a crucial mistake. He threatens to commit suicide. He doesn't dare to face up to his family. He doesn't understand that his life will only be enriched by facing up to his family. His wife will realize that he's less of a bore than she always thought. His children will see that their father is no paragon of virtue. They themselves have probably stolen the occasional Mars bar or bag of potato chips from the supermarket, or taken a couple of euros out of their father's or mother's wallet. *But you knew it was wrong, didn't you, Dad? Yes, I knew that, but it was stronger than I was.* Disgrace doesn't exist. Animals don't experience disgrace. It's a human invention. Those who live without disgrace are freer, closer to nature. A grown man is caught stealing money and electronic equipment. At the home improvement center he buys a length of rope, puts it in his satchel, goes to his employer and threatens to take his own life. It's a scene from a comedy. Only people with no sense of humor actually hang themselves after a scene like that. Stupid people.

In the speeches at Hans van Wezel's funeral, too, one heard mostly incomprehension and perplexity. A former classmate talked about the city manager's "keenness." I don't know if everyone picked up on it, but at the word "keenness" I'm sure the silence in the chapel deepened a notch. There were plenty of things you could say about Hans van Wezel, but keenness was probably the last trait you'd associate with that wet blanket. Unless his passion for cashboxes and stray laptops fell within the category of "keenness." While one of Hans's older sisters was giving her speech, I asked myself what he had told them at home. Nothing at all, I suspected. His sister related an anecdote about him: something about a sandbox and a puppy — and, for the first time, cautious laughter was heard in the chapel.

Then it was my turn. The sister wasn't very tall, I had to bend up the mike stand on the lectern first. I coughed, I cleared my throat. I leaned on the lectern with both hands, I had no notes to read from. I am the mayor known for his off-the-cuff speeches. I looked into the chapel, first at the row all the way in the back, then my gaze moved up, traveling over the people's heads, until finally it rested on the bereaved family. I looked at the city manager's wife for a moment, and she looked back at me, without lowering her eyes. She had not been weeping, her eyes were dry, she was sitting straight up in the uncomfortable wooden pew, she bore her sorrow with dignity. I had probably seen her before at some reception at city hall, I knew her name, her age, her date of birth. But I couldn't remember her face. It was not an unattractive face, but also not one you'd necessarily remember. A

75

woman like so many others. Women who marry a man because otherwise that man would have no wife. I looked at the daughters too. I knew their names as well, their birthdays, only from the big black notebook (I had looked them up that morning), but I knew which school they went to. I nodded to them, something that was meant to look like an encouraging nod — but encouraging in what sense, I asked myself the very next moment. Was it in the sense of *Chin up, it's a huge shock right now, but I'm sure you'll get over it. You all have a long and happy life in front of you, right?* I hoped that was the way it would go, that they would get over it, maybe even sooner than they could imagine at this point. But I also knew that wasn't true. The children of suicides never get over it. *I guess we weren't important enough to keep living for,* that was the thought that would accompany them from this day forward.

I tapped my finger against the microphone, as though checking whether it was turned on. Of course it was, the city manager's sister had just used it to give her speech, and that had been clearly audible and amplified. It's just a tic of mine, I always start my speeches by tapping on the mike. Stalling for time, getting into speech mode, the way a soccer player genuflects before running out onto the pitch, the way a tennis player bounces the ball a few times, adjusts his sweatband, and plucks at the seat of his pants before the service.

How much might the city manager have told them at home? I asked myself briefly as I leaned toward the microphone. Nothing — suddenly I knew that for sure. What was he supposed to tell them? *I got caught stealing things and they fired me, but I'm going to tell the mayor that I'll hang myself unless they give me another chance: that will make him change his mind.* No, his wife and children would never know about that. They would spend their whole lives wondering why he did it. Maybe they would come up with all kinds of wild speculations. Had the city manager been a habitué of sites with child pornography? Did he use his lunch breaks to drive out to the pickup spot for gay men along the big lake south of town? Did he make a detour after office hours to the western docklands, where he paid a Ukrainian streetwalker to suck his dick? Here, once again, scandal raised its hoary head. Which of those acts was scandalous enough to leave a woman widowed and two children fatherless?

I took a deep breath, one last time. While

the chapel descended into true silence —
when the mayor gets up to speak, that's of a
different order than when a former colleague or a big sister does — I paused for a
moment and thought about the question of
guilt. Did I feel guilty? Was I in some way
coresponsible for the city manager's death?
During the last few days, of course, I had
asked myself that any number of times.
Once, about ten years ago, I came back to
our house from some shopping in Hulst, in
Zeelandic Flanders. We used to have a
house along the dike in Graauw, at the edge
of the village. I always parked on the left
shoulder of the road, in the grass. This time,
though, a cat, which had apparently been
sleeping there, shot out onto the road and
ended up under the left rear wheel of the
car coming up behind me. The driver didn't
notice a thing and drove on. As I turned off
the engine and opened the door, my hands
were shaking. The cat was lying in the tall
grass right beside the road. It was writhing,
there was no blood, the cat didn't make a
sound. "Take it easy now," I said. "Calm
down, I'm not going anywhere, I'll stay with
you." The cat squinted and looked at me,
its body went on writhing. It was as though
the cat was smiling at me. I looked up and
down the road, but there was no one else

out on the street. "I'll stay with you," I said to the cat, but it was already still, it had stopped moving, the smiling eyes had closed.

If I hadn't laughed in Hans van Wezel's face a little less than a week ago, when he showed me that rope from the hardware store, his bereaved family wouldn't be sitting here today in the front pew of this chapel at Nieuwe Ooster. But was that observation the same as feeling guilty? Deep in my heart, I was convinced that people with the city manager's personality structure would all end up at the cash register of the hardware store sooner or later, to pay for their length of rope.

I turned my gaze to the back rows. I saw my wife, my secretary, a couple of aldermen and council members — it took a moment for me to finally home in on Maarten van Hoogstraten. He had taken a seat at a far remove from my wife, almost on the other side of the chapel, close to the door.

There you go, I thought. If they had nothing to hide, they would probably be sitting closer together or maybe even right beside each other. Now it was almost as though they were ignoring each other. They were acting like nothing was going on, which meant something was going on. It was clear as a bell, I realized; preposterous, in fact, that they themselves didn't see the kind of farce they were putting on for everyone here.

I spoke my first words. I addressed the dearly beloved, the family of the deceased, I mentioned his wife and daughters by name. "On this tragic day," I said. "A loyal employee on whom I could always count." It went well, it went smoothly, I was not quite on automatic pilot, not entirely, but whenever I stick to a certain pace then one sentence almost seems to trigger the next. I'm what people call a "gifted speaker," there's no reason to feign modesty about that. I always find the right tone, even at the funeral of a grown man who blackmails his employer with a length of rope and then, when he is laughed at, can't figure out anything else to do but carry through with his threat. I noticed it happening this time too; the chapel was quieter than it had been yet today, there had been more coughing during the earlier speeches, more shifting about in the pews. I saw it happen right in front of me, a man raised his hand to his mouth but didn't dare to cough. They were all wide awake. It isn't every day that you get to be present at a speech from the mayor. A politician with a nationally famous face. But you have mayors and then you have mayors, you have politicians and then you have politicians: most of them will bore you to tears. Anyone who has tried to follow a parliamentary debate knows how bad it can be. When the current prime minister is speaking, the chambers ring with vicarious embarrassment. Why does he keep on smiling the whole time? Why does he act so jovial when he really isn't? Who is he trying to fool with his boyish behavior? I have, as I said before, seen my own speeches, or snippets of them, on the nightly news any number of times. Don't get me wrong, I'm not a narcissist. I also feel a certain embarrassment when I see myself standing at a lectern. That lock of hair behind my left ear is sticking up just a little too much; someone, my secretary for example — my city manager! — should have warned me about that. My posture is perhaps a little stooped, I probably look a little too angry — but I stand my ground. People listen to me attentively. There were no scraps of paper or crib sheets on the lectern, I looked straight at the audience the whole time, talked off the top of my head. Not too hurriedly, not as though I wanted to get out of there as quickly as possible, and not too slowly, either, not so that the listeners started yawning one by one and sneaked a glance at their watches or telephones. No, for as long as it lasted I commanded their full attention. And I never go on too long. I know when to stop. You have people who love to hear themselves talk, preferably for as long as possible. They have no sense of their audience's attention span.

And then suddenly, without warning, I remembered the brief conversation I'd had with my city manager just a week prior. What else was I supposed to say, when he clicked open that satchel and took out the rope? What could I have said? *Hans, listen, it's not all that bad, a little money and a couple of iPads and phones. If you pay it all back and return the stuff, we'll forget about it.* But that was precisely what I didn't want. It was the combination of the worn brown satchel, the unmistakably brand-new rope, and Hans van Wezel's imploring, canine look — the look of a dog that hopes it will be the one the visitor to the pound takes home, and not the dog in the next kennel. "Put that rope away, you idiot! I won't let myself be blackmailed with a rope! Please, Hans, do me a favor, get out of my sight and never come back."

And that's what he had done. He had taken my words to heart, and never came back again.

It was possible, I thought. I could do it. It would come as a relief to everyone, not least of all the family. After the initial shock they could come to terms, as they say, with the planned death of their husband and father. After the dismay would come the rage. And then, probably, closure. *Maybe we're ultimately better off without the kind of idiot who hangs himself for a couple hundred euros and a few stray phones and iPads.* I hope you're satisfied with your decision, I thought. I hope you're somewhere and can see what you've caused.

But I kept my mouth shut. For the first time during my speech, I sought eye contact with my wife. Perhaps not because I actually needed to see her, but because I suddenly remembered telling her yesterday that I wanted to see a familiar face in the crowd.

It took me a couple more seconds to realize that she was no longer in the chapel. At least not at the same spot where she'd been a few minutes earlier — that was my first, optimistic thought, but I couldn't immediately locate her anywhere else. Automatically, I looked at the back row, the pew closest to the exit.

Alderman Van Hoogstraten wasn't in his seat either. Fast as lightning, I scanned each row. Every face. But not a single one of them belonged to my wife or to the alderman.

I began to wind things down. "We'll always remember our Hans as a particularly pleasant and conscientious colleague." The doors of the chapel opened, leaf-filtered sunlight fell on the gravel walkway. The gravediggers raised the coffin to their shoulders. My secretary popped up, to the left of me. "Lovely," she said. "Very good."

Birds warbled, white clouds floated across a blue sky. I put on my sunglasses and looked over my shoulder, but my wife was nowhere. The alderman, too, seemed to have vanished. I pulled my cell phone out of my pocket.

Where are you? I typed.

I was just about to send the text when I saw that I had two unread messages.

Sweetheart, Diana asked what was taking so long. She's waiting for me down at the Bijenkorf, the whole thing's dragging along so slowly here. I hope you don't mind. You were good. X

The second message had been sent less than a minute later.

Too good. That man was an asshole. See you tonight. X

8

It was on a weekday in mid-February, around one in the afternoon, when I felt the phone vibrate in my pocket. I had just stopped by Van Dobben for a liver-and-salt-beef sandwich and their "special" (tartar, hardboiled egg, onions, and a glop of mayonnaise on a soft white bun), and now I was crossing Rembrandtplein, on my way back to city hall.

Dad, I read on the display.

For about three seconds I considered not answering it, but I did anyway.

He came straight to the point. "Have you got anything going tomorrow?"

"All kinds of things," I said. "The usual end-to-end. So what is it?"

"I wanted to ask you to come with me and pick out a grave."

"A grave?"

"I saw this beautiful cemetery," he said. "In Ouderkerk aan de Amstel. But your mother doesn't want to go. 'What do I care where I am when I'm dead,' she says. You know how your mother is."

There were all kinds of things I could have said. I could have said that I was way too busy tomorrow. An obvious question would have been why this couldn't wait until the weekend. On the other hand, I can't deny that my curiosity was piqued. Never in his long life had my father talked about a grave or anything that had to do with dying. Being buried or being cremated: I can't remember the subject ever coming up.

"Tomorrow, early in the afternoon?" I said. "Shall I pick you up around two?"

One of my strong points is that I always know by heart most of my appointments for the next three or four days. Tomorrow at two I was scheduled for a visit to a scandal-stricken day care center.

"No, I'll swing by and pick you up," my father said. "Make sure you're on the square at two. I can't stop there for very long."

I wanted to object but couldn't come up with anything that fast. In the last five years, I had tried to reduce to a bare minimum the time I spent in the passenger seat beside my father. But it didn't matter anymore, he had already hung up.

Ouderkerk wasn't all that far away —

somehow this felt more like a plea than a reassurance.

Sunlight was flashing on the water the next afternoon as we drove out of town past the old windmill and the statue of Rembrandt kneeling in the grass with his sketchbook, along the narrow two-lane road beside the Amstel. It was, as I've said, mid-February, but it felt like spring — *the warmest February days since 1914,* I remembered hearing on the news the night before.

"What's that truck doing there?" my father asked; he had slowed for a curve, now he leaned up over the wheel and was squinting through the windshield, like someone trying to read the small print at the bottom of a contract.

I followed his gaze, but the only thing on the road in front of us was a group of cyclists. I was just about to tell him that there wasn't any truck, but he had already accelerated and passed the cyclists without knocking even one of them into the ditch.

"When are you supposed to go in for that physical, to renew your license?" I asked him, after letting about a minute go by in silence.

"What do you mean?" he said. "Why are you asking me that? You think I'm too old to drive a car?"

I decided not to answer him, to let him come up with it himself.

"End of June," he said at last. "That's why your mother and I are going to the South of France this spring, one last time. For the last time."

"The last time? What do you mean, the last time?"

"What's that sign say? How fast are you allowed to go here anyway? Sixty? Eighty?"

"Fifty."

He breathed a deep sigh. "I know, buddy. I can't read the signs anymore. I'll never pass that exam. In June they're going to take my license away. But I've never been in an accident. Never in my whole life. When I drive through a town, I slow to fifty. Out on the road I never drive faster than a hundred and twenty. It's the bureaucracy. Old people, they strip us of everything, one thing at a time. The subtext is clear enough: Please, drop dead, you're only getting in the way. You're taking up space a young person could use."

"But why did you say 'the last time'? You two can take the train to the South of France, can't you? Or fly? Why not just start flying now, instead of driving the whole twelve hundred kilometers?"

We were stopped at a light; when it turned green, my father's car didn't move. I was about to warn him, but at that moment someone behind us started honking.

"All right already!" he shouted, twisting his arm around to give the man the finger. "What's the big deal? You in such a hurry to get someplace where nobody wants to see you anyway, dickhead?"

Without using his blinker, he turned left over a bridge and then left again right away on the other side — again without using his blinker. He moved his face back up close to the windshield.

"It must be here somewhere. Past those houses, I think."

"So why did you just say 'for the last time'?"

"What?"

"What you just said: that this spring will be the last time you and Mama go to the South of France. I don't think you meant the last time by car, I think you really meant the last time."

"Here. This is it."

He pulled over to the right. I noticed that he tried to do it nonchalantly, but the front wheel hit something, a curb or some other obstacle, and we came to a halt beside a big tree — so close to it that there was no way I could open my door.

"When the summer's over, we're going to cash in our chips," my father said. "Your mother and I. We've been talking about it for a long time, and it seems like the best solution. So we're going to do everything one last time. Go to the South of France, have dinner at the Amstel Hotel, we've drawn up a whole list of things. In May I'll turn ninety-five. That's going to be my last birthday. I want to talk to you about that too. That we should make something special out of it. The whole family, a restaurant, something extra maybe, a boat ride, don't ask me, something everyone will remember later on. After that we pull the plug. Not right away. In September or October. Autumn, a nice time of year for a double funeral. In any case, before the Christmas holidays, at least then we won't have to go through that misery again. Luckily, our final Christmas is already behind us."

"But why, for Christ's sake? You're both in perfect health."

I tried the car door, but couldn't open it farther than ten centimeters or so.

"Which is why it's precisely the right moment," he said. "We've both lived our lives. We've had great lives. So why finish that off in a nursing home? Why let things get to

90

the point where the nurses have to help you take a shit? If you actually happen to make it all the way to the pot. All that misery, pal, I don't even want to think about it. And to be frank: as far as this goes, we've been thinking mostly of ourselves, but you should also stop and think what it can mean for you. For you and Sylvia. No needy, demented parents you have to go and visit every Sunday afternoon. No father who shits his pants during Christmas dinner, no mother who doesn't even recognize you anymore. Because that's where it's headed. Your mother is only a little forgetful these days, but those are only the first signs. Try to imagine what a load off your minds that would be. And what a lovely finale: a big, bang-up birthday party. And a couple of months later, a funeral. Nobody even has to cry. 'They lived a wonderful life,' write that one down already for your speech. 'They lived life the way it should be lived, right up till the end.' "

I protested a little — for form's sake, I admit; I told him a couple of times that it was a ridiculous plan, that they might live to be a hundred without seeing their health decline; but from the very start I couldn't deny that it sounded like an attractive idea

91

to me. A life without parents. Orphaned at sixty.

"What is it?" my father asked.

"I can't open my door," I said.

In the weeks just before this I had acted as normal as possible — as far as the situation allowed. I had vowed not to let it show, or at least not to ask any direct questions.

It was a lot harder than I'd figured. I had to be careful not to act *too* normal, because that would definitely arouse suspicion — from my wife, primarily; my daughter was another matter.

"Did you two have any luck?" I asked Diana the evening after Hans van Wezel's funeral. She was lying on the couch, her notebook on her lap, she had to take off her headphones first.

"What did you say?"

"I asked whether you two had any luck this afternoon. Buying clothes. Did you guys buy anything? At the Bijenkorf?"

"Mama was late. They were almost closed. It didn't matter. I was tired. We're going to go again next Thursday, then they do late-night shopping."

I could hear my wife in the kitchen: the sounds of clattering plates and cups — she was filling the dishwasher. *How late was she?*

I could have asked my daughter. *What time was it when Mama got to the Bijenkorf?* But I didn't. Ask no questions that might seem overly inquisitive. *What does it matter what time it was? How should I know?* I counted back. What time had it been when the grave-diggers raised the city manager's coffin to their shoulders? What time had I started in on my speech? My daughter put on her headphones again.

In any case, it wasn't like the *whole* story was made up, I thought with a certain amount of relief. My wife really had agreed to meet Diana at the Bijenkorf. But how much time had passed between my daughter's phone call or text message and the moment, just before closing time, when Sylvia actually arrived at the department store?

An hour? Half an hour? Had my wife and Alderman Van Hoogstraten spent that half hour French kissing, somewhere behind one of the big trees? I tried to picture it, but only half succeeded. The alderman was at least a foot taller than Sylvia, he took her face in his hands, his lips approached hers . . .

I tried to stop my imagination at that point, but by then the image was more powerful than I was. I kept looking, I couldn't take my eyes off it, the way you'll

93

watch open-heart surgery or an eye operation on TV, even though you know you shouldn't, the remote in your hand, your thumb on the button, ready to zap away, but you wait too long: the shot of the sawed-open rib cage, the surgeon's hands in their green plastic gloves holding the throbbing heart, the white eyeball hanging out of its socket, attached to the head by only a few bloody threads, will remain tattooed on your retinas for the rest of your life.

I saw hands fumbling beneath clothes. First only a coat, but then in the opening between two buttons of a shirt. Fingers — a woman's fingers — behind a belt, the shirt-tail half out of the trousers, a button popping; the fingertips — the nails — tickled the downy growth below the navel and then went down farther.

"What is it?" Diana asked.

I looked at my daughter; she had pulled her headphones up off one ear.

"Nothing," I said.

She sighed.

"You said something," she said.

I kept looking at her. I tried to smile. "No, really, I didn't."

"But I heard you, really I did." She shook her head, then slid her headphones back down and returned to her notebook.

■ ■ ■ ■

I went undercover in my own home. From behind my newspaper, I kept a close watch on my wife. I let my gaze glide over the articles, but I read nothing, only made sure I turned the pages every now and again. At the most natural pace possible. I was a plainclothes cop, the head of a family who had assumed the guise of a head of a family, who had adopted the appearance and behavior of a loving husband and father. It was a role that didn't differ essentially from the one I had been playing in this family for years. But from the New Year's reception on, and particularly after the city manager's funeral, it became a role. It no longer went automatically; I had to make sure I played it to the hilt, so you couldn't tell it from the real thing.

"When do your exams start?" I asked my daughter. "Monday, right?"

"What am I tasting?" I asked my wife as I chewed on a meatball; Sylvia's meatballs, made according to a recipe from her home country, from her own region, were one of my daughter's and my favorite dishes. "Mustard, or some kind of spice?"

I had to be careful, in other words, not to

play my role with too much pizzazz, not to lay it on too thick. Sometimes I caught myself on the verge of becoming just a little bit too much of a wonderful head of the family. Too attentive. Too interested. A father with an above-average interest in his daughter's social and academic life. A husband who tries to give his wife her way in everything. I knew why I was doing it: my senses were stretched to the limit, I saw and heard everything. From the tiniest shifts in my wife's behavior, I was trying to deduce whether my worst fears were based in the truth.

Yes, that's how it felt: as though everything was wide open. Not only my eyes and ears, but my taste, smell, and tactile functions also seemed poised to register even the slightest nuance. The sensation that accompanied eating a piece of chocolate was almost painfully intense. I stuck my nose in our cat's fur as it sat purring in my lap, and I knew for a certainty that I was smelling things I'd never smelled before: grass, flowers, earth — the odors the cat picked up as she wandered through the gardens behind our house. Everything I touched seemed electrically charged. It used to be that I sometimes got a shock when letting go of a metal door handle or the back of a chair;

now sparks flew even when I picked up a pen or a coffee cup.

Whenever I heard the ringtone of Sylvia's phone, I turned down the TV. I used to do that, too, but only to be accommodating. Now I did it mostly to hear who was calling. I had to watch out not to appear more attentive than I normally was, not to turn down the TV even lower than I used to.

Before the New Year's reception, before the city manager's funeral, I had not only been attentive but also grouchy and preoccupied at times; I had not always focused my full attention on the things my wife and daughter said or asked. I had listened with half an ear, nodded a few times by way of an answer, often realizing only too late that, had one of them insisted, I couldn't have told them what they'd just said.

But now I was no longer preoccupied. It was physically impossible for me to simulate a dreamy, vacant look. I tried to, by thinking about other things, but just as I had once tended to let my mind wander, now I was unable to do that — unable to pretend that my thoughts were elsewhere.

It started becoming obvious. "What's with the look?" my daughter would ask sometimes. "What do you mean, what look?" I asked. "You know, the way you just looked," she said.

And she was right. While brushing my teeth at night, I could see it with my own eyes. My look in the mirror could only be described as *intense.* Because of that, I no longer dared to look directly at my wife when I slipped into bed beside her at night. For fear that she would see it too.

"G'night," I would say, and quickly turn off my reading light. And right away I would ask myself whether I had ever, in the past — the very recent past, the past of only a few weeks back — turned off my reading light so quickly. Probably not, but the worst of it was that I wasn't entirely sure.

In the dark, I waited for the question I feared most. *Is something wrong?* Or was that, in fact, the last thing she would ask, because she was every bit as guilty as I imagined? And how would I respond to that question?

Mostly silence, though, was what came from her side of our bed. Sometimes she would read a little; at other times, after only a few minutes, I would hear her regular breathing shift into the quiet, reassuring snore that I had never, in almost thirty years of marriage, found irritating. Only endearing.

So I lay with my eyes open in the dark,

and came to the hideous conclusion that her snoring no longer sounded reassuring. That it was anything but reassuring. And then on to the even more hideous realization that it might never sound reassuring again.

"Never again," I whispered aloud, in spite of myself, and I felt my eyes sting.

Only when the first beams of morning light fell through a crack in the curtains did I finally fall asleep.

9

I was born in this city. Amsterdam, of course, is not a real city, except in the eyes of people from outside. We, the ones who were born here, immediately recognize the provincial from the way he moves, the way he walks, the way he holds his head. The man from the provinces who thinks he's ended up in a real city. He walks as though he were in Paris or Rome. He admires his reflection in the store windows and congratulates himself on his decision to exchange his provincial life for a stay in this city, which is not a real city at all.

That is how he sits at the sidewalk cafés, how he eats in the restaurants (always, and without exception, the wrong restaurants), how he strolls through the museums, visits the movies and the plays at the municipal theater: as though he has freed himself from the mud-and-manure pong of his native village, from the chains of a petty existence.

"I'll never go back there again!" he declares resolutely — but a man from the provinces in Amsterdam is like the prisoner who digs a tunnel only to discover that, instead of outside the penitentiary walls, it surfaces in the exercise yard. Amsterdam is a toy city, a ball pit for grown-ups, an open-air museum that exhibits traditional arts and crafts.

I could take the easy way out and say that it was mostly his accent that gave Alderman Van Hoogstraten away. But that would indeed be too easy. After all, my wife's accent gave her away too. You had people who started talking more loudly as soon as they heard her accent, as though they automatically assumed she must be deaf, or retarded. The same loud tone that ambulance personnel use when addressing an old lady along the highway. *Can you still hear me, ma'am? Hello, ma'am? How many fingers am I holding up?*

Whatever the case, it remained a strange and wondrous thing to hear Alderman Van Hoogstraten say something about Amsterdammers in a speech. Especially about Amsterdammers who included himself. "We Amsterdammers," he would say, for example — but the way he pronounced "Amsterdammers" reminded you more of pitchforks, pigs, and rubber boots in the mud. On the nightly news, people with accents less pronounced than his were subtitled often enough.

The alderman acted like a little boy visiting the big city for the first time. He had moved here about five years earlier, but still couldn't believe his eyes. He went on being amazed at all the neon signs, the number of motor scooters — he still jumped every time a tram screeched through a curve. At the same time, you could see how pleased he was with himself, that he had left the barnyard and the village pump behind and actually dared to sit at an outdoor café in this big city.

Why does someone cheat on their partner? Out of lust; for the sake of variety; because the opportunity presents itself. I crossed lust off the list right away. Even I, a man after all, the injured male party, the cuckold, could summon up enough objectivity to see that the alderman was no lust object.

What does Maarten van Hoogstraten have that I don't? Only a few weeks earlier, if someone had suggested I ask myself that, I would have said they were insane.

I wonder if — no, I know for a fact that I wouldn't have minded as much if my wife had started something with an American movie star. With Brad Pitt or Ryan Gosling. Matthew McConaughey? Or someone a little more her own age: George Clooney. Or ten, twenty years older, what do I care: Jack Nicholson, Clint Eastwood, Sean Connery. That would have been easier to accept, because each of those men is objectively, demonstrably better-looking than I am. More glamorous. In some ways, it would have been more to her detriment than to mine. She's trying to move up in the world, people would have said, being the wife of the mayor of Amsterdam apparently isn't enough for her.

But Maarten van Hoogstraten, no matter how you looked at it, was a few giant steps back. Less attractive, on the sliding scale of male attractiveness, than I was. In every way, in terms of both status and physical appearance.

What's more, the alderman stood for everything my wife despised. Normally speaking, she joked about people like him, or even laughed right in their faces. Maarten van Hoogstraten was a staunch environmentalist. He sincerely believed in global warming. And he was so passionate about it that he tried not to travel by plane. Whenever possible, he would pick a holiday destination you could get to by train.

"But what do you actually think?" I asked him one time. "Do you think the airlines are really going to change their itineraries because they know you're not on that flight or something? That they're going to say: *Let's cancel that route, Maarten van Hoogstraten is taking the train?*"

He didn't appreciate that at all. He tried to laugh it off a bit — it was right after the Monday council meeting and we were standing around with a little group in the coffee corner, but I could tell right away that it bothered him.

"Well, but if everyone thought about it the way I do, there really would be a lot fewer flights," he said.

Since when had my wife been able to stand the company of humorless men for more than ten minutes? The story about the rabbit and the chewed cable didn't seriously count as humor, did it? Maarten van Hoogstraten was an advocate of windmills. He wanted to ruin the whole Amsterdam skyline with those feeble sails on a stick. The urban planners on the project had played it smart. The whole thing was put together in a way that you could barely get an objection in edgewise. No turbines in residential neighborhoods or too close to buildings, no, all of it out at the edge: along the IJsselmeer, in Amsterdam-Noord, out along the ring road on the south side. The result, though, was that the windmills would be the first thing you saw as you came into Amsterdam. Just when we were off to such a good start creating a real skyline. A miniature skyline, true enough, but still. No self-respecting city could let itself be surrounded by windmills, not if you ask me.

Maarten van Hoogstraten believed in organic meat, he made a huge detour just to buy all his meat at an organic butcher shop, he didn't know yet that the organic meat myth had been debunked long ago. Organic meat was a direct appeal to the meat-eater's guilt feelings. But there was a price tag attached.

Since when had my wife been able to stand, for more than ten minutes, the company of men who used no deodorant because it's better for the environment? Because of the much-vaunted ozone layer. I'm not stupid, I'm perfectly aware that aerosols affect the ozone layer, but that's no reason to make the people in your immediate surroundings — your own biotope — suffer from an armpit odor most reminiscent of a stagnant pond full of dead frogs. I'm sure he used something: a deo-stick or roller from the health food store, a fragrance based on algae, seaweed, and ground sunflower seeds, but whatever it was, it wasn't very long-lasting. By the time lunch break came around, Maarten van Hoogstraten had already started stinking of himself. The greenhouse effect began with him.

That's what had always annoyed me most about the alderman: he had left his farming village for the big city, but he brought the countryside along with him. The windmills. The happy free-range pigs, rolling around in the mud. His own barnyard odor.

Last Thursday night, after a meeting that ran late, we went with a few aldermen, including Van Hoogstraten, for a nightcap at Café Schiller.

It's tiring to be the obvious pivot in almost every group. The motor behind every conversation. I know that sounds arrogant, but it's just my day-to-day reality. I've tested it often enough to know it's true. In all different kinds of company I have, at some random moment, suddenly stopped talking. At first the other people don't notice, they go on talking for a while as though nothing was wrong. But the conversation itself starts acting like a plane that suddenly runs out of fuel at high altitude. The engines fall silent, the aircraft begins its nosedive, the crash is inevitable. The people look at each other; occasionally they also steal a look at me. The silences between the sentences grow longer and longer. Then the first of them shrugs, looks at his phone, and announces that it's about time for him to turn in. Another one glances at his half-empty glass and takes a quick slug. A third one acts as though he's feeling cold and blows into his hands to warm them. But that's actually the way it is: they really do feel cold. For a while they have warmed themselves at the fire of my presence, my words; the motor that keeps the conversation running all by itself. It's as though they're standing around a campfire that went out without anyone noticing.

On the rare occasion, I've put it to the ultimate test. No more than rarely, because usually I'm relieved when people get tired of my company and go looking for entertainment elsewhere. In the ultimate test, I also take one last sip from my glass. I look around, as though I'm searching for new faces; the others have already started to turn their backs on me, by the count of three they will start to leave. I count to three. *One . . . two . . . three.* And then I suddenly say something. A belated comment that no one saw coming. "A city like Amsterdam shouldn't even want to have windmills," I say.

They've all remained standing; the ones who had turned away now make a half-turn back. I have to do my best not to grin, I see it happening before my eyes, how they look at me expectantly. They don't say anything, all they do is look.

"Windmills don't belong in a real city," I say, half a second before the silence has time to become painful. But even that's not completely true: no silence is painful in the presence of a strong personality like myself. The strong personality can let the silence go on as long as he wants; there is no one, after all, who dares to break it. Sssh, don't say anything, he's probably deep in thought.

That's the way it is. I am the prime mover behind the conversation. Every conversation. At Café Schiller I put it to the acid test again. Halfway through the conversation, I suddenly fell silent. From one moment to the next, I stopped talking completely, no more than a "yes" or a "no" when someone asked me something. After only a few minutes, they started shifting uneasily in their chairs. Their person-to-person chatting died out too. Every once in a while, they looked furtively at me. "Everything okay, Robert?" the boldest of them asked. "Are you sick?"

"No, I feel fine," I replied. "What could be wrong?"

No new round was ordered. One by one they got up, went to the bar to pay their part of the tab, then left. "Bye." "Bye." "Hey!" "See you on Monday." "Hope you're feeling better." That last farewell came from Alderman Hawinkels, the same alderman who had asked if I was feeling all right. I pictured them unlocking their bikes outside the café. Pictured them clustering together on the sidewalk for a moment. *What was with him all of a sudden? Is he sick? Aw, don't worry about it too much, he's probably just tired. The end of the week. You'll see: Monday he'll be right as rain.*

I thought about Alderman Van Hoogstraten. Would he look more concerned than the others? Would he have ideas of his own about my behavior? *Maybe he suspects something, maybe that's why he's so quiet . . .* While still biking home he would call my wife, or send her a text message. *I need to talk to you as soon as possible. I think he knows. About us.* A few moments of inattention would do it. His front tire would end up in the tram rails. The approaching taxi he would see only too late. At the funeral my wife would wear sunglasses, but at last I

109

would know where I stood. You can keep an extramarital affair under wraps for a long time, but sorrow is a lot tougher, it oozes its way out through every pore.

The following night, Sylvia and I had a fight. Not a little fight; we always skipped the gradual mobilization — the threats to neighboring powers, the cancellation of all furloughs, the summoning of reservists. From one moment to the next we face off, armed to the teeth. I can't remember what it was about. We'd had dinner at the little Chinese restaurant close to our house, the one we go to whenever we don't want to run into anyone. The place is always half empty. A few lonely diners, the occasional older couple. No lowered voices, no nudging each other when the mayor comes in — no pulling out the cell phone and asking to take a selfie with him.

As I worked on my wonton soup and Sylvia cut her *siu mai* into little pieces (a habit that I, according to my mood at the moment, find either annoying or endearing — in any case, a habit that could never cause a fight), everything was still clear skies and smooth sailing. Literally clear skies and smooth sailing, like on the afternoon before Pearl Harbor, the evening before the Six-Day War, the brilliant, cloudless morning of

September 11. No one's being mobilized. No suspicious troop movements have been detected. The element of surprise is the connecting factor here. By the time the marines come barreling out of their barracks, most of them still in their pajamas, some with their razors still in hand, shaving cream still stuck to their faces, the huge flagships of the U.S. fleet are already ablaze or have already sunk. What exactly happened between the time that the waitress cleared the table after the main dish (shrimp with Chinese mushrooms for Sylvia, *char siu* for me) and the moment that we paid the bill, I have no idea. A teensy mood shift as we walked home. A barely perceptible change in atmospheric pressure, as with an approaching blizzard or thunderstorm. A slight pressure at the back of the eyes: the harbinger of a splitting headache.

"What exactly did you mean by that?" Sylvia asked cuttingly. Maybe we'd been talking about Diana. Not about her new boyfriend, because Sylvia liked him. More like something about school or the quantity of alcohol Diana consumed during a weekend. My wife and I feel differently about that. On both counts, my opinions are a bit more liberal. So maybe it was about our daughter, but then again maybe not; it didn't really matter. The fact of the matter was that we made no real effort to keep our voices down as we crossed Rembrandtplein. By that point, we were already walking ten feet apart. Every once in a while my wife tried to walk faster, to cut me off, but then I picked up my own pace and caught up with her again. Then I did the same thing. I took such giant steps that within a few seconds I had left her twenty yards behind me. But when I turned my head as discreetly as possible, to catch a glimpse of her from the corner of my eye, I saw that she was making absolutely no attempt to catch up.

"Yeah, run away, coward!" she shouted right then. "Go on, run away again! That's what you always do when it gets too complicated, run away."

I stopped. I turned around and stuck my hands deep into the pockets of my raincoat, and I balled my fists. A few passersby had stopped too. A taxi coming from Reguliersdwarsstraat slowed; the driver rolled down his window and said something to my wife. "Keep moving, you!" she yelled. "Mind your own business!" I wondered whether anyone had recognized us yet. It wouldn't be too hard for someone to pull out his phone and film us. And then sell that film to the tabloids, for good money.

One evening, years ago, we'd had dinner at Sluizer on Utrechtsestraat. Out of the blue, with no warning, I felt the blood drain out of my face. I told my wife that I was going outside, I was afraid I wouldn't make it to the toilet in time, that I would barf all over our table. I edged my way past the tables. Conversations stopped, heads turned tactfully. I was probably moving too fast, I realized then. And despite the onrush of nausea and the dizzy feeling in my head, I had stood up too quickly. Outside, in the fresh air, I came to my senses quickly enough. I crossed the bridge to the Keizersgracht, unbuttoned my coat, and pressed my stomach against the cold metal of the railing. I took a few deep breaths as I stared down, at a couple of ducks floating there beside a half-sunken sloop. After about ten minutes I went back to the restaurant.

Then, a little less than a week later, during dinner with a good friend at another restaurant, the whole thing started. The good friend asked whether things were all right with us. *With the two of you,* he clarified, looking around and lowering his voice. With my wife and me, our relationship. He had heard something, maybe it was all a load of crap, but he thought it was better to check with me first. Two days later, it happened again. A reception at the Hilton. A friend of a friend, no more than a casual acquaintance really. "Everything okay?" the presumptuous acquaintance asked. "With you and the wife? No, it was just that I heard something. Something about a fight in a restaurant."

By this time, we were almost back at the house. And we were also walking next to each other again, albeit with five feet between us. In silence. I still had my hands in the pockets of my raincoat; Sylvia, intentionally or no — a soft rain had begun to fall — was holding her open umbrella right above her head, so I couldn't see her face.

At the front door we went on grumbling a bit. I stuck the key in the lock. My wife said something about how bullheaded I was, that I could never admit to being wrong, or words to that effect. Then we were standing in the entryway. I turned on the light. Sylvia closed her umbrella. Inside, in the entryway, our fight was suddenly over, like a storm from sea that peters out as it moves inland.

"That's not true," I said. "It's not true that I never admit it when I'm wrong."

"See, there you go again!" my wife said.

And then we both had to laugh; still with our coats on, we hugged each other, awkwardly at first but then with growing conviction.

"What in the world was that all about?" Sylvia said; through the cloth of my raincoat I could feel her fingers massaging my back.

"Don't ask me," I said; I tried to do something with my fingers, too, but her coat was too thick, so I pressed her against me even harder.

It was true: I had absolutely no idea anymore. The cause and course of our bickering were fading fast already, and as I followed her up the stairs, I couldn't help but smile.

What, after all, could this fight mean, other than that we still cared about each other? That my wife cared about me, I should say. Only uncaring couples stop fighting completely. At most, they sigh deeply, or roll their eyes meaningfully when the other starts to talk.

10

At this point, I should tell you about the Jericho — just so it doesn't pop up later in the story entirely unannounced. The Jericho is a 9mm pistol of Israeli provenance. There was a period, I hadn't been mayor for very long at the time, when this city seemed to be going off the deep end. A hit list had been drawn up, they said. If you were on a list like that, you couldn't be sure you were going to live to see the next day. I remember the emergency briefing with the police chief and the district attorney. A number of national politicians and prominent figures were in trouble. What I remember most clearly about that meeting was the thinly concealed disappointment on the faces of the DA and the police chief when they found out they weren't on the list. *Why him, why not us?* That's what I read in their expressions. *So aren't we important enough?* In the weeks that followed I saw that same disappointment on a number of faces, on a number of occasions. We'd had to promise, of course, not to reveal the names on the death list, but someone forgot to tell the press. They hadn't counted on *De Telegraaf.* Less than twenty-four hours after the triad met in my office, the whole list was published on their front page. Then I saw even more disappointed faces. The death list formed a clear parting of the waters between those who mattered in this country and those who were apparently so insignificant that they could be left alive. Seeing my own name on the list, I can't deny, had precisely that effect on me. *I matter,* I thought to myself. *I've become a target.*

I was given round-the-clock protection. A police cabin on stilts was erected in front of our house. For the first few months, four bodyguards went with me everywhere. Later that was reduced to two. Whenever I went out to dinner, we had to reserve two tables. Sometimes the hit-listers would run into one another; on the far side of the dining room, a national politician might have reserved two tables as well. We would nod to each other amiably from a distance, but often enough we couldn't help smiling. *We matter,* we said to each other with that smile. *We belong to the select group of twenty*

Dutch people who have to reserve two tables at a restaurant.

And then, suddenly, there was the Jericho. I was given my first target practice at the naval grounds behind the Maritime Museum. "For situations when you have only yourself to rely on," they told me. "It will probably never happen, but imagine they succeed in neutralizing all four bodyguards, then you can't be standing there empty-handed." Without meaning to sound swanky, I had an aptitude for it, for aiming and firing a pistol. "You're a good shot," my instructor said after the very first lesson. We practiced on sheets of cardboard with the outline of a person drawn on them with a fat black marker. "We're not out for Sunday brunch here," the instructor said. "We don't aim for the legs, we're not out to just injure someone. Imagine: There are four attackers. You have six bullets. That means you're allowed to miss twice. We aim all six shots at the head and at the heart."

I can't deny it, I got a kick out of the shooting lessons. The heft of the Jericho in my hand — I had never held a pistol before, and it was a lot heavier than I'd thought. And then the instruction to keep the barrel pointed at the ground once you'd removed the safety. But the best thing of all, really, was the shooting itself. The report. The recoil. Something that's more powerful than you are. I couldn't escape the impression that the Jericho had a life of its own, that it was trying to free itself from my grasp every time I fired.

After a few clips of six bullets each, I asked whether I could take out the earplugs.

"Why?" the instructor asked with a smile.

"Because in real life I probably won't have time to put in earplugs," I said. "I don't want it to take me by surprise. I want to know what it sounds like."

After that first lesson I lay in bed with my ears ringing, the same way they had rung long ago after a concert at Paradiso or the Milky Way. Afterward, my instructor congratulated me on my request to take out the earplugs. Most people never did that, he said. He showed me the cardboard sheets with the human silhouettes and pointed out the bullet holes. "Not bad for the first time," he said. "With six bullets, no one would have survived this. In the next couple of weeks, we're going to perfect that. In the end, each and every shot has to hit the head or the heart."

The day after our fight (and two days after the late-night beers with the aldermen at

Café Schiller), I was reminded of the Jericho as I took a leisurely bike ride down to the Maritime Museum, where a reception was being held for the French president, François Hollande. It was probably being so close to the naval grounds again that made the pistol cross my mind. Times had changed, the bodyguards were gone. For years, the Jericho had been lying idly in the bottom drawer of my desk. Empty. Every once in a while I opened that drawer and the loose bullets would roll with a hard metallic sound, like ball bearings, across the bottom.

François Hollande is not a big man. And even with the best will in the world, you couldn't call him attractive. I am a head taller than him. I felt for him. I have a couple of friends who are taller than me. I know how tiring it can be to have to spend a whole conversation looking up at someone. As though you're admiring frescoes on the ceiling. It doesn't feel right. The cramp in your neck and the feeling — which can never entirely be dismissed — that you're somehow less than the person to whom fate granted more height.

Our prime minister held a short speech. Then there was a stand-up buffet. That is to say: the usual snacks were spread out on a long table. Blocks of cheese, liverwurst — the slices of herring were served with the obligatory toothpicks with a little Dutch flag on them. Young men and women walked around with serving trays. Glasses of orange juice, water, red and white wine, the odd glass of flat beer.

After the prime minister's speech, François Hollande looked around. I saw fatigue in his eyes, boredom — he had already spent a whole morning in the company of the prime minister. During that brief, empty moment when no one seemed to be paying him any heed, I walked up to him.

I looked around to see if there was somewhere we could sit, but all the chairs were taken. And then there was my French. Which is, to put it mildly, no great shakes. English was out of the question. Like most French people, I suspected, François Hollande almost certainly spoke no language but his own.

I started off with the usual things. Whether he'd had time to see a bit of Amsterdam? Whether he had ever been here before? In Amsterdam? In the Netherlands? They were the questions you might ask any visitor or tourist you came across. *Did you find what you were looking for?* popped into my mind. *"C'est la première fois que vous êtes à Am-*

sterdam?" My French was up to that much, at least, but then François Hollande said something back that I didn't understand. I decided not to ask what he meant (*Quoi? Comment?*), not this early in the game, but simply to act as though I'd understood. *"Oui, oui, oui,"* I said, a bit too readily and a little too quickly. The French president looked at me questioningly for a moment; the wrinkles of a slight frown formed on his forehead. *"Ah, oui?"* he said then, pointing at the floor with his index finger, at a spot just in front of his shoes. *"C'est intéressant! Ici?"*

I cursed myself and my faulty French. For a moment I thought about Miss Kalb, my French teacher in high school. She was almost seven feet tall, and like all women that size, she was single. Miss Kalb drove a green Renault 4 — probably because it had such a high roof.

What was it that Hollande had asked me? Whether this was the same room where William of Orange had been assassinated? Or if Anne Frank had hid from the Germans in the attic above us? As far as I knew, he might have been asking where the first Huguenot refugees had been hanged, back in 1792. French dates, that was another thing! To start with, you never heard them right the first time, and after that you had to start the arithmetic. *One thousand seven hundred four times twenty and twelve,* the French said without blinking an eye, and then you were supposed to know right away that they meant seventeen hundred and ninety-two.

At that point, a girl came by with a tray full of glasses. My salvation! Red wine, white wine, orange juice, water. First take a glass, then change the subject right away. A little too quickly, I grabbed a glass of red. First of all, that was impolite, but second, I had now missed the opportunity to wait and see what President Hollande would choose — and then accommodate myself to him.

He took a glass of water. *De l'eau!* It was only a little past noon, it's true, but one of the things I've always found so charming about the French is that they never look at the clock before bringing in a carafe of wine. François Hollande took his glass from the tray, cocked his head, and smiled at the girl.

"Merci, mademoiselle," he said.

Then the girl smiled too. She was an extremely Dutch Dutch girl, pretty in the way to which our country holds the patent rights, in a way that ought to make the Dutch nation feel proud. So white, so blonde: creamy white. A full and rosy face that could have figured on a pack of butter.

She was as tall as me, she too looked down on the French president from a height. And she was, as I mentioned, blonde; her hair was tied back, but in a loose way that showed how much hair she really had: it was full and thick, with little curls, held together with an elastic band — at least that's what I assumed, for the elastic itself was hidden from view.

I realized that now — in a moment, once the girl had walked away, and if my French could handle it — I could try a jovial comment. *That's right, Mr. Hollande, they don't make them like that in France!* A comment that was sort of questionable, covered in a thin layer of machismo — but something you should be able to get away with when talking to a president who visited his sweetheart in the middle of the night with a crash helmet on.

The detail about the crash helmet had won me over for François Hollande from the very start. I had seen the pictures. The Dutch newspapers, with the exception of *De Telegraaf,* were much too reticent, so I downloaded a couple of French magazines on my iPad mini. That particular issue of *Closer,* the one that got the whole affair rolling, as well as *Paris Match.* Grainy photos of the president on the back of a motorbike, wearing a regulation helmet, shot from a great distance with a telephoto lens. Anyone who has seen the movie *The Day of the Jackal* knows that all you would have had to do was replace the telephoto lens with a rifle and a telescopic sight, and the French would have had to elect a new president. That was also the general gist of the articles that went with the photos, to the extent that I could follow them: that the president, with his puerile behavior, had placed himself unnecessarily at risk. But it was precisely these details, the explicitly boyish disguise and the even more juvenile mode of transport, that made me identify with François Hollande. He became a boy who snuck out at night with a flashlight, on his way to the girls' dormitory. In *The Day of the Jackal,* the assassin played by Edward Fox practiced on watermelons. He put a melon on a pole and fixed his telescopic sight. The watermelon was not merely punctured by the bullet and knocked off the pole; no, it blew apart completely, there was nothing left of it — that was the way the head of the French president (the movie was set in the time of Charles de Gaulle) would blow apart later on, you kept thinking during the rest of the film.

I looked at François Hollande's head and

raised my glass of red wine. *"Santé!"* I said. We clinked glasses: my wine against the president's water. If this man had been a bank teller, or the floor manager of a super-market, would any woman have turned her head to watch him walk past? No; if ever the eroticizing power of fame had been made manifest, it was here, in the bland face of François Hollande. It wasn't like with Mitterrand, Chirac, or Sarkozy. They were all womanizers, too, but with those three you could easily imagine that they would have gone around chasing women all their lives, even if they hadn't become the presi-dent of France. After seeing the nocturnal telelens photos of François Hollande on the back of the motorbike, I spent a long time looking at those of his sweetheart, Julie Gayet. An actress I'd never heard of before. In the few pictures printed by the Dutch newspapers, she looked fairly normal. Noth-ing special. No Carla Bruni. A normal, not even particularly young woman; exactly the kind of woman you would have imagined at the side of insurance salesman François Hollande. But in *Closer* and *Paris Match,* as well as in the French edition of *Elle* that I had downloaded in the meantime, there were other pictures of Julie Gayet. The photo of the actress on the red carpet at

Cannes, in a red dress with lots of bare back — just above the curve of her rear end you could see a tiny tattoo — made it particularly clear what a stunning beauty she was. There was yet another photo in *Elle,* which the caption said had been taken at the film festival in San Sebastián, in which Julie Gayet was sitting in an old-fashioned chair, probably in some hotel lobby, almost without makeup, in trousers, her legs crossed, wearing sports shoes. She was in her early forties, I knew by then, but in the picture in the hotel lobby she looked no older than twenty-eight. A girl, a very normal girl even, but of a normalcy that would make any boy want to go sneaking off to the girls' dormitory.

And then you had the two pictures that were in almost all the papers. A photograph of a conference hall and an audience, some party congress from the looks of it. François Hollande was sitting in the front row. A little farther along was Ségolène Royal, his ex. It wasn't completely clear which picture had been taken first. In the one, Hollande and Ségolène Royal, four chairs down, are listening attentively; in the other, the French president is looking up at a woman standing in front of him and to one side, with her back to us: Valérie Trierweiler, his girlfriend

— but for how long? Hollande looks ruffled, perhaps even irritated. *What are you doing here? Drawing attention to yourself?* Julie Gayet was also in both pictures. She was sitting two rows back from Hollande. In the one picture she is smiling, in the other she stares pensively into space. If you look closely at the two photos, at the actress's face, at her body language, to the extent you can read body language from a still photo, you see that she's probably just being herself — that above all. Doing her best to be herself, you might say. Meanwhile, though, we all knew that it had been going on for months. That Julie Gayet glanced in the mirror and let her hair down whenever she heard the motorbike on the street below. Maarten van Hoogstraten, too, had acted as normal as he could at the New Year's reception; this was the thought that forced itself on me now. The double-dealers always tried to act as normal as possible, and it was precisely that normalcy that sometimes gave them away.

From our fight the night before, I had drawn the conclusion that my wife still cared about me. Today I realized that this, in itself, didn't necessarily mean anything. Why, after almost thirty years, should Sylvia suddenly stop caring about me? Even if she had a secret affair going with an Amsterdam alderman?

It was at that exact moment, as I felt my face grow hot and my heart grow cold as ice, that François Hollande winked at me. He had turned his head to follow the tall blonde girl with the serving tray, the Dutch butter girl who had walked on and was now standing with her back to us, a few yards away. In that one moment it was not the French president on a state visit to Amsterdam who was winking at me, but the man in the crash helmet, the enamored president who slipped out a back door of his palace at night to pay a secret visit to his lover.

After the wink, he said something in French, something I understood right away this time, but which I won't repeat here, so as not to damage the French president's reputation.

I knew what I had to do. I winked back and I said something too. A comment that wasn't really my style — like a too-flashy article of clothing you put on even though you know better, a leather jacket with too many zippers and shiny press-studs. A comment that could pass muster only when you made it plain as day it was meant ironically . . . and even then, only barely.

François Hollande cocked his head a little

and looked at me. For a moment I thought perhaps he hadn't understood me, but then he started to laugh, raised both hands to his jowls, and pretended he was taking off a crash helmet.

11

The next day, my mother and I met for a late lunch at Oriental City on Damstraat.

"You look tired," she said after we had ordered and handed the menus back to the waitress. "You're not working too hard, are you?" She removed the paper wrapper from her chopsticks, took them between her fingers, and made a few pincer movements. "I'm sorry, Robert, that was a silly question. Of course you're working too hard."

Our table was on the second floor, at the window; sunlight fell at an angle across my mother's face, making her wrinkles look even deeper than normal. I had to admit, my father was right about what he'd said to me a few times in the past: she had indeed "aged beautifully." My mother had never struggled against growing old, she let nature take its course, the way you might decide one day to no longer mow the grass in a garden, to abandon the planters to their

131

own devices and let the ivy go ahead and overrun everything. That's why she now had the kind of face you rarely see on old people these days, especially not on older women. Just old, really old, with no structural alterations. No lifted eyelids that had then started drooping again anyway, no permanently amazed look in the eyes themselves, with pupils dilated to the size of egg yolks floating in ponds of oyster-colored sclera.

The faces of women who had undergone remodeling often had something empty about them; something had been erased for good — as though they had pushed the delete button, so that we can never really read the first (or second, or third) version of their life stories. My mother's face was more like a manuscript or typescript: old, yellowed, with countless strike-throughs and grainy, dried-up Tipp-Ex corrections, from a time when life stories were still written by hand or on typewriters.

A few hairs stuck out of a light-brown mole on her left cheek, and something almost like a downy mustache darkened her upper lip. But still, it was not an untended face. Something silvery shimmered on her eyelids, something that matched the silvery-gray of her hair. That silvery-gray was not her natural color. And that was precisely what gave her such sophistication. Had she chosen dark blonde or brown, the combination with her wrinkled face would have told everyone that it was dyed, the color would have accentuated her age rather than make her look younger. No, it was exactly the opposite: the way a man who is going bald can always shave his head, so my mother looked "younger than her years": years she did not try to muffle away by dying her hair a color that would have been biologically implausible in combination with the landscape of clefts and dry riverbeds that crisscrossed her face these days. "Erosion" was the first word that came to mind when I kissed my mother on her rough and, at the same time, remarkably soft cheeks.

Had the suspicion concerning Alderman Van Hoogstraten and my wife left visible traces on my own face? Could it really be? I asked myself. Traces I myself hadn't noticed, the way everyone who looks in the mirror on a daily basis thinks he hasn't grown any older? Only when we see people at greater intervals do the changes become noticeable. The age, the suddenly visible decline. Or a new pair of spectacles, for that matter. A different hairdo. "Have you lost weight?" we ask. We mean it as a compliment, yet still, caution is advised: the person in question may also have a nasty disease.

I rubbed my eyes, squeezed the bridge of my nose between thumb and middle finger. I knew my mother well enough: if she said I looked tired, I looked tired. There was no use denying it.

"Yes, I really am a little tired," I said. "A hectic schedule. Obama's visit. Then François Hollande. The windmill debate. You know how it goes. You have to play the perfect host. Sometimes that's no effort; other times, it just isn't my day."

"Yes, I know you. You can't hide it, you see it on your face right away. As far as that goes, you're the image of your father."

"So how's he getting along?" I asked, grateful for a chance to change the subject. "I mean, I saw him not so long ago, but I'd like to hear it from you."

I didn't know what I would do if my mother went on asking about my fatigue. *Is everything else all right, at home? With Sylvia? Is Diana getting along well at school?* It wasn't that my mother saw right through me. I wasn't an open book to her, but there was also no use in trying to put one over on her. If I didn't want to lie about something, I had to be sure to avoid the subject completely.

"Your father's getting old," she said.

"Really old, I mean."

For the last few years, this had become her regular approach to old age. By calling my father "really old," she herself remained out of range. In that way, the concern about my father getting old became our common concern: hers and mine. My mother and I were the "younger ones," we were younger than my father, she by a year, I by thirty-five, but we were above all in full possession of our faculties, with no physical complaints worth mentioning. There was only her forgetfulness, but so far there was nothing alarming about that.

"Oh, really?" I said as the waitress placed our starters on the table: *siu mai* for her, wonton soup for me.

The morning after my father and I visited the graveyard, I had suddenly asked myself what my mother thought about their plans for the immediate future. I assumed that the two of them had talked about it at length, that they had made the decision together. Whatever the case, it had never occurred to me to ask my father about it. *What does Mama think about this?* A simple question that I forgot to ask. I racked my brain: Could I have asked him that, but forgotten in the meantime? *Did the two of you decide on this together, this business about taking fate into your own hands? Did Mama think it was a good idea right away, or did she hesitate at first?*

No, I was pretty sure of it: neither of us had brought up my mother's thoughts on the matter. We had strolled around amid the tombstones and headstones. It was a lovely cemetery, with an old part and a new part. The old section was marked by thick, overhanging trees; the epitaphs on the headstones went back to the late eighteenth century. With me it's automatic — no, obsessive: I stop, I read the name or names, and then the dates. These were often family graves, or at least graves with a married couple in them. The man usually dies first. I always look at the final year on a gravestone, I think everyone does that. Only then at the date of birth — and then the arithmetic starts. How much older was the husband? How many years later did she finally die?

"Come on," my father shouted. "Stop dawdling! This is it."

We had arrived at the new section. Fewer headstones, more markers on the ground. The trees here were thinner. It reminded me of a new housing development. The same rectilinearity, everything seemed to have been laid out according to a street plan.

136

Gradually, the dates of death came closer — the people became older, too, lived longer on the average. In the old section the headstones were still carved from local stone, worn by the elements, green with moss, but here you saw more and more marble and decorative stone, apace with the increasing prosperity in the second half of the twentieth century and the first decades of the twenty-first. Somehow, it didn't seem fitting for my parents to end up in this new residential tract. Unfair. In view of their ages, they belonged in the old section, amid the listing stones, the worn letters, and the moss.

"You know how your father is," my mother said. "He thinks he can do anything. And not so long ago, he still could. You know how I've always depended on him. On his energy. A hike around the IJsselmeer? A monastery on a six-thousand-foot mountain in the Pyrenees? I'd let it cow me before I even started. But I knew there was no talking him out of it. He always gloried in that kind of thing. I didn't want to be a party pooper. And you know what would happen then? I would always be thankful to him. Somewhere halfway up the mountain trail I would stop, huffing and puffing, and look down into the valley, and then I knew that I would never have been there without him. I was sweating, I was covered in mosquito bites, I would rather have stayed down below, but I also knew that I should be glad to be standing there now, looking down from above. When we went to the beach, do you remember how your father was always the first one to dive into the water? Even when it was cold as ice? He'd shout: 'Come on, come on in, it's wonderful!' and I was always just relieved to be finally sitting on the beach — you were, too, I think. But there was no getting out from under your father's enthusiasm. Do you remember?"

"Yes, I remember," I said. "Sometimes it was exhausting, literally, just being around him. I always felt like a dud when I was with him. I *was* a dud too — compared to him. Everyone was more of a dud than he was. I know exactly what you mean. It was tiring, often, but you did end up in places you would never have ended up in otherwise."

At a cemetery, for example. To help pick out a grave, for the two of you — for my parents. But I couldn't remember whether he had told my mother about our visit. Wait — he'd said something, I remembered then, about how my mother didn't care where she ended up after she was dead.

The waitress set down two plates on our

hot plate, then lifted our platters from the trolley — a whole crab with ginger and spring onions for my mother, *char siu* for me — and put them beside the plates; she scooped some rice onto them and left.

"It feels weird to me somehow," my mother said. "To just stop all of a sudden, when there's no real immediate cause for it."

I put a dab of sambal on my plate, then jabbed a piece of *char siu* off the platter and swiped it through the sambal.

"There really isn't anything wrong, except for the fact that your father seems a little more fatigued than he used to be," she went on. "But that's normal, I think, being less energetic at ninety-four than you were ten years ago. Something really *has* changed. You know, Robert, I'm not sure I've ever told you this, but whenever one of us would have a birthday with a zero or a five at the end, your father and I would always drink a toast to the next ten years. We started doing that when we turned thirty; I think that we were thirty when we first started feeling old. 'To the next ten years,' we'd say, and clink glasses. But last time he said something different. The last time, when he turned ninety, he said: 'To the next five years.' I think he sensed, consciously or unconsciously, that

139

he wouldn't make it to a hundred."

"And what about you, Mama? Do you have that same feeling in your bones? I mean: you're ninety-three, right?" I tried to catch the waitress's attention. "Would you like some more wine?" I pointed to her half-full glass. "I'm going to have another beer anyway."

"You know what's funny about your father? Maybe I've told you this already, so if I did, just say so. I have a tendency to tell the same story two or three times. But I'm not demented enough not to know that. Which is why I always ask politely beforehand. So stop me right away if you've already heard it. Promise?"

"I promise," I said. What she said was true, I'd noticed it before. Last time I had my birthday, she called me the next day to ask whether she'd forgotten to wish me a happy birthday. But she never forgot anything important, and she could still remember the minutest details of things that happened a long time ago.

"It was on King's Day, last year," my mother said. "Your father and I were taking a walk around the neighborhood. It doesn't interest me in the slightest, all those children selling all that old garbage, I always find it a little sad that they have to get up so early

140

on their day off, just to get a good spot. But anyway, at one point we decided to stop in for a beer at that café on Middenweg, what's it called again? You see, it's that kind of thing . . ."

"Elsa's," I said. "Elsa's Café."

"Thank you, sweetheart, Elsa's Café. Anyway, we had a glass of wine, then another one, and we ran into the people who live across the street, they were there too. At one point I went to the ladies' room for a minute. Well, not a minute, there was a huge line. I was gone for maybe fifteen minutes. At first, when I came back, I couldn't find your father outside, there were so many people standing around. But suddenly I saw him, way off in a corner, talking to two girls, they couldn't have been more than nineteen. There was a band playing, fairly loudly, and I saw that he leaned over to one of the girls and shouted something in her ear. Apparently she didn't understand him the first time, because she put her ear closer to his mouth and he shouted again, and then she shrieked with laughter. And then she said something to that other girl, who burst out laughing too."

My mother was holding a crab leg between her fingers and snapped it in two; little pieces of white crabmeat flew everywhere, a few ended up in her hair. There were little particles of white around her mouth and on her cheeks too.

"I wormed my way through all those people, heading for your father and the girls who were laughing so loudly, but suddenly I stopped. Let him go, I thought. I'll keep my distance. That's what I did. There weren't any neighbors or friends around, so I just stood watching calmly from a distance. It was as though your father had forgotten all about me. After maybe half an hour he finally looked around, and then he saw me standing there. He waved, signaled to me that he was coming, but in the end it took another fifteen minutes before we were ready to go home."

I was about to say something, something about my father and women, both of us knew what he was like on that count. On vacation, back when I was only nine or ten, he had no qualms about turning around in his seat in some foreign restaurant, just to watch an attractive waitress walk by. "My, my, apparently there's no law against that here either," he would say. My mother would roll her eyes or wink at me; she had always found his behavior funnier than it was shameful.

"No, wait, I know what you're going to

142

say," she said then. "The best is yet to come. After that, when we were walking home." Meanwhile my mother had arrived at the part of the crab shell without the legs, the part that always reminds me of a spaceship, the black dots of the eyes are the cockpit, where the two pilots operate the legs. She picked up a little spoon and scraped out something green, and I looked away. "We were walking down Hogeweg, and I noticed he was wobbling a little," my mother went on, "that he had to try really hard just to walk in a straight line. He kept shaking his head and laughing under his breath. 'Did you see those girls?' he said then. 'The two I was talking to? That one girl was absolutely smoldering. The way she looked at me! With those big dark eyes. At first, I thought: What's she after? But she just kept looking at me.' And then he started talking about that other girl, about how she was much less attractive, but that's exactly why he'd done his best to keep her in the conversation, too, and he claimed that that had made the first girl 'smolder' even more, the way he put it. I asked him whether he actually believed what he was saying. Whether he realized what age those girls were, whether he remembered how old he was himself. But he said: 'I can't help seeing what I see, can

I? I've got eyes in my head, don't I?' We were walking close to the curb right then, he took a wrong step and fell halfway between two parked cars. When we got home I made two grilled-cheese sandwiches for him and put him to bed. 'The whole room is spinning,' he said. 'Just like it used to.' And then he fell asleep with his glasses on."

We walked together down Damstraat, to the tram stop on Dam Square. "It's strange to think about it," she said. "Having lunch with you like this, I think: Why does this have to end? Why not just go on having lunch at Oriental City every two weeks for the next five years? But there's also something to it, to stopping at a point when things are still pleasant. Now things are still pleasant, I mean. If you have to spoon-feed your mother pieces of crab later on, that's going to be a lot less pleasant. For you. Maybe I won't even notice anymore. Or maybe I will have lost my taste for it. Did he tell you about the new car?"

"New car?"

"He started talking about it about six months ago. That we needed a new car. He came home with all kinds of brochures, don't ask me what it was, I couldn't care less. That's what I told him too. 'What's

144

wrong with the car we have?' I said. 'It still runs fine, doesn't it?' And for a long time, I thought he'd dropped the idea completely. But a little while ago he started in about it again. 'We've got the money,' he said. 'So let's go to France in style this time, for the last time. In a convertible.' I guess I must have looked at him like he was out of his mind, because he hasn't brought it up again. But do you know what I mean? First those girls, then this. I don't begrudge him his little pleasures, but on the other hand I think it's so incredibly childish. I almost find him sort of pitiful, and I don't want to think that way about your father."

The No. 9 tram stopped in front of us. I leaned over to kiss her, and as I did I used my thumb to wipe some of the white crabmeat off her face.

"I know what you mean," I said. "But I wouldn't worry about it. Cars, girls: most men have that during their midlife crisis. Maybe it's only happening to him now. Maybe he's just sort of a slow starter."

12

A few days later, Sylvia and I left for four days in Paris. It had been a year since we'd gone there together, but that had been an official visit. Now we had all the time in the world, and could do whatever we felt like.

Our hotel was in Saint-Germain-des-Prés, on Rue Saint-Sulpice. We always went for breakfast on the glassed-in patio of a brasserie on Boulevard Saint-Germain. By the third morning, the waiter knew our orders by heart: a croissant for Sylvia, a *sandwich au jambon* for me, and two cafés crèmes. (On our fourth and final morning I felt like having a croissant, too, but I ordered my usual anyway, because I didn't want to disappoint the smiling waiter.) Then, after breakfast, we would take off walking. With no plans, no destination, and above all with no city map. First across the Seine, then left past the Louvre, one morning by way of the Rue Saint-Honoré, the next through the Jardin des Tuileries to the Champs-Élysées.

You saw them lying around everywhere. Sometimes in doorways, but more often right in the middle of the sidewalk. Whole crowds of children, most of them between the ages of two and six. A mattress, a few dirty blankets, a couple of garbage bags and plastic sacks with their possessions.

"That's really going far too far," my wife said as we passed a sleeping woman with four sleeping children. "See how little those children are? You can't do that, can you?"

I could have said something about how maybe she had no other choice, I could have said something about the economic malaise in Europe, in the world, but I didn't.

"It's like they have no sense of pride," Sylvia said. "Beggars, okay, you've got them everywhere. It's not pleasant, it shouldn't even exist in a rich country like France, but this is different. They're not even begging. You see that? Do you see a hat or a paper cup anywhere? But that's not necessary, of course. They get their money in other ways."

I said nothing. We had stopped before the display window of a Louis Vuitton shop. The window held only one bright-red handbag, on a bed of black velvet. From the corner of my eye, I looked at the woman on the mattress. She had just woken up and was rub-

147

bing a dirty hand over her face, which was none too clean either. Her hair was covered with a dark-brown checkered scarf, her upper body shrouded in a dark-green vest, it looked like only the top layer of many. The children slept on, three little girls and a boy, it was ten thirty in the morning. For a moment I wondered what time they had gone to bed last night, in order to sleep so late, and shook my head inadvertently.

"Would you like it if I bought you a bag like that?" I asked, just to change the subject. "If I were to give you a fire-engine-red Louis Vuitton bag, would you throw your arms around my neck?"

I was deeply aware of the contrast between the bag in the shopwindow, which probably bore no price tag because it was so screamingly expensive, and the dirty woman with her sleeping children ten meters farther along. If you were to use this in a film script, people would say you were laying it on way too thick. A tendentious scene; haven't we, here in the West, missed the mark completely when we spend a month's salary on a handbag while little children are sleeping out on the street? Or was it not the Louis Vuitton bag that was the real symbol of decadence, but this unwashed mother doing this to her own children?

"The women draw your attention," my wife was saying, "while the children are trained to cut open your bag or ruffle through your pockets with their nimble fingers. And no, sweetheart, you wouldn't please me with a bag like that. It's not that it's ugly, in and of itself, but it's the brand. You have to ask yourself whether you're the kind of person who walks around town with a Louis Vuitton bag. And I'm not that kind of person."

We strolled down the Champs-Élysées to the Arc de Triomphe, then crossed and strolled all the way back again. At a brasserie in a side street, we went for the menu of the day. I asked for *oeufs durs mayonnaise* as an appetizer, and the waiter complimented me on that. "An excellent choice," I understood him to say. Then he said something else: about Parisians or Paris, a complete sentence spoken with a grin, of which I actually understood only the word *manger.*

"I've never understood what's so special about that," Sylvia said, once the waiter left. "Eggs boiled for more than five minutes, a glop of mayonnaise on top, and there you have it."

"I think it's wonderful. An ice-cold hard-boiled egg, and they make the mayonnaise themselves, don't forget that."

"It's just sort of a childish dish. Like a hotdog or a fish stick. But okay, that's the way you are too: childish."

She said it with a smile, raising her glass of beer in a toast, and now she winked at me as well. I raised my own glass too. It was one of those thin glasses on a stem, the kind the French call a *demi.* It felt ice-cold to my fingertips, it was covered in little drops of dew, and the head on it was impeccable, almost a pity to drink out of, like walking across a lawn covered in fresh snow. I knew my wife was only teasing me about the childish dishes I ordered — she had said nothing yet about the steak tartare I'd chosen for the main course, but I knew that was coming. I saw her teasing (and her smile, her wink) as a reassurance. Would she still tease me (and smile and wink) if she were having an affair with Maarten van Hoogstraten? Wouldn't the teasing be the first thing she'd stop doing? Or was she only putting on a five-star performance? Was she only trying to act the way she always did, insofar as that was possible? Simply because otherwise it would be the first thing I'd notice: that she no longer teased me about the food I ordered, no longer raised her glass in a toast, smiled, winked?

From the moment we left Amsterdam, I

had kept a close eye on her. No, not close: Casual. Nonchalant. In the Thalys on the way down I'd leafed through an issue of *Vrij Nederland,* without reading a word. Then, with a sigh, I took the marker out of my book: page 170, a hundred and fifty left to go. When you watched a movie, you knew within ten minutes whether it was good or whether it was a piece of shit. With a book, that took a little longer: you gave the author the benefit of the doubt for fifty pages or so, but by page 170 you knew it was hopeless, that things could only get worse.

In order not to be too conspicuous about only pretending to read, I turned a page once in a while. Meanwhile, from the corner of my eye, I watched my wife, who seemed to be completely absorbed in her issue of *HELLO!* Had she done her hair up in some special way? Had she put on more, or precisely less, makeup? Had she lost weight in the last few weeks? Weight loss, a different hairdo, more lipstick: these, according to all the popular magazines, were the most obvious external symptoms of adultery. But I noticed nothing out of the ordinary, not in her behavior during the train trip either. As far as I could tell, she wasn't checking her iPhone more frequently, and on one occasion she laughed out loud at a WhatsApp message, from a girlfriend, she said, a fellow countrywoman who had sent her a funny video. I heard trumpets blare, a loud male voice speaking in her native language. Fortunately, she didn't ask if I wanted to see it, she knows how I detest ostensibly funny videos that people share for want of a sense of humor of their own.

When she went to the restroom, she just left her iPhone on the fold-down table. I could have taken a quick look at it, could have scrolled through the messages in search of one from Maarten van Hoogstraten. *I think about you all day, sweetest! What are you wearing? I'm lying in bed, I'm taking off my boxers now while I think about you, will you take off something too?*

But it was all purely theoretical. I wasn't going to look at her phone, of course not. Because I never did that. Because she knew I never did that. You couldn't just start looking at your wife's phone all of a sudden, just like that. Not because she would notice right away, but simply because it was not done.

And then again: Would Sylvia be foolish enough to put Maarten van Hoogstraten in her list of contacts, under his own name and with his own profile photo? No, my wife was most certainly not that foolish. Unfortunately, no. No, he would be in there without a photo and under a different name (a woman's name!). She would delete all his messages right away. It was even more likely that they would have agreed not to send any messages at all for the duration of her stay in Paris.

But would they be able to keep that up? Can people who are infatuated with each other put up with not hearing anything from the other person for four days? No, that was impossible. One whole day, maybe — half a day, I corrected myself, thinking back on my own infatuations. Despite all the promises not to call and not to send amorous messages, those promises would — within a day and a half, tops — become too much to bear. It was simply too early to verify at that point, I decided, we had been on the train for only ninety minutes. Once we arrived in Paris, I would resume the close surveillance of my wife.

There Sylvia came, walking down the aisle, occasionally reaching out to steady herself on the backrests. Maybe I was imagining it, but she really did look slimmer, I told myself as she sank down into her seat.

"I heard a beep," I said. "I think you have a new message."

■ ■ ■ ■

On our second day in Paris, though, there were still no visible signs of an affair. Perhaps, I reflected once again as the waiter placed my steak tartare in front of me and served Sylvia her *faux-filet* with *pommes dauphine,* it was precisely the *absence* of any visible sign or signal that should confirm my worst suspicions. The completely normal way my wife was acting, the mildly mocking smile and the way she shook her head as she viewed my steak tartare, as she always did when I ordered this particular dish, could be a deliberate tactic. *No phone calls, no text messages, no mail.* In my mind I saw them whispering it to each other; my wife was naked, her body covered with a sheet only to the navel, her hair fanned out as she rested her head lightly against the alderman's hairless chest. *He would notice right away, I would have to keep my phone with me all the time, even under the shower. When he hears a beep, he'll ask who the message is from.* Yes, that was true, that's how it always went. My wife's phone beeped every hour, sometimes more often. At breakfast, at least three times. I didn't even have to ask, I only glanced up from my newspaper or paused before sipping at my café crème. "My sister," she would say, or: "My little brother." There was only one sister who she called "my sister," and that was the eldest one. Her elder brother, though, she always referred to as "my big brother." Her younger sister was called "my little sister." We sat down to breakfast at ten, which was still too early for a message from our daughter, from Diana. Independently of each other, though, we always looked to see what time she had still been online the night before. Last night, that had been a quarter to two. "Isn't that kind of late?" my wife had asked when she came out of the bathroom. "For a normal school day?"

"Hmm, but it's Friday, she doesn't have a class until the third period," I replied. I always kept better track of those things than Sylvia did — or no, I didn't keep track at all, I just knew them. I also knew Diana's average for German at the moment.

We're not going to send a single message. It's only four days, Maarten.

My wife laughed and began cutting her *faux-filet.* "It's a miracle you've never come down with a salmonella infection," she said. That's what she said whenever I ordered steak tartare. And maybe it really was a miracle. How many kilos of raw meat had I

155

gobbled down in the last half-century, without ever ending up in a hospital? I'd had food poisoning, I knew what that felt like. Oysters, mayonnaise, meatloaf: all dishes that had, at some point in my life, produced in me a near-death experience. But steak tartare had never made me sick.

My wife's teasing remark today could, as it had at many points in the last few months, mean precisely one of two things: either she had decided to act as normally as possible and was pulling it off extremely well, or she wasn't acting at all and was truly behaving normally. Squinting slightly, I examined her face in profile (we were sitting beside each other at the little round table, so we could both look outside) as she chewed intently on a piece of *faux-filet.* There was nothing amiss, I told myself. Everything was what it was. I had been imagining the whole thing. We were alone together in Paris, the way we'd been alone together so often in a foreign city, in Madrid, in Rome, in Berlin, in New York. We were doing what we always did, what we enjoyed doing so much together, lunch with beer and wine, and later perhaps a glass of calvados along with the coffee.

I had seen them during this trip, too, the Dutch people you could always pick out right away, their length, their far-too-blond children, even in Paris they stuck to a sandwich or a slice of pizza for lunch, washed it down with cola or water. They didn't live. They didn't know that you could also enjoy life in the middle of the day. From five o'clock on, it's okay, then the Dutchman promptly drinks himself into a corner. After the fifth glass it's not about enjoyment anymore, with a certain fury he drinks himself as quickly as possible into an exuberant, uninhibited, and noisy version of himself. The locals give a wide berth to clusters of screaming Dutchmen. The Dutch people who make you ashamed to be Dutch.

"What's wrong?" Sylvia asked. "Doesn't it taste good?"

At that very moment, her telephone beeped. She laid her knife and fork beside her plate and opened the red case. I kept looking at her as she peered at the screen. Her expression didn't change; she seemed lost in thought, as though she couldn't quite place the message or its sender.

"I have to handle this right away," she said. "I have to make a call." She slid back her chair. "It's too noisy here. I'm going outside for a moment."

This time she'd said nothing about "my little sister" or "my big brother." I had to

157

get up, too, to let her pass. I looked at her questioningly; it was only normal to look questioningly at my own wife when she received a message that seemed to demand a quick response.

"A girlfriend," she said as she wormed past me. "A girlfriend, but you don't know her."

I kept looking at her, trying with all my might to suppress any glimmer of disbelief or suspicion, as far as one can consciously suppress something like that. "I'll explain in a minute," she said.

And then she was gone. A few seconds later I saw her out on the street, at first it looked like she was going to turn left, but then she seemed to change her mind: if she moved to the left she would end up right in front of our table. She was holding the phone to her ear. I was still standing, I had to lean down to see her. To the right of the brasserie, around the corner, there was another sidewalk restaurant with a sun-porch. She talked. She paced back and forth, but it was just a little too far away, I couldn't see whether she was smiling, whether she was agitated. Then she stopped and looked straight in my direction. I didn't know whether she could see me, I waved to her, but she didn't react. I sat back down. I

158

looked at my own plate, the half-eaten steak tartare, then at hers. *I told you not to text me here. But still, darling, it's nice to hear your voice.* Sylvia hadn't finished even a third of her *faux-filet,* hadn't even touched her *pommes dauphine.* Her lunch was getting cold, fast. What could be so important that it couldn't wait until after the main course? I tried to remember whether she had ever mentioned a girlfriend I didn't know, or whether in our shared life, in which we knew almost everything about each other, there was even room for an unknown girlfriend. My wife always called her friends by their names. No, I was certain of it now. Never, not once, had she said, *I'm going to meet up this afternoon with a girlfriend, someone you don't know.* I rose halfway to my feet again. My wife was standing there. She was no longer pacing back and forth. A truck was just turning the corner; she held the phone in one hand and pressed the other against her right ear to block out the noise. As far as I could tell from this distance, she looked serious. Focused. I sank back in my chair. What was Maarten van Hoogstraten saying to her? *I can't stand to be without you this long. I had to hear your voice.* I looked at my half-eaten steak

159

tartare, then at my wife's plate of tepid *faux-filet* and cold *pommes dauphine,* and felt an enormous rage rise up inside. Where did Alderman Van Hoogstraten get off, coming in from five hundred kilometers away like this to ruin our lunch? I felt tears welling up. Don't! I told myself. That's the last thing you should do, make a pitiable, ridiculous figure of yourself. A cuckold trying to make his own wife pity him, what could be more disgusting than that? But it was hard to stop. Suddenly a picture loomed up before me, a picture of Maarten van Hoogstraten lying on a bed. His own bed. He was wearing white boxers. He held the phone to his ear; his other hand was in his underpants. *What are you wearing?* he asked my wife. *All I have on are my underpants. I'm thinking about you now. I'm thinking about you with no clothes on, the way you came out of the shower that last time in the hotel. I thought I was going to explode. Shall I take off my underpants? Shall I tell you where my hand is? What I'm doing with it now?*

No tears came, the rage had won out. No sentimental tomfoolery! "Fucking hell," I said. Out loud, apparently, for the waiter who was walking past the table right then stopped and looked at me.

"Monsieur?"

160

I pointed to my empty beer glass and mumbled something that might or might not have been proper French. There was really no need for me to express myself clearly, though, the waiter understood. *"Encore un demi, monsieur,"* he said, and hurried off.

Suddenly, Sylvia was back; this time she squeezed her way between the table and the plate-glass window and dropped down into her chair.

"Oh, oh," she said. "What a mess." She picked up her glass and took a sip. Then it was empty. She looked around, but the waiter was somewhere outside our field of vision.

"I just ordered a beer," I said. "He'll be back in a minute."

Then she looked at me for the first time since she'd come back. I searched her eyes for a clue; not just her eyes, but also her cheeks — a blush that might betray the provocative nature of her phone call.

"What's with you?" she asked.

"What do you mean?"

"Your eyes . . ." She moved her face up closer to mine. "They're all red. Have you . . . have you been crying, Robert? At least, that's what it looks like."

I raised my hand to my eyes, squeezed the

bridge of my nose. "I . . . There was something . . ." I nodded at my plate of half-eaten steak tartare. "There was something in my steak. A really hot little pepper, I bit into it and it brought tears to my eyes."

She shifted her gaze questioningly from my left to my right eye and back again. She looked at me doubtfully, then smiled; it was a pitying smile. *How can you come up with such a stupid lie?* her look and her smile said. *Did you really think I'd fall for that?*

"So what was that all about?" I asked quickly, to draw attention from my teary eyes. "I mean, what was with this girlfriend? I don't know her, that's what you said."

I had been planning not to ask about any of this. I had been planning to let a silence fall, once Sylvia had come back. I had hoped to examine her closely as she became entangled in her own lies. Watch her pretend to have carried on a phone conversation with an unknown girlfriend, instead of having helped Maarten van Hoogstraten — with a few whispered, titillating words — to cream his boxers with a little shriek.

And even as I was thinking that, I wondered for the first time whether I could distinguish between the two, whether I would really be able to tell the difference between my wife's made-up version of the phone call and the actual facts. Between an imaginary girlfriend and a girlfriend of flesh and blood.

Sylvia narrowed her eyes to slits, sighed deeply, and looked away from me.

"You don't know her," she said, picking up her knife and fork and cutting into her cold *faux-filet.* "But what a story!"

She started telling me. She had met this girlfriend of hers at the Dutch conversation lessons she'd been going to for the last six months or so. That much was true. She wanted to perfect her Dutch even further. "I make too many mistakes with the simple things," she'd said. "*De* and *het, die* and *deze,* what a terrible language you people have! Anyone can learn English in six weeks, but you can keep on doing this your whole life, and even then: after one word, you people already know that you're dealing with some idiotic foreigner."

The girlfriend's name was Sadako, she was from Japan. She and her Japanese husband had been living in Amstelveen for the last year. The husband was almost never around, his company sent him all over the world. And now, recently, Sadako had the strong impression that he wasn't always traveling alone. Something about a photograph, my wife said; he had sent her a

163

picture of a dinner party in San Francisco. A table at a restaurant, about eight people, men and women. Everyone in the picture was looking into the camera; the chair beside Sadako's husband was vacant. He also sent another picture, one he'd apparently taken himself, because he wasn't in it. In that one his chair was empty, but the one beside it was now occupied by a woman. A real beauty. Sort of Asiatic, too, although Sadako couldn't make out what country she was from. Not Japan, in any case, maybe Thailand or Vietnam. But it was actually something in the picture itself that aroused her suspicions. The first photo, the one with her husband in it, had been taken so that you could see the entire group; in the second photo, though, the one Sadako's husband had taken, three of the faces on the right side of the table were out of frame. As a result, the woman in the chair beside the one where Sadako's husband had been sitting was in the exact center of the picture. Her husband had sent them right after each other, first the one he was in, then the picture with the woman in it. Sadako had not been able to avoid the impression that the second photo was sent by accident, that he hadn't been paying attention, she told Sylvia. But that wasn't all. Two days later, her husband sent her another photo. This one showed him in a seat in an airplane, an aisle seat, on a flight from San Francisco to Dallas. He was going to a conference there, he told Sadako in the message. The window seat was occupied, but the one in the middle was vacant. Sadako had uploaded the photo from her phone to her laptop and used photo-editing software to blow it up as large as she could. Her husband wore glasses, he was smiling, the eyes behind the lenses smiled along with him — the unsuspecting eye would assume that he was smiling at her, at Sadako, his wife back in Amstelveen. But in fact, of course, he was smiling at the person (the woman!) taking the picture. Meanwhile, Sadako had zoomed in so far on her laptop that one lens of his spectacles filled the entire screen; it was no longer completely in focus, but sharp enough to see the reflection in the lens, the reflection of a woman, a woman taking a picture of Sadako's husband with his own telephone. The face reflected in the lens was too small to recognize, of course, but according to Sadako it was clear enough to see that it was a woman — a woman with her black hair hanging loose, just like the woman who'd sat beside him at the table the night before. It was that loose hair that put an end to Sadako's hesitation. Stewardesses, after all, never wore their hair loose, always in a bun or ponytail, and often enough tucked away completely beneath an airline company cap.

As I listened to my wife — with one ear, for I was actually paying more attention to how she told the story than to the story itself — I wondered whether she could possibly make up something like this on the spot. Whether she could possibly have dreamed up this story between the time she broke the connection with her lover and the time she returned to our table. It seemed improbable to me, it was too detailed for that. It was always possible, of course, that the story itself was true, that she'd heard it somewhere else, and that she had decided in a blind panic to use it now in order to allay any suspicions I might have. But even so. It also had to do with the details about the girlfriend. The girlfriend I didn't know had now become a Japanese girlfriend. A Japanese girlfriend with a name. Sadako. Why would my wife, if she were to make up a girlfriend, make up a Japanese girlfriend?

"It's so horrible," Sylvia concluded her story. "And I feel so sorry for her. Her husband is coming home in two days. She knows almost no one in Holland. That's why she called me."

More significant, perhaps, than this story that would have been almost impossible to make up, more significant than the unnecessary detail of the girlfriend's nationality, was the improbability of my wife making up a story precisely about an adulterous spouse. A story about an incurable disease would have been more like it: a girlfriend I didn't know who failed to respond to one course of treatment after another. Or was this an essential part of her strategy? With a juicy story about a faithless Japanese husband, she didn't have to dodge the subject. A real adulterer, after all, would avoid this particular subject at all costs. For fear of giving themselves away with a blush, fluttering eyelids, or other body language.

I looked at my wife. She looked back at me without batting an eye, a slightly mocking smile playing at her lips — perhaps the mocking smile of a woman amused by her husband's gullibility.

"I would notice it right away," she said.

"What?"

"If you did that. If you cheated on me like Sadako's husband. I would be able to see it on your face, you wouldn't be able to keep it a secret for more than a couple of hours."

I said nothing. She smiled, no longer

167

mockingly, more like tenderly, as though she had caught a child telling an innocent fib.

"Did you really bite into a pepper, is that why you had tears in your eyes? Or are you going to tell me the truth?"

I didn't quite blush, but if I didn't say something fast I was going to turn red as a beet.

"I was thinking about us," I said. "About how happy I am. With you. How happy I am to be here with you, in Paris."

As I said it I thought about Maarten van Hoogstraten, his hand in his underpants, his sticky fingers.

"Me too, darling," my wife said. "I'm always happy when I'm with you. Every minute of the day."

PART II

13

In the mid-1980s my best friend Bernhard and I went on a trip through a few countries, countries I won't mention here by name. Suffice it to say that they lie to the south, east, and southeast of Belgium — past Paris, in any case. One of those countries is the one where my wife was born.

I don't mean to bore anyone with a load of autobiographical detail. With what you might call my "political career" — although at that particular point in my life there was hardly anything like a career. If anyone's interested, you'll find it all on my Wikipedia page. Student union chairman, political party member, alderman, state secretary, mayor. The Wikipedia page, by the way, also mentions my wife's nationality. Her name, her real name, is misspelled, with an *e* in there somewhere where there should actually be an *a*. The first time I noticed it I resolved to change it — to have it changed

— but that never happened. In fact, I never thought about it again until this very moment. How many times in your life, after all, do you look at your own Wikipedia page?

Back then, Bernhard Langer was already the most brilliant Dutch physicist and astronomer of his generation. In his field of expertise — black holes, the Big Bang, the rapidly expanding universe — his only competition was from the likes of Stephen Hawking. In fact, though, there was no real competition: Bernhard was good friends with Hawking, who was ten years his senior. They visited each other regularly, and in scientific publications they were often mentioned in the same breath. At thirty-two, Bernhard could have become the youngest rector magnificus ever at the Delft University of Technology, but he opted for adventure and accepted a position in the United States, first at Princeton, later at Harvard.

We took off from home on a Saturday in July, with no real fixed plans. We briefly considered heading north: it was already stiflingly hot in Holland, which made us fear the worst for our southern and eastern destinations. But we had no desire to see boring Scandinavian forests, to visit countries where the food was bad and the alcohol prohibitively expensive.

There were certain advantages associated with our country of origin. Advantages that would disappear if we went north. The farther south we went, the more we towered above the local population. When we went into a café or restaurant, all heads turned in our direction. We were both blond, Bernhard even a tad blonder than me: at one in the afternoon, with the sun straight overhead, the color of his hair almost hurt your eyes. We were aware of the eyes — all eyes! — that were pinned on us until we sank our tall bodies down into our chairs. In those days, the corner of the world in which we found ourselves was one where very few tourists came. A neck of the woods that I, without giving away too much, will call "the interior." *The blazing interior:* the guidebook strongly advised against visiting these parts in July and August. But I found out all of that only later, after I met Sylvia. At which point the travel guide suddenly seemed laden with meaning.

Back in Amsterdam, I stuck my nose into the pages of the book and it was as though I could smell her. Lavender. A whole purple field full of it. The lavender blossoms were motionless, there was not a breath of wind, at most they shimmered in the heat. Honeybees, bumblebees, and other insects with large yellow abdomens, striped in red and black, insects we didn't have in Holland and whose names we therefore didn't know, buzzed from flower to flower.

I have no trouble admitting that, of the two of us, Bernhard was the more attractive. About ten centimeters taller than me, but also more muscular, above all broader; on the dance floors of black-light clubs with revolving disco balls, he took the initiative right away. He always went straight for his mark, while I have always been more the sort who hangs back. From a great height he would bend down toward the girl on whom he'd set his sights and shout something in her ear. The most hideous clichés were deployed, clichés I myself could never have used, but he got away with it. The girls thronged around Bernhard and looked up at him — and the simple fact that I was standing beside him made them look at me next.

"The later it gets, the prettier they all become," he said in Dutch, and winked at me. But then he said it again, this time in English, to the girls! And instead of turning their backs on us, the girls giggled, they came and stood even closer. One afternoon, somewhere in the second week of our trip through the interior, we were sitting with three girls on the lawn beside our hotel swimming pool when Bernhard began first to pat the nonexistent pockets of his swimming trunks, then to feel around under his towel.

"What are you looking for?" asked the girl sitting closest to him, perhaps not even the prettiest of the three, perhaps the one I would finally end up with.

"A smile," Bernhard said; and when she actually did smile at that, he added: "But I've already found it."

"If you ask me, that little one likes you," he would say to me, in Dutch again. Or: "The dark one is looking at you the whole time, Robert. You'd be nuts not to strike now."

"The little one" or "the dark one" was consistently the least attractive of the two (or three, or four) girls who had come to stand around and look up hopefully, imploringly at us, at Bernhard: the second choice, Bernhard's second choice, the last one you would ask to dance. He himself had set his sights on the main prize, the local Miss Universe, the girls who were just beyond my reach.

The second-choice girls were not necessarily ugly, far from it, at most a little less exceptional beside their blindingly beautiful girlfriend. When you removed Miss Universe from the equation, there was actually nothing to complain about. In principle, those girls had nothing to be ashamed of. They were all little, and they were all dark. "The little one" or "the dark one" was perhaps half a centimeter shorter and a barely perceptible half a shade darker than the first choice.

I had, in other words, no problem with the situation and the division of roles, it was highly tolerable. Happiness, I told myself back then, and I still tell myself today — or perhaps one would do better to speak of satisfaction, rather than happiness — is bound up closely with the acceptance of your own head. Your own body. Your build. There are plenty of things you can do about that body. You can lose weight when you think you're too fat, you can lift weights when you become embarrassed by the way your ribs stick out. But there's not much you can change about your head. The head has a mind of its own. It grows bald when it feels like it. It grows fatter, older, spottier, in a way you'd never thought possible. Visible to all, and not least of all to yourself. You can't hide your head by pulling a T-shirt or a sweater over it. It's there all the time, every hour of the day and night. It looks at you in the mirror. *This is it,* it says unblinkingly. *You'll have to make do with this.*

I was able, as I've said, to get along with my own head. I knew myself well enough to know which category that head put me in. In our own country, both Bernhard and I were nothing more than average, with our blond hair and our height. Or, to put it differently: in Holland there were already too many like us walking around, it was easy enough to pick a better specimen. And here we weren't at a seaside resort or some other tourist attraction, we were — I can't emphasize this enough — in the interior. There was no competition from countrymen or other blond gods from the north.

One evening — close to midnight — during the third week of our trip, I was lying on the bed in our hotel room with a headache when Bernhard suggested we take a stroll around the modest little town where we were staying. I groaned quietly. "Do we really have to? There's nothing happening here anyway." There were only three restaurants and four or five cafés, we had noted that afternoon, and we planned to travel on to the capital the next morning. "Come on, don't be such a wimp, Robert." I can't remember whether, after that, he said something like "you only live once," or whether he stuck to the umpteenth repetition of his favorite saying, "The later it gets, the prettier they all become." I also can't recall why I finally got up at last and went to the bathroom to hold my head under the cold faucet. The feeling that I might miss something, probably: I had that feeling around the clock back then. A big difference from these days. Which may be the greatest perk of getting older. I'm no longer afraid of missing something. I know that I won't miss a thing.

I looked at myself in the mirror. At my head, which hurt and pounded gently somewhere at the back of my eyes. I pushed back my wet hair and tried to press it as flat as I could against my skull, but knew it was wasted effort: no one would fancy this head. I didn't fancy it myself much, so why should anyone else feel differently?

We arrived at a deserted square we had come across earlier that afternoon. In front of a café were three white plastic tables and five or six white plastic chairs, none of them occupied.

"I don't know," I said in reply to Bernhard's questioning look. "Maybe we should look around a bit first?"

Bernhard patted his pants pockets. "Well, I'm going to get a pack of cigarettes anyway," he said. "You wait here?"

On the other side of the square were a few more empty chairs and tables.

"I'll head over that way," I said. "If that's nothing either, maybe we'd be better off having a drink at the hotel."

I sauntered across the square. Dirty yellow light was coming through a dusty window; you couldn't tell if there was anyone inside.

I was standing there between the tables with my hands in my pockets, trying to adopt an air for no one in particular — *I'm waiting for a friend. He's buying cigarettes* — when the door of the café swung open and two girls came out. As is usually the case when two girls are out on the town together, one was prettier than the other. It would be going too far to say that the other girl was ugly, no, far from it, at most a bit less extraordinary — "unexceptional" was the word that popped into my mind: the girl who would have been meant for me if Bernhard and I had been standing there in front of the café together.

But I was alone. I caught myself taking a longer look at the ordinary girl and, only after that, at the girl Bernhard would nor-

179

mally have snapped up.

They were talking, but when they saw me they slowed and smiled at the tall, blond Dutchman standing there, amid the empty tables with his hands in his pockets.

"Hello," said the prettier, the bolder, the more self-confident of the two. She held her head tilted a bit to one side, causing her bobbed black curls to hang loosely on one side of her face; a lock fell over one eye on the other side, a lock that she brushed back behind her ear in a single smooth motion. "Are you lost?"

For the course of half a second, I tried to come up with a snappy answer, but it was hopeless. I *was* lost. I had looked into her black pupils, and into the broad whites around them when she opened her eyes questioningly wide. *Are you the one?* I felt like asking. That was all I knew right then: that she was it. *For all time* — that was what flashed through my mind. *After this, there will never be another.*

At that very moment I felt a hand on my shoulder.

"Well, well," Bernhard said in my ear. "Can't leave you alone for a minute, can I? So, are you going to introduce me to your new girlfriends?"

And then he said it, or rather, whispered

it, although strictly speaking there was no reason to do so at all.

"May I congratulate you, Robert? It is indeed just like they say: the later it gets, the prettier they all become."

14

"Can I bother you for a moment?" Sylvia asked. I hadn't heard her come in, she was suddenly standing there at the foot end of the couch where I was lying, reading the newspaper. In her left hand she held an open black book that could only be a Moleskine pocket diary.

"I was just thinking," my wife went on, without waiting for an answer. "Do you have any appointments on Friday?"

"I don't know," I lied. "I'd have to look at my agenda."

I knew very well, though: I had nothing going on that Friday. But I wanted to keep it that way. I had so much going on already. Days with nothing at the end of them were rare in my profession — but they were the happiest days of all.

"Bernhard and Christine are flying back to Boston on Sunday," my wife said. "And I'm going out with Miriam and Louise on

Saturday. So I thought, maybe we could invite them over for dinner on Friday. At least, if you still want to see Bernhard."

I very much wanted to see Bernhard, but I wasn't sure if I felt like having dinner with the four of us. Whenever I met up with Bernhard, I tried to say as little as possible. I talked just enough to hide the fact that I wasn't saying anything at all. That was how the roles were divided between us. He talked, I listened. I thought that, except for me, he had very few friends who could listen to him so well. And I thought he was perfectly aware of that. Purely for form's sake, he would ask me a few questions about Sylvia and Diana. About the issues at play in a big city. Then he would bust loose. He needed almost no encouragement. As though you'd held a burning match to a pile of dry twigs.

I wasn't sure whether I felt like having dinner with the four of us, because maybe I wanted to talk to my best friend alone. On the other hand, though, Bernhard was perhaps the last person I would want to talk to about my suspicions.

I saw it in my mind's eye: a restaurant. The way I visualized it, it was at Dauphine, across from Amstel Station. That's where we tended to meet when he was in Holland for a few days. First I would let him go at it, let him blow off steam about his black holes and the distances between stars, his continually expanding universe. Appetizer. Main course. Only after dessert would I suggest that we take something along with our espressos. Grappa. Cognac. Calvados. *Bernhard, there's something I need to talk to you about. Something about Sylvia . . .* And that was where the film broke down.

Of course, in all these years I have asked myself more than once what would have happened if I had been standing on that little square in front of that café on that dark, empty evening with my friend Bernhard. Whether perhaps things would have followed their natural course and I, as always, would have settled for the runner-up. At the most decisive moment in my life — in our lives, Sylvia's and mine — my bride-to-be had had no material for comparison. She had seen only one tall, blond Dutchman standing there amid the tables, with his hands in his pockets.

She too had looked at me, looked into my eyes, and knew at that same instant that I was the one and only, as she would later swear to me — swear again and again, at least five times a year to this very day.

Sometimes I thought about it this way:

You see a house for sale, you are given a tour of the rooms, it's a rather pretty house, spacious, light, lovely wooden floors, a view of the park. You sign for it. And then — your decision can no longer be reversed — you are given another tour. Of a different house. The rooms are just a little more spacious, a little lighter, there is a fireplace (the other house didn't have one), but what clinches it is the view: this house is on the beach, blue sea as far as the eye can see, white sails in the distance. You try to recall the house you saw earlier. You liked it, didn't you? Yes, but then you hadn't seen this house yet. You know that you could have had this house, too, but now it's too late. You've already signed for the other one. You try with all your might to get the original feeling back, to find the first house as lovely as when you first saw it. But it doesn't work; for the rest of your life you'll think only of the fireplace and the endless blue sea.

"But Bernhard's a handsome guy, isn't he?" I dared to ask her for the first time, two weeks after we'd met. Bernhard and I had stayed in town a few days longer, then he'd gone on to the capital on his own. "To travel on with a man in love, you don't want to do that to me, Robert," he said, and he slapped me on the shoulder, kissed Sylvia

185

and the other girl — her big sister, eighteen months older than her, as it turned out — three times on the cheek and wished us all the luck in the world.

"Yes, he's a handsome man," Sylvia said. "But not my type."

"So what *is* your type then?" I asked — for the first time; in all the years that followed I've asked the same question maybe a hundred times.

"*You're* my type, darling. But of course you knew that already. And if you ask me, you knew that already on that first night, when you stood there waiting for me with your hands in your pockets."

I couldn't hear that often enough; each time it was a confirmation of what Sylvia and I had seen at the same moment in each other's eyes.

But I was never entirely sure about it. Sometimes, in bed at night, when I couldn't sleep, I would play the other version of the same film. A version that also began on the little square, but now with two main characters instead of one. *If you ask me, the little one likes you, Robert.* Then Bernhard stepped up to Sylvia. He acted like he was searching his pockets.

What are you looking for?

The chirping of crickets. Violins soar.
A smile, but I've already found it.

15

That Friday evening, I caught myself keeping an even closer eye than usual. On Bernhard and Sylvia. All those years, I had gone on believing firmly in the film version with the happy ending, the one where Bernhard wasn't Sylvia's type and she had chosen me 100 percent. I may have been the house without a fireplace, the house with a relatively ordinary view, but I was the house where she felt most at home.

Meanwhile, though, Alderman Van Hoogstraten had appeared on the scene. Nothing more than an apartment along some backstreet, the living room looked out on a brick wall. What type was he? Why would Sylvia suddenly feel like moving into something smaller? A cold-water flat in a dumpy neighborhood?

We talked about the usual things. About the children (Bernhard had four from his two previous marriages, and one boy, five years old, with Christine), about living in America, in Boston, about American politics, President Obama, and the civil war in Syria. Sylvia had made her famous casserole, the big hit of her native region, and during dessert — a caramel pudding baked in the oven to give it a thin, fragile crust — talk turned to Amsterdam.

"What strikes us most when we walk around town here, after almost a year in Boston, is all the foreigners," Christine said.

A brief silence descended; Bernhard didn't seem to catch the faux pas and merely nodded to confirm his wife's story, but a broad grin had appeared on Sylvia's face.

"Oh, God, no, of course I don't mean it that way!" Christine said, laying her spoon down beside her caramel pudding and taking Sylvia's hand. "You're, you're . . . different. And besides, how long have you been here anyway? No, I mean the masses of foreign tourists. It wasn't that way ten years ago. And now you have certain streets . . . Damstraat! We walked down Damstraat yesterday, you hear almost no one speaking Dutch there anymore. And the canals are really awful too. The line for the Rijksmuseum, the one for the Anne Frank House circles all the way around the Old West

Church these days. You added it up, Bernhard," she said, turning to her husband. "How long do you have to wait in line there?"

"Oh," Bernhard said, "it was only a rough estimate. But three and a half hours, for sure. Yeah, you have to be pretty determined."

"What do you think about that, Robert?" Christine asked. "I mean, I imagine that, as mayor, you must be pleased for the city. Pleased about all the revenue those people bring in. But what do you really think about it? You don't want Amsterdam to turn into a sort of Venice, do you, where all the natives move away and the ones who stay behind have no choice but to work in the tourist industry?"

Before I could reply, however, I heard the key turn in the lock of the front door, and a few seconds later Diana and her boyfriend came into the dining room. While Bernhard and Christine were getting up to hug Diana and kiss her cheeks, I tried as hard as I could to remember the boy's name. But I couldn't. In fact, it didn't matter all that much; I would only have to give him a different name here anyway, an alias, like the one I've given my wife. Again, upon hearing the name of my daughter's boyfriend, everyone would know right away who we were dealing with. Preconceptions stuck to his cultural background, too, like dust particles to a staticky wool sweater. *That explains a lot,* people might not quite say aloud, but they would definitely think it when they read newspaper reports of a shooting or stabbing involving people who shared that particular cultural background.

"Diana, aren't you looking lovely!" Christine said as she hugged my daughter. "And you're so big! Sorry, I'm sorry, I know I sound like some maiden aunt."

"And you are . . . ?" Bernhard held out his hand to the boy and tossed me a questioning glance.

"This is . . . ," I started in — but fortunately Diana's boyfriend spoke his own name, and I vowed to myself never to forget it again.

"Pleased to meet you, sir," the boy said.

"Would you two like some of my delicious dessert?" Sylvia asked.

"No thanks, Mom," Diana said. "We're going upstairs to watch the rest of *True Detective.*"

"Goodbye, ma'am, sir," the boy said before they got to the stairs. "Very nice to have met you. Sylvia," he said to my wife. "Sir." That last one was directed at me.

191

"What a nice girl she's become," Bernhard said once Diana and the boy had left. "Or actually, not a girl anymore, a young woman already."

The nuance did not escape me. Bernhard always talked about pretty or ugly women, no other category existed for him. Nice wasn't really part of his vocabulary.

I was a proud father, of course. After Sylvia — no, besides Sylvia, Diana was the prettiest woman in my direct surroundings. She had her mother's eyes, the same deep, dark sheen to her black hair. *Raven-haired* — if that adjective applied to anything at all, it was to the color of my wife's and daughter's hair. But she was definitely no fashion model, even the proud father could see that. My wife's native language had one adjective more than our own to denote someone's attractiveness. The sliding scale of attractiveness that began at the bottom with *repugnant, ugly, unsightly* and then rose by way of *nice* (as in "what a nice girl") on its way to *attractive, pretty, beautiful, irresistible* . . . What comes after *irresistible*? *Ravishing,* perhaps?

In my wife's language there is, besides *beautiful, attractive, ugly,* a second term for *attractive* that means something different than it does with us. Our *attractive* actually means only one thing: that someone may not be a ravishing beauty (fashion model), but that they still look very good. With the emphasis on *look*. In our language, *attractive* has to do only with appearances; in my wife's language, it is concerned primarily with the inner person. In other words: someone may have a nose that is too large, that throws their whole face out of kilter, they may have buck teeth and all-too-prominent gums, skin that is blemished by spots, hairs, or eczema, a body that could stand to lose twenty kilos, but despite all these glaring defects they can be extraordinarily *attractive.* First of all, because of what are actually outward traits anyway: an irresistible smile that makes us forget the teeth and gums, a glance that forces us from the very first moment to stare only into those eyes, and pushes the surrounding face into the background, a voice so dark that all our fibers tremble at the sound of it, a voice that touches something deep inside us, that transports us — beside us in bed at night — to a country beyond the horizon where we wish we could spend the rest of our lives.

Attractive, in my wife's language, makes up for a great deal, perhaps for everything: one leg that is shorter and thinner than the other, or that even stops completely just below the knee, missing fingers, or a thumb that looks more like a finger or claw of some other species of animal than our own broad, human one. The almost total absence of hair growth in men, the almost total absence of breasts in women.

"Yes, she's nice isn't she?" said Sylvia — the proud mother who I knew was now using *nice* to mean *attractive,* attractive in the sense it had in her own language.

"I'd actually like to . . . ," Bernhard started in, pulling a pack of Marlboro Lights and a lighter from his pocket. "But I don't know whether you would . . ."

"Please, go do that in the garden!" Christine said, before Sylvia or I could open our mouths. Bernhard glanced at me, a little like a child who has just dropped a glass and broken it.

"I'm pregnant," Christine said.

For a few seconds all was silent, a silence broken only when Sylvia put her dessert spoon back on her own plate.

"We're going to have twins," Christine said.

16

We sat in the deck chairs in our garden, both of us smoking our second cigarette. It was perhaps a bit too cold to be sitting outside, but I had vowed not to go in until I had told Bernhard about my suspicions concerning Sylvia. As mentioned, I'd had doubts about whether I should do that at all, but this evening, after a couple of beers and half a bottle of wine, those doubts had disappeared into the background. Bernhard was my best friend. The day after tomorrow, he and his pregnant wife would leave for Boston. I would let him finish talking first, wait calmly for a pause in his discourse.

"There are things we, as humans, simply can't fathom," Bernhard went on; his talk had started a while ago — exactly where I couldn't remember anymore, probably with the vastness of the universe, with light being sucked into a black hole. "Think of it this way: It's basically the same as if our eyes couldn't perceive colors. As if we saw everything in black and white. In a world like that, a tulip is a light gray."

This was what Bernhard had mastered like no other: making the world around us exciting again. We could go out to dinner with a group of friends and spend the whole evening talking about soccer, women, politics, and the rise or fall of property values, but once Bernhard got rolling we all became little boys again, lying with our heads together in a field, chewing on a blade of grass and staring up at the blue sky. Boys who first try to pick out animals and other shapes in the clouds floating by, but go on after that to fantasize about what might be behind those clouds. How far away is the sun that we feel warming our faces? How long will it go on shining? Into eternity. But what's eternity? Does eternity go on existing after you're dead?

"A deaf-mute person, for example, knows that sounds exist," Bernhard went on. "Because we, the ones who can hear, have told them so. But now try to imagine that we were all born deaf and mute. You and me, Sylvia, Christine, all of us. We don't have the faintest idea what sound is. We pound a hammer against a piece of iron, but we don't hear it. We speak to each other in sign language, that's all we know, that's the way we've always done it. The wind doesn't rustle through the trees. The waves hit the beach in total silence. As a matter of fact, we don't need sound at all. Besides being empty, the cosmos is above all silent. It's really interesting, as a thought experiment. How would the human race have evolved without sound? Would we have invented the same things? Or would they have been very different things, to help us get ahead in a world enveloped in silence? Would Columbus still have discovered America? And would that still have happened in 1492? Or fifty years later? How would we experience a war without sounds? Or a soccer match? We can't be deafened by incoming artillery anymore, because we're already deaf, we have been all our lives. The referee doesn't hear us shouting 'boo,' because there's nothing to shout. He can't blow his whistle for a penalty either. But otherwise everything's the same. The grass still smells like grass. The soldiers are still chased out of their trenches and run to their deaths. But they don't scream when an artillery shell punctures their chest. The dying soldier doesn't scream for his mother. He thinks about her, he still does that. He uses gestures to tell his comrades to leave him behind, that they should leave him here amid the blown-apart carcasses of the horses, the pools of mud and the barbed wire. With gestures he makes clear to them what they, if they get out of here alive, should tell his mother: that he didn't suffer."

I leaned over to my friend to light his next cigarette and asked myself — not for the first time — how long he would have stuck it out with Sylvia if it had been him rather than me who had appeared on the scene first, amid the plastic tables on that dusty little square. In a separate reality, he would have had time to utter his corny opening lines. At the disco, which bore no signs of being a disco on the outside, where we went for a drink next, it would have been me rather than him who sat on the uncomfortable wooden bench beside the dance floor, next to Sylvia's elder sister. I wasn't like Bernhard; after a lot of waffling I probably would have asked the sister to dance. But would I have put an end to my travels for that sister, because I couldn't imagine living a life without her? And how long would it have been before Bernhard had had enough of Sylvia? A day? Two days? A week? Or would he actually have married her in my stead? Would I have been his witness to their marriage, rather than the other way around? And — and here my imagination ground to a halt at times, in the middle of the night, on those half-sleepless nights when I stared wide-eyed at the ceiling and listened to Sylvia's breathing, still reassuring at that time — would I simply have married the sister out of desperation, in order to at least be able to lead that parallel life, apart from but still close to the woman who really should have been mine?

The wedding was held eight months after we met. In her hometown, at my request. I don't know what it was, but I wanted to have as few people there as possible. As few people from Holland, in any case. Bernhard was, as I've said, my witness, but the rest of my circle of friends I left in the dark as much as I could. From the start, I also tried to discourage my parents from traveling off to the remote interior. "It's really far away," I said. "There's nothing there, her parents' house is small, you won't be able to stay there, there's only one hotel, but it's not a place you'd want to spend the night." What I forgot was that my parents, particularly my father, only felt encouraged by stories about remote, hot interiors and uncomfortable hotel rooms. "If our only son is getting married, we'll be there," my father said.

"And that's that." My mother asked one last time about the beds in that hotel, whether they at least had clean sheets — I could have convinced her to stay at home, but my father had already gone to a special travel store and bought a hiking map of the surroundings. "Not far from there, there's a medieval footpath to a twelfth-century Crusaders' fortress," he told my mother, "on a mountaintop six thousand feet high." My mother only looked at me, sighed deeply, and lowered her eyes.

I should be honest about my reasons for not wanting to get married in Holland. Sylvia's parents hadn't even considered the possibility, they simply assumed that their daughter would celebrate her wedding in the place where she was born. For me, the main point was not to introduce my bride-to-be to the Netherlands all too quickly. To the Dutch, to be more precise. Dutch men. So far, besides me, she had seen only Bernhard, a man more handsome than me by any standards, even though he wasn't her type. There, in that hot interior of hers, we were the only tall, blond gods from the north, but in Holland she would immediately see that there were thousands of men like me. Better and worse versions of me, but all just as tall and just as blond.

Wouldn't there be, even if only from a purely statistical standpoint, plenty of better versions among those thousands who might also be her type?

Of the wedding party itself, I remember mostly the things that *didn't* happen. I don't know exactly why it was, probably my own prejudices, but I had been half-expecting certain rituals that made you hope for as few lookers-on as possible. No countrymen, in any case. Countrymen who would go on for years telling juicy anecdotes, anecdotes that confirmed the preconceptions, stories in which the national character of my wife's compatriots would serve as the radiant focal point. I knew full well that, had I been the only Dutch guest at our wedding, I myself would have wanted to go on for years dishing up anecdotes like that. I didn't doubt that for an instant. But in the end, nothing I had feared actually happened. Or rather, nothing that could have made me dread the presence of my countrymen.

On the spit in the garden, it's true, an entire animal carcass revolved slowly — the carcass of an animal that could still easily be recognized as such, with legs, a head, and a tail, and here and there the remainder of a patch of hide that went up in flames, crackling and spattering fat all around, but as far as I could tell there had been no unusual cruelty involved in the animal's demise. (I won't name the species of animal here either; some species would rule out certain countries as the one my wife comes from.) There were also no rituals involving blood or intentional mutilation. No dishes were shattered, no glasses were thrown into the fire, the women were not separated from the men before the ceremony. It's true, there were children running around the party grounds till far past midnight, until sunrise; in Holland a babysitter or overage relative would have brought them to bed long before that. An overage relative whose presence was no longer really considered desirable — in our own country, older people are seen mostly as annoying busybodies who you hope will piss off as soon as possible. In my wife's hometown, the children ate and drank and danced along with us, the littlest among them fell asleep in the grass, but even the oldest relatives and villagers stuck with the party until the break of day. And finally, no bloodied sheets had to be hung out the window of our bedroom as proof my wife was still intact — all mine; that I was the first man to take her in his arms on that same particular night.

■ ■ ■ ■

"The most important challenge facing us since time immemorial has been the question *Why?*," Bernhard said; behind the glowing cone of his cigarette, his face remained largely hidden in shadow. "Not just for the scientist, for all of us. First we explored the world, then the universe. We put people on the moon. People may land on Mars within the next fifty years. But believe me, what we find on Mars will hardly outclass our visit to the moon. Only more craters and rocks and dry riverbeds through which water may or may not have run long ago. It's just farther away, that's all. On the whole, an expedition to Mars will turn out to be a disappointment. No, our real objective is a lot closer than that. In fact, it's all in here." Bernhard tapped his finger against the side of his head. "In our minds. We have to be willing to think further than we've ever thought before. We have to be deaf people, but deaf people who want to be able to hear. For a deaf person who assumes that all mankind is deaf as well, hearing would be the greatest conceivable discovery. That's where we have to get to. We have to stop wanting to travel farther all the time, but only to travel inside. We have to want to think what has been unthinkable until now."

Till then I hadn't said a word, at most an affirmative grunt to show that I was still listening. I was reminded of Bernhard's wedding; not one of his first two weddings, but this latest one, with Christine. In the last twenty-five years, marriages in the Netherlands have been celebrated only ironically, and Bernhard and Christine's wedding was no exception. It was held here in Amsterdam, in the accommodations shared by both city hall and the opera house, in a special wedding room done up in green and orange pastels with a crooked chair sticking out of the wall. The table on which the marriage vows are confirmed stands atop a turntable, which revolves slowly during the signing of the register. The waiting list for this wedding room stretches out into eternity. But what are the crooked chair, the weird colors, and the turntable meant to say except that we shouldn't take this marriage seriously? It's marriage with a wink and a nudge. We get married, but in fact it doesn't amount to anything, of course.

It was at the end of our own wedding party when it happened. Most of the guests had gone home. I walked out to the edge of the garden, and then farther still, past the chicken coop and the little shed where Sylvia's parents kept their canned vegetables and cured meat, where the garden tools hung on the wall and the homemade sausages from the beams. There was no fence; the grass faded seamlessly into a plot of fallow land where only a few thistles and low shrubs grew amid the boulders. Here the terrain dipped at first, went down into a dry ditch, then climbed steeply on the far side. There was a little path there, I knew that, Sylvia and I had climbed it before. After a few hundred meters uphill you reached a point, a sort of hollow in the rocks, where you could see her parents' house and almost the entire town far below.

I had no real plan. No, in fact I did. But it was a plan that started taking form only once I had sunk to my knees and then carefully — one foot behind the other and my hands searching for a hold on the hard ground — began crawling down into the ditch. I was going to follow the winding path up to the hollow in the rocks. I was happy. At that moment I knew for sure that I had never been happier in my life. I felt a need for perspective, for distance, if you will. To the extent it was possible in the dark, I wanted to look down from that hollow, from that height, on my new life. On my newly won happiness. But I had barely reached the bottom of the ditch when I heard someone behind me quietly speak my name.

"Robert . . ."

Shall I throw caution to the wind and give my wife's eldest brother a name that really fits him? The problem, though, is a different one. His real name fits him so well, fits him so perfectly, like a custom-tailored suit, that you can't take it off of him with impunity. I'm quite content with the names I've come up with for my wife and daughter; in fact, the more I use them the more their real names recede into the background. Sylvia and Diana — I've already become attached to those names, it will be hard to ever say farewell to them.

Sylvia's older brother was called what he was called, I don't know how else to put it. He *is* his name, just as Jesus Christ, John F. Kennedy, and Mick Jagger *are* their names. They can never be called anything else. Conversely, no one else can ever bear their names. We would probably start giggling nervously and adopt an incredulous expression if someone were to introduce themselves by one of those names.

So, until I come up with something better, I will call him "her brother."

Before I go on to tell you how all of them there, without exception, pronounced my name wrong — not only did they place the stress on the wrong syllable, it actually sounded as though they needed more air in order to pronounce the unfamiliar vowels and the consonants that cluster together so tightly in our language — and how they also spoke that name with a certain irony, in thinly disguised disbelief, as though they didn't want to accept that a name like mine could really exist, I should first say that I have given myself a different name here too. That seems only fair to my wife and daughter. And you will all agree that it was not badly chosen. Everyone knows my real name, all you have to do is superimpose my alias on my real name. So now think about my real name and try to imagine how that would be pronounced by a foreigner in whose language consonants serve only as a bridge between vowels. A language in which the consonants are the screws that hold words and sentences together: without the screws the words would fall apart, but screws should never draw too much attention to themselves. They shouldn't stick out. A word with two vowels and five consonants, three of which are also huddled together in fright, is a poor excuse for a word — or at least it will make anyone who doesn't speak Dutch laugh out loud.

"Robert . . ."

He sat down on a stone. I clambered back up. We sat together like that at the edge of the dry ditch, its bottom hidden in darkness. From a crumpled pack of the popular local brand — tobacco that smelled like asphalt and literally took your breath away at the first drag — he offered me a cigarette. He lit mine, then held his lighter under his own.

During the second and a half that it took, I looked at his face in the light of the flame. Like all men in that country, and perhaps even more in this part of that country, in this town, he looked at least ten years older than his age. It was hard to say why. It was not simply the sum total of more grooves and wrinkles, of a few more blemishes and moles than in the average Dutch face, of the generally less-well-tended teeth, one of which was missing already. It was also not because these faces were more bronzed than our own, more weathered by life out of doors and the strength of a sun unfiltered by clouds or mist. These men actually did their utmost never to expose their faces directly to the sun. They stayed in the shade as much as possible, meals here were always eaten indoors, the tables on the restaurant patios were there exclusively for tourists. A casual glance might make you think that their faces aged more quickly than ours, that they had been through more, seen more. In comparison with most Dutch faces, that might be right. The uninhibited good cheer with which the average Dutchman viewed the world was something you wouldn't find around here. Unmarked faces, faces without a history, like the ones you saw in Holland, were found here only among children, but even they often had more grown-up faces, so you could see exactly what they would look like when they grew older. No, I would have tended to say — and by then I had the right to an opinion, eight months had passed between first meeting Sylvia and our wedding day — that these faces were above all *tired.* Worn-out. Not only from working too hard, or from a life lived too hard, but perhaps tired of life itself. Of the passing of time. Even at an early age — Sylvia's brother had not yet reached thirty-five — life and time had etched an old man's face over the top of his own. Time here had taken an advance on the future, and made the faces years older than they actually were.

Could it be, perhaps — I asked myself this

back then, and I go on asking myself to this very day — that we consider people with faces like that more capable of anything? Or less, when it comes to feelings of compassion, mercy, general courtesy? Wasn't I simply the milquetoast, here in these surroundings, in this unrelenting heat amid the boulders and the thistles? The kind man from the Far North who would be of no use to anyone in times of war? Who wasn't much use anyway, in this hard world of the interior. A tall, gentle blond man, a sissy who helped the women clear the table, carry the plates to the kitchen. Who, God help us, picked up a dish towel and helped to dry the glasses and plates? What had gotten into this man anyway? Had he come here to be a good example to these weathered men?

I've asked myself that often enough, and I'm very much aware that preconceptions raise their heads here too. For a man who considers it only natural to cut an animal's throat (as efficiently as possible, by the way, with no unnecessary cruelty) as something that goes with life itself, like love, birth, and death, would it constitute a smaller step for him to place that blade against the throat of a fellow human, a smaller step than for us — for me, a grown man who would start to gag if they asked me to pluck a chicken? In all these years, no one at Sylvia's parental home has ever asked me to do that: they probably sense quite astutely that I dry plates and glasses, but that you shouldn't ask me to do something as rudimentary as plucking a chicken. In the same way you don't send a child out to disarm a landmine.

And wasn't that same gentleness (that milquetoast air, that sissified behavior) the principal reason Sylvia had fallen for me? Because she preferred a man who would help her with the dishes to a man from her own village who would have her serve him at the table, and boss her around like a barnyard animal — even if he probably wouldn't cut her throat?

A man with a face too old for his body, short and squat, often too fat as well, the kind of man a woman couldn't really get excited about (Sylvia's words). Admittedly, you saw it there much more often than here: an unsightly man with short legs and a fat belly beside a local beauty queen. "Can you believe it?" Sylvia would say whenever we passed a couple like that. "I could have ended up that way. I don't even want to think about it."

"Are you glad, Robert?" her brother asked, blowing smoke from his nostrils and laying a hand on my shoulder. "No, sorry, I am using the wrong word. I meant 'happy.' Are you happy, Robert?"

Her brother's English was better than anyone else's in the family, including Sylvia's. He had asked whether I was 'glad' but corrected himself immediately. *Are you happy, Robert?* They had trouble pronouncing the *h* around here, it always came out as a long, guttural *ch,* making "happy" sound like *chèppie,* but this was not the moment to correct someone's pronunciation.

"Yes, I am happy," I replied. "Very happy." I caught myself pronouncing the *h* as a guttural *g* both times, as though not to embarrass my new brother-in-law. In the same way that I, a man who grew up on the south side of Amsterdam and therefore spoke standard educated Dutch, would catch myself putting on a slight Amsterdam snarl when addressing the cat-calling Ajax supporters from that windy podium in the parking lot — to reduce the distance, I suspect, to try to be "one of the guys." Not really on purpose, mind you, I actually thought it was a bit ridiculous; I did it without meaning to.

There had been language problems with Sylvia's parents too; from the start of our relationship, Sylvia and I had spoken a grab bag of fractured French and English. But her parents spoke nothing but their own language. A common language, in fact, wasn't even necessary. When Sylvia had first stood across from her parents in their little living room with this tall, gangly Dutchman at her side, she had taken my hand. I saw it on their faces, read it in their eyes. Disappointment. They really did their best; her father slid back a chair from the kitchen table and gestured to me to take a seat, meanwhile barking something at his wife, upon which Sylvia's mother placed an opened bottle of wine and four glasses on the table.

It was eleven o'clock in the morning. I took little sips of wine and smiled until my jaws hurt. Now that we were seated, the difference in height was less apparent. Standing in the living room doorway I had felt ashamed of my height, I ducked automatically when I entered the room, but most of all I towered two or three heads above both her parents. Sylvia is not tall either, but she's certainly not short, she was at least a head taller than her father and mother. It was definitely humiliating, especially for her parents, for her father who had to tilt his head back all the way to look me in the eye, her mother who didn't even dare to do that and so kept her eyes fixed on a spot no higher than my knees.

But it was humiliating for me, too, in the way that you can carry your own discomfort around with you like an almost visible physical defect. When someone has a hunched back or an ugly scar, people later tend to remember mostly the hump and the scar. Hump and scar take on meaning in retrospect. One realizes that one could not expect much good, after all, from someone with a hump or a scar.

What was I doing here with my excessively tall Dutch body, for Christ's sake, in this house, in this country where I had no business being? Of course, I had come to carry off their daughter, their pretty daughter. All the foreigners, after all, went gaga over the women here. They didn't have them at home, women like this. Real women, with femininity oozing out of every pore. In Holland they had become extinct long ago.

Later, Sylvia would tell me that her parents had above all viewed me as someone who was "different." What they regretted most was that she was not going to marry a man from her own region. After that, they had admitted that it wouldn't have been so bad if I had at least shared their daughter's nationality or background.

"He seems nice," her mother had said. "But he's awfully foreign."

And what, in turn, had their daughter seen in me? Why had she chosen this beanpole, instead of a real man from the village? The fact that I wasn't a real man was written all over me: that stupid smile, above all, and the way he takes those little, hurried sips of wine. You'll see, next thing he'll take all the glasses into the kitchen himself and insist on helping with the dishes.

"I am glad to hear that," Sylvia's brother said, kneading my shoulder gently with his fingers. "I can see that you have a good heart. That you will be a good husband for her. But I want to tell you one thing, Robert," he added after a brief silence. "If you ever do anything to hurt her," he said — his fingers had stopped kneading and tightened their grip on my shoulder — "if you ever do anything to her, then I know where to find you. Then you'll have me to deal with."

"Basically, there are two major issues our brains can't cope with," Bernhard said. "The first one is the universe. The coming into being of that universe, and its finitude. Or rather, its infinitude. When it comes to that, science really has no answers. They never get further than some new theory about the dawn of the cosmos. That it all went a lot faster than we'd assumed till now, that the universe itself is therefore expanding much more rapidly than we'd thought, that first there was this huge clump of matter, which then blew apart. And so forth and so on. But the most important question is the one that's always skipped over: the why of it. In other words: What was there before the universe came into being? Where did that matter come from, all of a sudden? Why does science always start counting from the moment of the Big Bang, and never before that? And why does that same science never look farther than the boundaries of the universe? Why doesn't science look *beyond* the boundaries? If the universe is finite, what comes after that? Outside of that? Simply more of the same? Or nothing at all? And what are we supposed to imagine by 'nothing at all'? Those are the two mysteries which our brains are simply too limited to cope with. Here, we're like the deaf people who can't imagine what hearing is like.

"It's precisely that same vacuum that religion fills," Bernhard went on. "The universe stops at the same point our understanding does. What lies beyond the borders of the universe? What happens to us after we're dead? In essence, it's the same question. It's beyond our comprehension, we say. And that's exactly it. What we can't get to with our comprehension, we fill in with our imagination. With a hereafter. Or with a scientific explanation, like with the universe. Scientists laugh about the Creation story. About a God who created the world in seven days. Ridiculous, they say, but they forget that their own scientific explanations never begin with nothing either. There's always matter, out of the blue. But for the sake of convenience we don't bother ourselves about what came before that. Before the Big Bang, and before matter came along. Meanwhile, we've grown accustomed to thinking in terms of billions of years, in billions of light-years. But we don't worry our heads about the time before the universe came into being. Because we don't even know if there's anything there to worry our heads about. In fact, we don't know anything. The universe is infinite. Infinitely empty, that above all. The distances can't be expressed in miles. Again, you can ask yourself: What's the point of it, of all that space? I've never been religious, I wasn't brought up that way either, you know that. But do you remember that time — what was it, twenty years ago? — when we drove through Death Valley? We headed north out of Los Angeles, and then you had the exit with that big sign warning you that the next service station was a hundred and fifty miles down the road."

"Yeah," I said. "And those two jets dogfighting, way up in the sky."

"Yeah, that. I remember that too. Then there was this huge salt flat, and that was it. No houses. No other cars. I think we didn't see another soul for the rest of the afternoon."

"Right. We even got kind of scared. We thought: What if the car breaks down out here?"

"That was completely realistic, that fear. It still happens. Just a couple of years ago. A mother and her little boy. Camping out at Zabriskie Point, but then the car wouldn't start. And that family in the camper in Montana. It was fall and they were going from the city to their house in the woods when all of a sudden it started snowing. They found the camper the next spring, when the thaw set in."

Now I remembered something else from that trip across the salt flat. We had talked about God, about how it was easier in a desolate spot like that to understand why people believed in a God. And after that we switched from God to guns. To the right to bear arms. In Holland, people always laughed about the Americans and all their guns. All those pistols and rifles you could buy anywhere, even at the supermarket. But those same Dutch people must never have driven into Death Valley from the southwest. There is nothing there. No houses, no trees, no bushes. Just a dirty-white cracked plain and the bare mountains in the distance, without a soul in them either. Dusk was already falling, and everything changed color slowly, from a soft pink to a deep purple. If there wasn't a God, then there wasn't anything at all, we both thought. And then we realized that we would feel a lot more comfortable driving into that deep, deeply hostile landscape with at least one gun in the car.

And now I thought back on Sylvia's brother. The moment when he had stopped kneading my shoulder and made me promise never to do anything to hurt his sister. I had looked at his face, at his eyes in the dark, at the glowing tip of his cigarette. For half a second I wondered whether maybe he was joking, whether the brother of my wife — the woman I had married only a few hours before — might be pretending to be serious. That I was the object of a practical joke, and that I would be the laughingstock of the family for the rest of my days if I took his threat seriously. I took a couple of deep breaths; I waited for the moment when he would start kneading my shoulder again and burst out laughing. *Hey, I had you by the balls for a minute there, didn't I, Robert? Come on, admit it. You really believed me.*

But there was no laughter. I might have been imagining it, but it felt as though his fingers dug into my shoulder with renewed strength.

"I would never do anything to hurt her," I said. "Never. Sylvia is the love of my life. It would be absolutely impossible for me."

I clearly remember what I thought at that moment. On the one hand, this confirmed all the preconceptions at a single blow (*that's the way these people are, it's in their blood*); on the other, I was thankful to Sylvia's brother. I had started something new, a new phase in my life in which the waffling was over once and for all. I had not just married the love of my life; it also really mattered. This was no marriage with a wink and a nudge.

"I'm glad to hear that, Robert," he said quietly — and almost right away his fingers began kneading my shoulder again.

17

I didn't really know what I wanted. No, that's not completely true: I knew, above all, what I *didn't* want.

What I didn't want was to go snooping around, gathering evidence. That's the way things usually went in real life. Betrayed husband goes snooping around. He tries to crack the password to her computer (daughter's name, pet's name plus the last two digits of her year of birth). For the moment at least, his wife's e-mails don't provide a clue. Maybe she has a second, secret e-mail account. Or, at an unguarded moment, when she leaves her iPhone lying around the house the way she so often does, he can thumb back through her WhatsApp logs. But will he actually find anything? Wouldn't she have taken the necessary precautions long ago, wouldn't she have deleted the damning e-mails and text messages as soon as she read them?

I remembered that movie where the journalist punches in the last route recorded by his murdered colleague's car navigation system. But my wife didn't even have a driver's license. In any case, that wasn't what I wanted, I realized then, a couple of weeks after our dinner with Bernhard and Christine. I would keep my eyes open, I promised myself. From behind my newspaper I would go on watching her. During our shared meals, around the family dinner table or, like recently, with the three of us at Café Schiller, I would join in the innocent patter and meanwhile register the intonation in my wife's stories, the way a seismologist records the first vibrations of the earth's crust.

Solid evidence would be sure to destroy things. An incriminating e-mail or explicit text message would cause irreparable damage. For the rest of my life I would be able to reproduce the text word-for-word. At unsuspecting moments, those words would work their way to the fore and go on sullying our future — our future together, I allowed myself to think now, the happiness we'd regained. Three or four years from now I would watch from the beach as my wife waded carefully into the surf, and suddenly the text *More and more kisses! See you on*

Monday, Maarten would appear as a caption at the bottom of the screen. As long as there was no evidence, I reasoned, anything was still possible.

And as long as everything was still possible, the whole thing could also suddenly be over. That's the agreement I made with myself. The agreement I wanted with all my might to make with myself. If — between today and a point in the not-so-distant future — it should suddenly be over, I would never go on blaming her. I didn't know if I was capable of that, but it was worth a try. I would give her the benefit of the doubt. Maybe it had never happened at all. As long as I didn't start in about it, it had never happened.

The past, though, that was what troubled me most. To what extent had our shared past been tainted by this? I thought about the things we'd done together in the last few months. Whether they still held the same meaning, now that they were covered in a shimmer of suspicion. The possibility of a double life. My wife who smiled at me — but a smile meant only to throw dust in my eyes.

Last autumn, we went to the Kröller-Müller Museum together for a long week-end. Four days off, just the two of us. On

223

short vacations like that we usually went to our house in the country, or to Barcelona, London, or Paris, but this time we headed into the Dutch backcountry. Sometimes Sylvia complained that she had never seen the Netherlands at all. "I know Amsterdam," she said, "but I've never seen the rest." That wasn't completely true; during her first couple of years here we went everywhere: to Schiermonnikoog, to Groningen, to South Limburg — but after those first couple of years we had indeed stopped doing that. Traveling around the Netherlands is like running on the treadmill at the gym: when you get off after half an hour, you're still right where you started.

We walked around the galleries. Truth be told, I rarely look at the works on exhibit. My impatience wins out over my feelings of guilt about my lack of interest. My wife is very different when it comes to this. There was a long corridor with little galleries on both sides. I prefer to walk past galleries like that as fast as I can, at most I poke my head inside and then pull it back, like a doctor in a hospital who's walked into the wrong room. But my wife goes into each and every gallery. She stands and looks at each individual painting for more than two minutes on the average. I could call that loitering, but I know that's not the case: I'm the one who goes too quickly, no two ways about it. On the rare occasion I'll follow her in half-heartedly; I stand beside her, looking at a dark painting in which a brightly lit ship is docked at a quay half-hidden by mist. I look along with her, I try to see the ship, the mist, through her eyes. Following her example, I lean forward to look at the little information card posted on the wall, giving the painter's name, the title of the painting, and the year in which it was made. When my wife is finished reading the card, she doesn't walk away; she takes a step back and looks at the painting again. For me, reading the card is the last stop, the final mandatory act before bidding a definitive farewell to the painting, but for her it seems to be a summons to take another look — through other eyes, with new information. By that time she has usually forgotten all about me, but sometimes she'll look over and smile gratefully: the same grateful smile she gives me when I've waited patiently in front of the dressing room at the boutique.

"Lovely, isn't it?" she says then. Or: "You can almost hear the silence through that mist." For me, that's the signal to turn to the next painting. Or rather, to let my gaze glide over all the other paintings in the gallery. In parting. More ships. A battle at sea. A shipwreck. Starving sailors on an island in the Barents Sea.

After a while, I would end up a few galleries away from her. When you don't stop in front of each painting, you see something very different, though: all of art history in a nutshell. That's the way the galleries at the Kröller-Müller were laid out, from past to present. From paintings with recognizable boats, skating scenes, and fruit bowls to paintings that gradually turned their backs on the recognizable world. By way of fading contours, riverine landscapes made of hundreds of dots, and ballerinas composed of square planes and cubes to a total lack of recognizability. Squares. Colors. Lovely colors, true enough, lovely squares too — but it was time to wind up my visit to the museum and get back to the outside world, which was still recognizable as ever.

I went back six galleries and found her on a bench before a painting of a group of men and women, a few of them holding parasols, who were picnicking on the grass along a riverbank. Still painted recognizably as people, as grass and a river, but with a first, tenuous distortion of reality. The faces almost without the familiar features, precursors of the abstract planes, circles, and squares, the grass not the color of grass but lighter than that, the light alkaline green of pistachio ice cream.

In fact, of course, I didn't look at the painting first, I looked at my wife. I had seen the painting before. It was the painting where I'd dropped out, the gallery where I had left her behind.

She was sitting on the bench, typing something into her phone, she hadn't seen me yet. I stopped and looked at her face.

She was smiling. She smiled as she wrote. Our daughter, I thought — I thought at the time, an eternity ago. Sylvia and Diana often texted each other when they were apart for a few days. That's why Sylvia was smiling, of course, because she was thinking about Diana as she wrote. Or because Diana had just written something funny that still had her smiling.

At that moment she glanced up from the screen of her iPhone and saw me. In retrospect, I can't say that she looked startled. No, she looked more like someone who has just woken up, who doesn't know for a brief moment which bedroom, which bed, she's in.

"Hey . . ."

Even without the hindsight, I remember how her smile began to fade when she caught sight of me. That she blinked her eyes, like someone suddenly opening the curtains in a darkened room.

I nodded at her phone. "Diana?" I asked. Our daughter was at home alone, the new boyfriend had yet to arrive on the scene. "Everything okay with her?"

My wife shook her head. "No, a girlfriend. But you don't know her."

A girlfriend. But you don't know her . . . Where had I heard that before? No, I hadn't heard it anywhere before. I would hear it *later,* about six months later, at the Parisian brasserie.

The girlfriend I hadn't known back then in the museum, was that Sadako too? The same imaginary or real Japanese Sadako who was already, or only six months later, being cheated on by her husband? By her *imaginary* husband, I couldn't help thinking now. An imaginary girlfriend with an imaginary husband — a nonexistent act of adultery.

With Sylvia and me, it's very simple: Wherever we are, it's nice. Wherever the two of us are together, we're happy. Our interests are quite different, but our interest in each other always remains at the same high pitch, wherever we are. Paintings, in and of themselves, may not interest me much, but a painting with Sylvia standing in front of it is always more than just a naval battle, landscape, or still life with fruit and a dead hare.

Wherever we were, it was nice; that was the thought that forced itself on me now. Back then, yes, during those four days in autumn. In my thoughts I heard myself formulating a hideous question. A question to which I was not completely sure I wanted to hear the answer. *How long?* was the question I hoped I would never ask. *How long has this been going on?*

I was afraid of defiling the past. Deception that tarnishes the present, I could probably live with that. I was already living with that. But not the past, please, not the past.

How many of those moments could I now reconstruct, in retrospect? How many did I want to reconstruct? Moments that might now mean something different.

The time she walked out of the room before answering the phone. That other time, when she . . . No, I didn't want to think like that. I didn't want to color in the past, to color it in retrospectively with incriminating moments. There were, as I've said, at least no outward signs of adultery. No sudden and inexplicable weight loss, no excessive makeup — and then, out of the blue, I suddenly thought of something else.

How many people knew already? How many girlfriends had she already told about it? *I have to tell someone, I'll go nuts if I keep it to myself any longer. Can you keep a secret?*

How many people had Maarten van Hoogstraten told already? That was my next thought. How many colleagues, secretaries, town hall messengers, doormen already knew all the ins and outs of the affair? The affair that would make waves if leaked to the media. The cuckolded mayor. Even worse: the oblivious mayor. Almost everyone at city hall knew about it, he was the only one who hadn't figured it out.

That happened sometimes. An old high school friend I still see on occasion. About ten years ago, his wife became involved with the husband of a couple they were on friendly terms with. Everyone knew about it. For years. I knew. Sylvia knew. But were we going to open our friend's eyes to the truth? No, he had to find out for himself, didn't he? Was he blind or something?

The simple fact that the media hadn't picked up on the affair yet, I thought then, might mean there was no affair at all. Or that no one had noticed anything.

No, I would leave everything intact, I decided. The past, first and foremost. The past contained no omens, as long as you

230

didn't go looking for them. Or, to put it differently: all omens — including the smile on her face in that gallery at the Kröller-Müller Museum — could, by the same token, be no omens at all.

As far as the present was concerned, from now on I would do things differently. What's more: I already *was* doing things differently. I had already tried the undercover agent approach. But as of today, I would be the mole in my own life. Visible and invisible, at one and the same time. The last person people would expect to be the mole.

From now on, I would do nothing but observe Maarten van Hoogstraten, too, in a way he wouldn't recognize as being observed. I mustn't change my behavior, my attitude toward him, otherwise he might suspect something. I didn't like him, I had never liked him. So I shouldn't suddenly act buddy-buddy with him or laugh at his lousy jokes. My expression had to show the same faint aversion as before. Aversion, if not quite contempt, although it was awfully close. Naive people drove me crazy. Maarten van Hoogstraten radiated the unrestrained cheerfulness of the ignorant. Of those who do not get it. His face, those oversized blue eyes, were on the side of the right. Against pollution. Concerned about global warming. The rising sea level. All of which were indeed things you could be against, things you could worry about. But people like him were awfully sloppy about the way they profited from issues like that. They borrowed credence from them. They were in the right — so how could you possibly contradict them?

Are you in favor of flooding? Would you rather see the sky darkened with pollution? And then, without blinking an eye: *So, are you against the fair distribution of wealth, doesn't it bother you that more and more people are dying of starvation so that you can enjoy a steak? Do you want to ruin our lovely planet even further?*

Even though you had never said anything like that at all. You wouldn't dream of it. You gave in to the terror. The terror of what was generally accepted as right, the terror of perpetual correctness.

No, from now on I would block his every move. I had always blocked his moves, but from now on I would do so less openly. I would adopt an interested expression when he unfolded his plans for a wind-turbine park at the city's edge. At regular intervals during his plea I would nod understandingly, raise my hand to my chin, and look

232

attentive — as if I were actually listening to him.

As if that wind-turbine park ever stood a chance in hell, I thought the next moment — and was startled by my own laugh, which was just a little too loud.

18

All signs indicated that the female journalist across from me in my office was about to ask one final question, when there was a knock at the door and my secretary stuck her head inside.

"We're almost finished," I said.

Mrs. Schreuder and I always agreed beforehand that, one hour after an interview started, she would knock on my door to say that I was expected at the next meeting or at the opening of a new bridge. But my sense of time told me that that hour wasn't over yet. It was a tough call, though; to my taste, all interviews last too long anyway. I always tried to outwit time by not looking at my watch, and my secretary always popped in to rescue me earlier than I'd expected.

"It's your father," she said, glancing at the journalist.

"Tell him I'll call him right back."

Mrs. Schreuder raised a hand to her mouth, cleared her throat, and looked at the journalist again. "He's not on the phone. He's . . . he's here. He's waiting outside, at the reception desk."

This was something new. This had never happened before. In all my years as mayor, he had never shown up unannounced at city hall.

"Just tell him that I'll be . . ." But I didn't finish my sentence. Something, a premonition that felt as though my heart had sagged a few inches, made me get up out of my chair.

For the space of half a second, I thought about asking the journalist whether she would mind waiting in the hall, so I could talk to my father in here — but that was not a good idea. Maybe she would want to include it as an "atmospheric detail" in the interview. Maybe it would annoy her. A hint of that annoyance would seep into the article.

"Do you have a moment?" I said, smiling at the journalist. "I'm sure this won't take long."

She didn't smile back at me: she glanced at her iPhone, which she was using to record our conversation, and tapped the screen with her thumb. "I was actually more or less finished," she said. "There's just one little thing . . . No, go ahead. I'll wait."

My father was standing beside my secretary's office, his hands in his pockets, in front of the king's portrait in the hall. That portrait was originally meant for my office, but I couldn't stand the thought of seeing that face first thing each morning. I knew what would happen then. In the course of time, maybe after only a couple of weeks, I would grow accustomed to that face, and I wanted to avoid this at all costs. In our former home we'd had a bathroom from the 1970s, brown tiles with a floral motif. That's the first thing we'll rip out, we told each other during the viewing. But it didn't happen. We kept postponing it. Renovating a bathroom is different from painting over floral wallpaper. You can't shower there for a few weeks, you actually have to look for a place to stay temporarily, or else you have to let the builders come in while you're on vacation. What happened was that we grew accustomed to taking a shower in a bathroom so hideous that it hurt your eyes. And we never used the tub — you never wanted to stay in there long enough for a bath.

After a while, we couldn't help but feel that something of the bathroom's ugliness had seeped into our inner selves. And so the king's portrait hung in the hall now. I hurried past it each morning, the way you skirt someone at a party whom you'd really rather not see.

"Robert . . ." My father tried on a grin, but I saw right away that he wasn't his usual self. His eyes darted back and forth from me to my secretary, who had come out with me and was standing at her office door.

"Come on," I said, laying a hand on his shoulder, "let's go down this way." I looked to one side and nodded to Mrs. Schreuder, a reassuring nod: *It's all right, I'll be back in a flash, I won't let the journalist wait too long.*

"I won't beat around the bush," he said, even before we had turned the corner to another, wider corridor; at the end of it, on the right, was the canteen. We could sit there, if there weren't too many people, but I suddenly wondered whether that was such a good idea. "We're going to move it up," he said. He had stopped walking, his hands were still in the pockets of his trousers, the kind of trousers my father had worn almost all the time for the past ten years: khaki, with lots of zippered pockets down the seams, active trousers, trousers to wear when you're working in the garden or clambering over boulders in a dry riverbed.

I knew right away what he was talking

about, of course, although I'd tried to think about it as little as possible in the last few months — thought about it so little that there were moments when I forgot about the whole plan. At those rare moments when I *did* think about it, my only conclusion had been that they had probably called it off. During our visits to my parents' house, or on the occasional Sunday afternoon when they came by our place, no one had brought it up again.

Just in case it actually was going to happen, though, I'd told Sylvia about their plan; not right after my father and I visited the graveyard in Ouderkerk, but much later, almost too late, while I was already parking the car in front of their house, just before we were going to ring my parents' bell.

"By the way," I'd said as casually as I could. "My parents may start talking about something that's fairly bizarre, to put it mildly. Just so you don't act too amazed. I meant to tell you about it before, but I never got around to it."

And I told her. Sylvia just shook her head. "What is it with you?" she asked, and I knew that by "you" she meant, as she did so often, *you Dutch people.* "Why can't you let life go the way it goes? Why does everything have to be arranged, from cradle to grave? I don't get it, I really don't, you people have lost all touch with reality."

"But people who are in a lot of pain and know that they don't have long to live . . . ," I sputtered, for form's sake, because I knew she was right.

"That's different. Are your parents in pain? Is their suffering unbearable? You know what it is, Robert? It's really childish. It's just clamoring for attention. They say they want to leave life in a dignified fashion. But it's nothing but vanity. They want to avoid having you watch them go into decline. They want to stage-direct your memories. These are energetic parents who go hiking in the mountains. Not parents you have to lift out of bed and take to the toilet. There's nothing dignified about it. It's a misconception that going downhill is undignified. A deathbed, troubled breathing, last words, a final sigh: that's the real dignity. Here, in this country, it's all about toys. A theme park. Even death."

During that visit, though, no one talked about the plan, and not on later occasions either. "So?" Sylvia would ask from time to time. "Is it still going ahead?" And after I told her that I didn't know, that neither of my parents had mentioned it lately, she would say: "See what I told you? It's just clamoring for attention."

But now my father was walking here beside me — we were almost to the door of the canteen — and he said: "Sometime in the next couple of weeks. We don't have an exact date. There are a couple of things we have to arrange first, and we're not going to let that rush us. There's no hurry."

"But . . . ," I started in, but I didn't know how to go on. Three of the tables in the canteen, I saw, were occupied by about ten council members, aldermen, and civil servants. I stopped in my tracks. My father walked on; in the doorway, he turned to me.

"But I thought the two of you were going to France first," I said.

"What are you standing there for? I thought you were going to buy me a cup of coffee."

I tried to sneak a glance at my watch, but he noticed right away. We had found a table at the window, the one farthest from the others. Out of earshot, or at least that's what I hoped — but my father had never been very conscious of his volume. *Not so loud, not so loud,* my mother often said. *We can hear you just fine.*

"You have to get going already?" he said. "This won't take long. I just figured it wasn't something to tell you about over the phone."

Two civil servants, at a table a little farther along, looked over and nodded to me.

"Anyway, about that vacation," he went on, after sipping quickly at his coffee. "Your mother and I have talked about that at some length. It just didn't feel right. Why go on a trip when you know it's going to be the last one? Too melodramatic, we realized that all of a sudden. Kind of like a prisoner on death row being served his favorite meal, I've never understood that either. If they asked me, I'd say forget it. The things they ask for are usually pretty banal, too, I read an article about it once. The biggest steak you can buy, or a Double Whopper with cheese and bacon from Burger King. This coffee is tepid."

He knocked back the rest of his cup and set it down on the saucer with a loud tick. People at the tables farther back were looking at us now too.

"But . . ." I really had to watch out now, not to start every sentence with a "but." When someone was planning to put an end to their life, it was probably natural to try to talk them out of it, even if they were almost ninety-five. The fact is, at the same time I felt something else: the same thing I'd felt

241

at the graveyard in Ouderkerk. A slight tingling in my fingertips and at the back of my neck. The foreboding of something new. The end of an era.

"And what about your birthday?" I said. "I thought you were at least going to celebrate that."

He took his cookie from the saucer and breathed a deep sigh. The cookie was packaged in see-through plastic, which he yanked on a few times. Then he rubbed it between his fingers and tried again.

"What the hell!" he said. "Do they really have to do that? Does everything have to be wrapped in plastic? A cookie, for God's sake! We talked about that too," he went on. "You have landmark years. Seventy-five. Eighty. At eighty-five it starts feeling uncomfortable. As though someone who has come back three times for a standing ovation comes back again for a fourth. After that, it starts getting normal. Ninety, if you think about it, is already an obscene age. Yeah, I know, I'm guilty of it too. I've asked people: How old do you think I am? But I stopped doing that a couple of years ago. Besides, a birthday is always an ordeal. Back then, it was because of all the people who showed up. These days, it's because of how many people don't show up. It's turned into a contest. A knockout race. And, right, I've won. No one shows up anymore because there's no one left to show up. So who am I doing it for anyway? For you guys? For your mother? Give me a break! It's no landmark anymore, Robert. We've reached the finish. There's no use sprinting another hundred meters."

I said nothing. I fumbled with my left sleeve, tried to pull back my shirt and coat a little, so I could check my watch.

"Yeah, I know, you have to get going," he said. "We're finished anyway. No vacation. No birthday. No more Christmas dinners. No New Year's. What a glorious prospect! Paradise exists, even in this lifetime."

"And what about Mama? I'd like to ask Mama —"

"You don't have to look so pained. We're not gone yet. Meet up with her. Come by the house. Give her a call. Call her tonight."

"Tonight? But you said 'sometime in the next couple of weeks.'"

"Only after a manner of speaking. Don't take everything so literally, Robert. Just one thing, though: Don't make a big, dramatic thing out of it, neither of us wants that. No teary farewells. We want it to go as naturally as possible. As of today, you know what's going on. But we'll just keep on acting

243

normal, as though we're going to see each other again tomorrow or next week sometime. So call her tonight. Talk to her. You both know how things stand. We both think it will be a fine way to die. The way I always hoped it would be. You go for a walk in the woods. That evening you sink down in your easy chair with a double whiskey. And the next moment you're gone. 'Do you want another whiskey?' your wife asks. But no answer ever comes."

I looked at him, I tried to look him straight in the eye, but my father averted his gaze and looked out the window. He took off his glasses and rubbed his eyes.

"And then a couple of practical points," he said. "On the day itself I'll send you a text message. Then you have to wait twenty-four hours and then come and take a look. Do you still have a copy of the front-door key, or would you have to look for it forever? I brought one with me, just in case."

When I got back to my office a little less than fifteen minutes later, the journalist didn't seem annoyed; she was keying something into her phone, and looked up only once I was sitting at my desk again.

"Sorry about that," I said, glancing at my watch by way of formality. "That was sort of urgent."

"No problem," she said. "We're pretty much finished. In fact, there's just one thing I wanted to show you."

From her bag she took out a sheet of A4 paper in a clear plastic pouch, stood up, and laid it on my desk.

Pictures, a photo series: it took a few seconds before I realized what I was seeing. There were about ten photos in all. In the first one, a policeman in riot gear, carrying a wicker shield and with his truncheon drawn, was rushing out from between two parked cars. Old-model cars, I saw, cars that told you right away that the photos had been taken somewhere in the early 1970s. I wasn't exactly sure what they were, Fords perhaps, or maybe Opels? Squarer, more blockish than they are these days; all cars are roundish now. Standing in the middle of the street were three men, just boys maybe, wearing heavy knee-length coats and scarves. The scarves were pulled up over their noses, all three of them were wearing motorcycle or motor-scooter crash helmets. In the next two photos you saw the policeman swinging his truncheon, but the boys didn't run away, it looked like they were dodging the blows and actually crowding around the man. Then there were a couple

245

of photos with the cop on the ground, halfway between the parked cars; he still had his shield, but he'd lost his truncheon. One of the boys had something in his hand, a brick, his arm was raised high. In the final picture you saw the boys running away. All you could see of the policeman were his legs, sticking out from between the parked cars.

"Okay?" I said to the journalist, who had taken the chair across from my desk and was looking at me attentively. "What am I supposed to do with this?"

"You don't have any idea? You don't recognize anything?"

I looked at the photographs again. There were no faces to be seen, not the policeman's, not the three boys' either.

"Does the name Mark Vader mean anything to you?"

I shook my head.

"It was front-page news back then. A nasty story. During a demonstration against the war in Vietnam, Mark Vader, an agent with the Special Patrol Group, is thrown to the ground by three men, just boys really, and receives blows to the head and the back of his neck with a brick. He remained paralyzed for the rest of his life."

It started coming to me: headlines, the

general outcry about the "defenseless" policeman being beaten when he was already down.

"Yes, I remember now," I said. "And those pictures, they were in the paper then, too, weren't they?"

"The series won an award at the time. World Press Photo of the Year in the news category. The culprits were never found. They never turned themselves in either. They could have, though. Or else people could have found out who they were. All it would take was for one of the three to start bragging in a café about being in the winning World Press photo. But that didn't happen either."

I suddenly sensed the direction this was taking. I felt it at the back of my neck, first cold, then hot, the hairs on my neck standing up.

"Okay?" I said. "But what does this have to do with me?"

I was on my guard now. I was sitting here across from a journalist, after all. A journalist who was going to describe my reaction in a full-spread article in her paper. An interview with the mayor of Amsterdam. A revealing interview. Even if I denied everything, the denial might still be used against me. Where there's smoke, there's fire, that's what they say. It was like being accused of sexual intimidation, of rape, of storing a distasteful brand of pornography on the hard disk of your computer. You could deny everything. Someone else had messed with your computer, the woman who accused you of rape is erratic and has been out to get you for years, your hand accidentally touched that buttock in the elevator — but there are no other witnesses, it's your word against hers.

"One of the three boys has come forward, after all these years," the journalist said then, not surprisingly. "Anonymously. He doesn't want to turn himself in, he just wants to tell his story."

I said nothing; I pretended to be examining the photos again.

"This man," she went on, "says that you are the boy with the brick. The boy who beat Officer Mark Vader into a wheelchair."

I leaned my elbows on the table, clasped my hands, and rested my chin on them. I tried to smile as I looked at the journalist.

"My my, is that what he says?"

"Yes, he's a hundred percent sure."

I'm not the demonstrating type. Once in my life I took part in an anti-Vietnam protest and shouted "Johnson, murderer!" But that was an otherwise peaceful demonstration. Later, in the early 1980s, I had a girlfriend who demonstrated against everything. Everything that was fashionable at the time: nuclear power plants, cruise missiles. To keep the peace, I once marched along in one of the big demonstrations against the stationing of cruise missiles. Out of love for her. But I hated it. Especially the cheerfulness. The cheerfulness of all those thousands of people who never for a moment doubted that they were demonstrating for the right cause.

While I looked at the journalist and kept smiling, I ran through my options.

This was not me. I was not the boy with the brick in the photo. If I denied it, that was what the paper would say. *Mayor denies dealing fatal blow.*

"So this man now claims that he is in these pictures, along with me?" I said.

"That's right."

"And that I am the boy with the brick?"

"I take it you're now going to try to tell me that this isn't you? That that boy — this man — is mistaken? That he laid that policeman low back then along with two completely different people? And that that one boy may look a lot like you, but in reality it's someone else?"

I looked straight at her, I was still smiling,

249

I had to give it my all not to blink my eyes. Blinking always makes the papers.

I wanted something else, though. I wanted the journalist to remember it all clearly, later on. To put my response, in all its details, into her interview.

"He's not mistaken," I said without blinking. "It was a long time ago, but I remember it as if it were yesterday. Yes, that's me. I'm the boy in the pictures. The boy with the brick."

19

I'm old enough, I remember the days when you were still allowed to smoke on planes. Only in the last ten rows, so there was always a cozy crowd of smokers back there. The ones who hadn't been able to get a smoking seat stood in the aisle. Those were always the ten most convivial rows on the plane, in the same way the most convivial people at a party always gather in the kitchen. Smoking and flying: the ideal combination. As Allen Carr writes in his bestseller *The Easy Way to Stop Smoking,* it is particularly those moments of stress associated with boredom that get us smoking: driving, talking on the phone, flying. I started again during the Christmas holidays. On the sly, I was almost going to say, but there was nothing sly about it.

"You've started smoking again," Sylvia had said not long before that, when she kissed me good night.

"Yeah," I said. "Not much, a cigarette every now and again. Does it bother you?"

She sniffed, put her nose up close to my lips, and sniffed again. "Actually, I think it's nice," she said. "I think it smells nice. Manly."

Ever since then I'd stopped being furtive. At least as far as my wife was concerned. We decided, though, that it was better to keep it hidden from our daughter. So as not to set a bad example. I would wink at my wife whenever I announced that I was going to take the garbage out to the container on the corner. I waited for the day when my daughter, too, would ask me the inevitable question. But so far that hadn't happened. My daughter and I kissed each other at least once a day, a peck or two on the cheek. When we did that I would hold my breath, the way you do when they pull you over for an alcohol screening. Briefly, at one point, I thought about buying a dog. There were moments, after all, when there were no full garbage bags to take to the corner. "I left something in the car," I'd say then. "A dossier, I have to run through it for tomorrow morning." My wife and daughter would be sitting beside each other on the couch. My wife would glance up for a moment and frown when I winked at her. There was little chance that my daughter had even heard me. "It wasn't in the car," I would say for form's sake, when I came back ten minutes later. "It's probably upstairs somewhere."

That's right, now that I'd started smoking again there were moments when I wished we had a dog. When you have a dog, there is no need to fib. "I'm going to take the dog for a walk." What could sound more natural than that? While walking the dog, you could easily smoke three or four cigarettes. I still remember what it was like, back before I quit. Time took on another perspective. After walking the dog for twenty minutes or so, a nonsmoker has had enough. When you're waiting for a tram or a bus, you experience that same, automatically decelerating sense of time. Everything takes too long. Time coagulates. There is only the waiting. But waiting in and of itself is nothing. At the bus stop I always lit up a cigarette. Or, even better: I rolled a cigarette. I still remember how disappointed I would be when the bus or tram would show up after the very first puff. When you smoke, you make time go to work for you. The smoker never waits. The smoker smokes.

Diana was about seven when she first started talking about a pet. *Yeah, yeah, of course,* we said, *that's wonderful, but who's going to take care of it? You? And what kind of pet are we talking about?* we asked, even though we already knew the answer. A dog. "I really wish I could have a puppy." *And who's going to let that puppy out? Are you going to do that?* "Yeah, sure," she said, "every day." *But a dog has to be let out twice a day. How are you going to do that? Before you go to school? Then you'll have to get up half an hour earlier.* We went on like that. We went on so long that the dog slowly disappeared from the picture. As I remember it, most of those conversations took place in the car, Diana in the back seat, her face in my rearview mirror. How the expression on that little face changed from cheerful and hopeful to disappointed and resigned. I could never keep looking at it for very long. A dog was not feasible. But were there pets that might be feasible, or just barely? When I brought up the goldfish, there was no reaction from the back seat. When a turtle was mentioned, she bit her lower lip. Boring. A guinea pig? A hamster? I hated the thought of it, I'd had a friend in elementary school who had guinea pigs (or were those hamsters?). The stench from the sawdust-lined terrarium brought tears to your eyes. And there was a little wheel that the hamster (or guinea pig) ran itself silly on, for hours on end, until one morning my friend actually found it dead on the treadmill. Deep in my heart, I was proud of my daughter for refusing to settle for a goldfish or a turtle. A rabbit? Rabbits? We went to a pet shop, where the salesman talked us into buying two ("then they're not as alone") pygmy rabbits and a hutch. It was a hutch on legs that we set up outside on the patio, close to the sliding doors, where we could see it from the dining room table. The rabbits stared out through the mesh in the door, and that was really almost all they did. Diana felt sorry for them, so we occasionally gave them run of the garden or the living room, where they crept under the couch right away, all the way to the back, so the only way you could chase them out was with a stick or a broom. But it was above all their total lack of interest in my daughter that finally put an end to their stay with our family. "I think they don't know who I am yet," my daughter said hopefully at first, when she would take one of them in her arms to cuddle and the animal would struggle to get away and then bite her on the finger.

Another thing was that the rabbits started growing; within two weeks they were twice their original size. The hutch was actually too small for them now. Still, it took a few weeks for us to realize that one rabbit could only turn around if the other one did so at the same time.

"Pygmy rabbits?" Sylvia said, and I could tell she was trying hard not to laugh. "Did you keep the receipt? I'd go back to that pet shop if I were you."

But of course I didn't. There was no use. The mayor coming in to complain about a pair of overgrown rabbits? Twitter and Facebook didn't exist back then, but the good old, perhaps even more reliable "grapevine" did. No, the rabbits would have to disappear from our lives without a stir. Found dead in their hutch was probably the best solution, but of course we weren't going to actively facilitate that by denying them food or water.

Deliverance finally came in the form of one of Sylvia's girlfriends, who lived outside of town and had a run with chickens and a goat and a few other obscure creatures. "Rabbits in the city, that's not really right," she said, pushing a fresh leaf of lettuce through the wire door. The rabbits were not interested.

One week later, we said farewell. Diana — purely as a formality — shed a few tears as the woman slid the cardboard box into the back of her Volvo. I put an arm around her, squeezed her, and mumbled something about the "better life" they would have in the country.

Maybe we should have made the leap to a dog right then and there. But that second chance to fulfill our daughter's dearest wish was one we ignored. The cat we have today made its appearance on her very next birthday. Months beforehand, Diana had already come up with a name for it: Eminem. And when it turned out not to be a tom, she changed the name, without thinking about it for more than three seconds, to Emmy.

The garbage bag in the pedal bin was still too light to act as a credible excuse, so I gathered together a few old newspapers and magazines too. A plastic bag from the Albert Heijn supermarket with five empty bottles (two red wines, two whites, and a Grasovka vodka) and the picture was complete: another breadwinner, just doing his part around the house.

"I'm going up to the bins on the corner," I said, sticking my head around the kitchen door. Per usual, my daughter was lying on the couch with her laptop on her lap, a pair of headphones clamped over her ears. My wife had her back to me, she was standing in front of the bookcase, her head tilted a little to one side — she was running her finger over the spines of the books.

"Any idea where *Anna Karenina* is?" she asked without turning her head. "We have it, don't we? I just can't seem to find it anywhere."

Our bookcase is one of those good resolutions incarnate that have never been carried out. Alphabetical order. By country. By genre. For a long time, I kidded myself into thinking that I would systematize it soon, but I've postponed it so often that I'm now simply resigned to the mess. Sometimes I go looking for a book, too, then I start at the top left and skim over all the spines until I've found it. A mind more orderly than my own would pick that book off the shelf right away — but something would be lost then, too, I tell myself in an attempt to gloss over my procrastination.

"I suddenly thought: I read that book years ago, when I was eighteen, I think," Sylvia went on. "I remember almost nothing, except the story. If I read it in Dutch this time, that might sort of give me something to hold on to."

I took a step into the room, intentionally bumping the bag of empty bottles against the door. This time my wife really did turn to look at me.

"I'm going to take these up to the corner," I said, lifting the supermarket bag and the garbage bag. My wife and I looked at each other. I tossed a meaningful-looking glance at our daughter, then looked at my wife again. I could have winked, but I didn't. Diana might look up from her laptop at that very moment and wonder what the winking was all about. "I'll be back in about fifteen minutes," I said. "Then I'll help you look."

On my way to the containers, two cyclists passed me from the other direction, a boy and a girl — in their early twenties, I guessed. They were busy talking, the girl laughed at something the boy said, and when they came past the boy looked over at me. I saw it happen before my eyes, the way it happened so often, the whole thing took no more than a couple of seconds: something in the boy's eyes changed from looking to brooding. He saw a famous face but couldn't quite place it. An actor? An anchorman? A politician? As they rolled past I turned my head to follow them and saw the boy lean over to the girl. They both looked back at the same time. Yes, now they knew, that's right, it was him. I raised my hand, the one holding the half-empty garbage bag. They smiled and waved back — and then they biked on. How nice. How normal. The mayor taking out his own garbage.

When I got to the containers, I found what I usually found there. A couple of torn-open garbage bags, the contents of which (orange peels, wet coffee grounds, flattened milk cartons) had already spread halfway across the sidewalk. There were shards of glass, too, from a mirror that had apparently shattered, or else been kicked to pieces by children, a couple of planks, and a microwave oven. The remarkable fact of the matter is that in the major cities of the world — Paris, London, Madrid, Barcelona, Rome, Moscow, New York, and I should know, I've been to all those places myself — the garbage is collected on a daily basis, that is to say, every day, but in Amsterdam that happens only once or twice a week. In all the other cities I mentioned, that collection also takes place at night, so that daytime traffic won't be held up by garbage trucks stopping at every corner. Amsterdam is one of the filthiest towns in Europe, yea, in the whole Western and Westernized world. In Tokyo you never see a scrap of paper on the street, in Paris and London the streets and sidewalks are hosed down each day, even when it's been raining. In Rome, unemployed young people empty the trash containers that the tourists have jammed full of empty pizza boxes. I could never claim that household rubbish was a policy spearhead for me. Boris Johnson, my London colleague, had recently spoken disparagingly of Amsterdam, particularly about all the filth on the streets: I needed to call him about that, but still hadn't gotten around to it. What, after all, was I supposed to say? He was absolutely right, of course. Here in Amsterdam it was Wim Pijbes, the general director of the Rijksmuseum, who sent a letter to a leading daily newspaper complaining about how all the trash blowing around was going to chase away the tourists. Tomorrow I had a lunch date with him, we were going to discuss the festivities surrounding the opening of the new Rembrandt exhibition, but the litter he'd talked about would undoubtedly come up as well.

With a sigh, I put the half-empty garbage bag down beside the two torn ones. I knew without even checking that the swing-up mechanism on both containers was jammed. Then I tossed the pile of newspapers into the paper igloo, pulling my fingers back — the way I always did — just in time to keep the lid from falling shut on them. Should I light a cigarette yet, or wait until I'd thrown the empty bottles into the bottle bank? I stuck my hand in my left pants pocket and, to my horror, pulled out only the pack of cigarettes, no lighter — or had I tucked the lighter into the pack?

I felt a wave of desperation rolling in. I had walked up here with the garbage and the bottles because I wanted to be out of the house when I made the call I was going to make. In fact, all I had done was cover up one lie with another.

Strictly speaking, I could of course have withdrawn to my study or to our bedroom, but then my wife or daughter might walk in on me. (*Could you just take one more look? I really can't find* Anna Karenina *anywhere.*) What's more, I couldn't smoke in the study or the bedroom. And during this phone call, I *had* to smoke, no two ways about it. Allen Carr was right: stress combined with boredom.

I hadn't told Sylvia about my father's visit to city hall this morning. And I'd said nothing at all about the journalist and the photos that showed someone other than me beating a policeman into a wheelchair for the rest of his life. Ever since the conversation with my father, though, the interview and the photos had seemed of lesser importance. In fact, the photographs suited me just fine. If I were caught doing something, something unworthy of a mayor, it wouldn't be nearly as bad. The embezzlement of public funds, a 100,000-euro kickback for granting a harbor concession to a transshipment company, coke abuse, an orgy, whores from the Dominican Republic at an after-party in city hall — all of that would be bearable. I would be brought down. I would have to resign my post. Or not. Mayors get away with a lot. I thought with envy of my former colleague in Toronto. Rob Ford had stepped down already by then, but before he did he got away with everything: drugs, public drunkenness, and obesity had only boosted his popularity. In any case, a scandal affecting me as mayor was far preferable to the broadcasting of an affair between my wife and an alderman like Maarten van Hoogstraten. In the event of a political scandal, my fall wouldn't damage us personally. A down-and-out, unemployed former mayor, but still the one with that lovely (foreign) wife. That couple who you could tell from a mile away were still deeply in love. ("In love!" Bernhard had said during our recent dinner at home. "In love, that's ridiculous! You don't think anyone believes that? After six months, the infatuation is over, everybody knows that. Something else takes its place: fondness, mutual respect." Then he had glanced over at his wife, but Christine was pretending to fish a piece of cork out of her wineglass.) A couple totally wrapped up in each other, who needed no one else.

I hadn't told Sylvia about my conversation with my father that morning; I wanted to call my mother first. To arrange to meet her, tomorrow or the next day, in the course of the week in any event. I wasn't sure where we should meet, though. Her favorite Chinese restaurant might be a weird place for a final goodbye. Something like a park, perhaps. Or the beach. There was no "beach weather" predicted for tomorrow, but then a deserted beach with lots of wind, gray waves, and whipping foam might be even more fitting for a talk about parting and a self-selected death.

"Good evening." The voice, which seemed to be coming from right beside my left ear, put a rude end to my musing. When I turned my head, I found myself looking at a man in his sixties. A broad smile, the reflection of the streetlamp in eyes that sparkled with amusement. "I'm sorry, I didn't mean to startle you," the man said. "But I wanted to throw away my bottles, too, and you're standing in the way." He gave me what you might call a searching glance. For the second time this evening, I saw it happen right in front of me; at that moment, TV footage and newspaper photos were probably being shuffled around in the man's mind. *I've seen this face before, but where?* "Oh, now I know," he said, and he breathed an audible sigh of relief. "Sure, I've seen you around before. On the bike. I live over there." He pointed to a spot on the far side of the canal. "I see you biking past sometimes, when I look out the window."

"Excuse me," I said, stepping aside. "Help yourself."

"No hurry, I'm in no hurry. Why don't you go first?"

The telephone in my pocket started vibrating. *Bernhard,* the screen said. Not a good moment. I ditched the call.

"Look," the man said, pointing at the bottle bank. "Do you see this? Not so long ago there was a bottle bank with one hole for green glass, one for brown, and another one for white, meaning transparent. I don't know how you dealt with that? Did you obediently put the bottles in the hole they were supposed to go in? I live just across from here, like I said. I have a perfect view of the bottle bank. Once every two weeks, or maybe once a month, I don't remember, they came and emptied it. A hell of a racket. But I paid attention. Maybe we were all good little boys and girls and put the wine bottles in the green hole and the gin bottles in the white one, but when they hoisted up that bottle bank to empty it, they dumped everything into the truck, all together. From my bedroom window I could look right into the bed of the truck, but there weren't three compartments for green, brown, and white glass. All the colors were dumped onto a pile. So why did they want us to separate all those colors, if it didn't make a damn bit of difference afterward? Now we've got new bottle banks where all the colors go in one hole. So why did I go to the trouble all those years to separate them?"

My phone buzzed again. Maybe it was the voice mail, I thought, maybe Bernhard had left a message, but when I looked at the display I saw his name again. I hesitated for a moment — then ditched the call again.

"It would be easier to take, though, if they'd only do something about this," the man went on, pointing at the garbage lying around the containers. "I don't know how many times I've had to go back home with a full garbage bag because the lid was stuck or the container was completely full. Three flights of stairs back up. Sure, it's a privilege to live here on the canal, but I don't have an elevator and my balcony is small, so the garbage bags really start stinking once the sun hits them. And if you leave them beside the container, you can get a fine. It happened to me once, the city's got officials who walk around and cut open the garbage bags, and I guess they found something. I don't remember what it was, a tax assessment, don't ask me, but that's how they got my address. In fact, it was a dual offense; tax assessments are supposed to go in the paper igloo."

When he fell silent for a moment, I breathed in deeply, through my nose. I could smell it, right through the odor rising off the torn-open garbage bags. It wasn't a stench, not even a sweaty smell. No, men like this one would always be sure to put on clean clothes, to shower regularly and shave each morning. It was more like the antiseptic odor you smell in hospital corridors, a cleaning product meant to hide other odors.

I could ask him about it, indirectly of course, after making a wager with myself that I would undoubtedly win. But the man began talking again; he had now started tossing his bottles into the bottle bank. "You're allowed to do this now, see, but after I got that fine I started throwing all my bottles, the green ones, the brown ones, and the transparent ones, into the same hole of that old bottle bank, as a sort of final act of defiance. Someone called me on it once. A lady on a carrier bike, you know, one of those eco types who always know better. 'Hey,' she yelled at me. 'You're throwing the green ones in with the brown bottles, you're not allowed to do that!' "

My phone vibrated again, and I pulled it out of my pocket. "Bernhard, have you got a moment? I'll call you back in five minutes."

It was quiet at the other end, then I heard my friend's voice, as clear as though he were standing right beside me.

"Robert, I need to . . . You remember what we were talking about before? In your garden?"

At that very moment, the man dropped two bottles into the container, one right after the other. With all the banging and the sound of breaking glass, I couldn't tell whether Bernhard had said something else. I turned my back on the bottle bank and pressed two fingers against my left ear.

"Listen, Bernhard, I can't right now . . . I'll call you back in five minutes . . . in ten . . ."

And before he could reply, I hung up.

"I won't keep you any longer," the man said. "Come over for a cup of coffee some-

268

time," he went on, pointing at the far side of the canal. "That house over there, sort of behind the tree, the third floor, my name's not on the door, but there are only three bells. It's the top one, so you can't miss it." He mentioned the house number. "Anytime in the morning, doesn't matter when; well, not *too* early, not before eleven. I tend to sleep in, ever since my wife died."

Bingo! I thought, despite myself. I'd seen it correctly, smelled it correctly; this man lived alone, and probably had for years.

"I'm sorry to hear that," I said, and right away I heard the artificial undertone in my voice, the phrase borrowed from American TV shows — and badly subtitled to boot — to express one's condolences. "I mean, your wife, have you been . . . Have you been living alone for a long time?"

I felt my face getting red, I could tell that I might start blushing. A couple of years ago I was on *Time* magazine's list of the one hundred most influential people in the world. As the only mayor, and the only Dutch person too. People who had made their mark on the year gone by. I checked it later. I was not only the first, but also the only Dutchman to ever make the list. (And the last one to date.) But here in Holland, that fact produced mostly laughter or a shake of the head. It had to be some kind of mistake. The American weekly probably hadn't heard about all the cups of tea I'd drunk in Amsterdam's mosques. About the downward spiral the city had gone into during my mayoralty. All those years the Rijksmuseum had been closed. Seven years, no less! *Unworthy of a metropolis,* my detractors smirked. Meanwhile, though, the Rijksmuseum has opened its doors again, and that shut them up. On the outside it still looks like a train station, but inside, everything — from the majestic entrance hall to the cloakroom and the restaurant — is of a grandeur more reminiscent of the British Museum and the Louvre. There, in front of *The Night Watch,* is where we received Barack Obama. In what other metropolis could an American president have his own helicopter land on the square in front of the door?

"Thank you," the man said. "What I mean is, there's no reason to be sorry about my wife. I've been alone for eighteen months now, but I think about her every day. In my dreams, she's still alive. We still sit at the table together and walk down the beach side by side. Every time I wake up in the morning, I have to get used to the fact that she's not there anymore. At first that made me sad, but then I realized that I was mostly feeling sorry for myself. My wife and I were happy together for more than thirty years. That's what I want to hold on to. Thirty years, that's tens of thousands of happy moments, almost too many for me to go back and remember during the years I have left. Wherever my wife is now, I'm sure she knows that her absence makes me sad. On the other hand, though, she wouldn't want me to let that sadness drag me under. At first, right after she died, I tried that, I tried to let it destroy me. I wore the same clothes every day, I stopped shaving, I started drinking, and I started smoking again. Then one afternoon I was lying in bed with the curtains closed, a bottle of whiskey and a full ashtray on the nightstand beside me, when suddenly it was as though I was lifted up out of my own bed, and I saw myself lying there, way down below. And, at the same time, I heard my wife's voice. 'Don't be such a baby, Richard!' she said. 'Look at you feeling sorry for yourself. But it's not just about you, it's about the two of us. Now that I'm not around anymore, you're the only one who knows how happy we were together. Think about us, Richard. Think about us every day. And stop acting so piti-ful. Come on, get up, take a shower, put on some clean clothes, get started on it this evening, treat yourself to a meal at our favorite restaurant. You can think about us there, about all the happy times we had there together. Wipe your eyes if you need to, but don't sit there blubbering. You should be thankful and happy that you can still remember so much about the two of us together.' "

During his story my phone had started vibrating again; it didn't seem fitting to answer it right then. But the man had apparently finished talking, and I pulled the phone out of my pocket quickly.

"Robert, listen," I heard Bernhard say. "I don't have much time. Can I talk to you for a minute?"

I made a quick calculation, it was six hours earlier in Boston.

"Bernhard, I'm . . . I'm standing outside," I said, glancing quickly at the man. Something in his expression had changed. In his eyes I saw the tired, dull look of someone who realizes that, inevitably, parting and loneliness are waiting at the end of every conversation.

To my relief, though, he raised his hand, nodded to me, and walked away. "Okay, go ahead," I said to Bernhard. "I can . . . I'm alone now."

"You remember what we talked about a while ago, in your garden? About the infinitude of the universe, and also that other mystery, about our own deaths?"

"Mm-hmm," I said, but Bernhard wasn't waiting for a reaction from me, he had only paused for half a second — and I was merely interrupting him during the intercontinental, second-and-a-half bounce.

"Well," he said again, after he had waited for a couple of seconds to see if I was going to say something else. "It may happen sooner than I thought."

20

I was lying on my back, in my own bed, with
my eyes closed; beside me, I could hear my
wife's measured breathing. I had already
gone through the whole bag of tricks in an
attempt to get to sleep, but it was no use.
As a child of eight or nine, when I couldn't
get to sleep, I often lay down on the cold,
hard floor beside my bed. I closed my eyes
and pretended I was riding a horse on a
cold, stormy night. At last, the lights of an
inn appeared through the trees in the
distance, but the innkeeper shook his head
dejectedly. The inn was full. There were
about thirty people sleeping in a room big
enough only for fifteen, they were bunched
up together, every square centimeter was
taken. Careful not to wake anyone, I tiptoed
over the sleeping people. There! There was
one little spot left, on a mattress in between
two grown-ups, just enough space for an
eight-year-old boy. If I scrunched up as

tightly as I could, it ought to work. Then I crawled back into my own bed, thankful for the place to sleep and the warmth of the blankets. I crawled all the way up against the wall, I thought about the cold, about the horse and the rain outside — and after a few seconds I fell fast asleep.

These days I try it by traveling, by reconstructing a trip. Last night I reconstructed, day by day, the trip I took with Sylvia through the western United States more than twenty years ago. Diana wasn't born yet, during our first happy hour at the hotel in Las Vegas we drank five margaritas each, after that there was the heat of Las Vegas, and the Chinese restaurant in St. George, just over the Nevada–Utah border, where the waitresses started vacuuming the floor while we were still on our appetizers, and the gray, glassy shrimp in hoisin sauce were cooked to death and so tasteless that all we could do was stammer that it was "too much." The Chinese owners put the remains in a doggie bag (our very first doggie bag, but certainly not the last one on that trip), which we tossed, almost choking with hysterical laughter, into the first dumpster we saw. The next day, in Kanab, there was an electrical blackout in the middle of a thunderstorm. There were two restaurants in town, both of them cooked with electricity. Like St. George, Kanab is in the state of Utah, where the drinking laws remind you more of a Muslim country, rather than anywhere in the West. The Mormons, who call the shots in Utah, drink no alcohol at all, but had come up with a slightly more flexible solution for out-of-state tourists: they were allowed to order beer or wine in a restaurant, but only along with their meals. At the first restaurant we went to, they apologized for not being able to cook for us until the electricity was restored. *Oh, but then we'll just have a beer until the lights come back on,* we tried. No, that was impossible. Only along with your meal. We had been driving all day through hot desert country, the area around Kanab had served as backdrop for a lot of Westerns, there was a poster of Clint Eastwood behind the bar of the restaurant, wearing a cowboy hat, holding his horse's reins loosely in his right hand. To the left of the poster was a floor-to-ceiling refrigerator with a glass door. Behind the glass, which was steamed-up now, we could see the bottles of Budweiser. At the second restaurant it was the same song and dance, there they also had a refrigerator with a glass door behind the bar. Theoretically, it would have been possible to leap over the bar, yank open the door, and make it out onto Kanab's dusty main street with a six-pack of frosty cold Budweiser. But it would have been a mistake to assume that a restaurant owner in these parts didn't keep a revolver or a rifle under the bar. A *Bonnie and Clyde* ending or, even more likely, an ending like in *Butch Cassidy and the Sundance Kid* — the two of us going down amid a hail of bullets. The next morning, we bought a cooler and enough bags of ice and bottles of Budweiser to protect ourselves against prospective lightning bolts and religious lawgiving.

And after that? After that, we drove to the North Rim of the Grand Canyon. That is where the fatigue set in. How many landscapes of dry yellow-and-red rock can one see before one starts longing for green pastures, dark forests, and babbling mountain brooks? Standing at the rim, we had taken each other's hand and decided that we'd looked at enough rocks for the time being.

Ignoring Bryce Canyon National Park and Zion National Park, we drove to Cedar Falls, where we bought a four-person tent at the local Walmart for eighty dollars. I was lying there in bed, trying to remember the name of the little spot on the Utah–Colorado border, beside the Colorado River, where we had set up that tent for the first time, when out of the blue, as though it had suddenly leapt out from a darkened doorway, a very different memory forced itself on me. Or rather, the memory of a memory, one I'd had not so very long ago, earlier that evening in fact, as I was gathering together the garbage bag, the empty bottles, and the old newspapers.

The rabbits . . . Earlier in the evening I had thought about our rabbits. The pygmy rabbits that had played such a brief role in our family life. And only now did I think about the New Year's reception, about my wife tossing back her head, that's how hard she'd laughed at Alderman Maarten van Hoogstraten's story about the rabbits — or at least how hard she'd wanted me to believe she had, that evening at Café Schiller.

How easy it would have been to make up a story when the ingredients for that story came from her own life, our own life! The rabbits left to run free in the living room (the alderman's living room, or our own?). The gnawed TV cables. Had our rabbits gnawed through the TV cables, or had they only hidden under the couch? Wasn't it strange that Sylvia hadn't even mentioned our own rabbits, that evening at Café Schiller?

I made a mental note of it. Tomorrow I would ask Maarten van Hoogstraten about the rabbits. Not explicitly, but in a roundabout way. We weren't on close terms, even at lunch or during cocktails we mostly exchanged bits of information about administrative matters. It would, at the very least, be odd — suspicious, I couldn't help thinking — if I were to suddenly ask the alderman about household matters, about the pets in his family, or the lack thereof.

And at that very same moment I thought of something else. What if I were to find out, tomorrow morning, that Alderman Van Hoogstraten had no rabbits? What then? What other conclusion could I draw but that my wife had made up the whole thing? That she had been lying to me?

I rolled onto my side, my back to her. Do I want to know this? I asked myself. *Rabbits?* I heard the alderman say. *No, we don't have rabbits, never have had either.* But then what had my wife been laughing about so loudly at the reception? And what had made Maarten van Hoogstraten's apparently hilarious story unsuitable for her to talk about?

How good was she at this? To what extent

were they all good at it, there in her home country, I thought then, unable to stop myself. To what extent was lying an inalienable part of their culture — was it in their blood?

In some cultures, lying is a survival tactic, no more and no less than that. The merchants who travel from village to village, prizing their wares, lie just as baldly as their eternally haggling prospects. Sylvia, too, couldn't buy a piece of worthless antique furniture without talking the price down by 90 percent, not even here in Amsterdam, at the flea market on Waterlooplein. *I'll give you two euros for that toaster,* she says to the stallholder who is asking for twenty. At moments like that I always move away a little, not only because I'm the mayor — the mayor with a wife who's haggling over a toaster at the flea market outside city hall — but because it embarrasses me. I hate rummage sales, including and above all the rummage sale on King's Day. As far as that goes, though, Sylvia and I are in complete agreement. "A country that celebrates its national holiday with a rummage sale!" she said, the first time the two of us sauntered together along the unregulated street market in our neighborhood. "Really, Robert, isn't that a bit dismal?"

As with the red rock formations in Utah, after Yellowstone National Park it was the conifer forests and icy mountain streams we became sick of. Getting to the sea, reaching the Pacific, became our sole objective. Soon after Missoula we drove into Idaho, then followed the whole length of the Columbia River, without stopping in Portland, all the way to the coast. There, on the oceanfront boulevard of the town with the fitting name of Seaside, we recorded our happiness for the first time on that trip. Or actually, someone else did; the picture shows both of us, and I'm sure it wasn't made with the timer. A passerby probably, someone who saw us sitting there with our camera and offered to take a picture of the two of us. I would have done the same. I would have offered too — and if they didn't have a camera with them, I would at least have stood and watched them from a distance for as long as possible.

We are sitting on a bench together, with the beach and the ocean as background. On the stone balustrade behind the bench, in between our heads, sits a huge seagull. Sylvia is wearing sunglasses, I have on a white

281

New York Yankees baseball cap. What the photo shows is perfect happiness, the married couple who don't need to smile at the camera, because everything about them, even without the smile, tells you that these two need no one but each other. In fact, they are granting a favor to the one taking the picture: he is allowed to look at them unabashedly for a few seconds, and then to immortalize them on film.

That thought was replaced right away with the memory of another picture, another picture that also portrays happiness without frills or special lighting. It was taken a few hundred kilometers farther south — we stuck to the coast for the rest of our trip — across the state border, in the northernmost part of California. In Redwood National Park.

Sylvia is standing at the side of the road, her hands on her hips, among the huge sequoias. She is wearing a blue dress with white polka dots, her head is tilted slightly to one side, the sunlight is first filtered by the branches and foliage and only then does it touch her. She smiles at the photographer. At me. It's the look in her eyes, in combination with that smile. It's a smile that promises everything. About us. About our future together. And the look in her eyes is real, I

don't know how else to put it, she's not pos-
ing, she smiles and looks at me.

A few days later, in our hotel room in
Santa Barbara, the water in the glass on my
nightstand suddenly started moving.
"Look," I said to Sylvia. At first we thought
it was a freight train, or a truck thundering
by in the street below, but the streets were
almost deserted, the tracks too far away.
Then the glass itself began to move, it slid
an inch or two closer to the edge. It looked
like a scene from a documentary about
paranormal phenomena, but at the very
same moment we realized what it was. "An
earthquake," Sylvia said without a trace of
panic in her voice. Afterward, we talked
about it often. Our room was on the fifth
floor; if the hotel had collapsed floor-by-
floor, like a film in slow motion, it would
already have been too late to run outside. It
was a good feeling. A good feeling to experience that together. Not fatalism, more like
acceptance.

In the twenty years after that, I often told
the story about the earthquake. And I
always laid it on a bit thickly. In fact, it had
been nothing more than a tremor, one of
many felt there as regular as clockwork —
when we excitedly tried to share our experience with the people at the hotel desk, they

283

acted as though they didn't understand. The two desk clerks shook their heads pityingly at these naive tourists. Everyday fare this was, a little shaking, nothing to get wound up about. But in our stories at countless dinner tables, at an equal number of boring birthday parties, Sylvia and I turned it into a real earthquake. We glanced at each other conspiratorially when I talked about how the ceiling lamp had swung back and forth, and she finished the story with the water glass falling to the floor and shattering.

For me, the real story we brought home from our six-week vacation was that photograph of Sylvia beneath the sequoias. The only real souvenir. Of course, I could have had the photo enlarged and framed. I could have hung it on the wall. But I didn't want to do that. In fact, what I didn't want was for other people to see her like that. I wanted to keep her for myself.

And so it ended up somewhere at the bottom of the box of photos. The same box with all the other pictures of our trip through America, which we went on thinking we would have framed someday. The endless freight train: in a landscape of nothing but dust and thistles, we parked the Chevrolet at the side of the road. The engineer blew the whistle at us by way of a greeting, I waved back, and Sylvia took one picture after the other, three boxcars at a time. Once we got home, we laid them out on the living room floor of the house we lived in then. Most of the photos overlapped each other by an inch or so, but that could be solved with a pair of scissors: the line of photos of that freight train stretched out for more than six meters.

I got out of bed and went downstairs. What I was about to do bore the scent of mortal danger. Maybe it would be wiser not to. But once I pulled the box of photos out of our junk closet, there was no going back.

In the ground floor hallway, I opened the closet door and saw the box almost right away, in the same spot where it had been last time, under the stack of old LPs, half hidden by the stepladder.

Turning on a single light in the living room, I groped around in the box. A vacation in Majorca, Diana wasn't quite two, her chubby little face beaming at me from the baby carriage; the Mexican restaurant in Santa Barbara where we celebrated my fortieth birthday; a few boxcars . . . And suddenly there it was, sooner than I'd expected, the photo of Sylvia amid the five-hundred-year-old forest giants in Redwood National Park.

I looked at her, at her face, and then at her eyes — I looked her in the eye. I tried to look at her the way I had looked at her through that viewfinder more than twenty years ago. I read the promise in her eyes, then I looked away and then looked again.

It was like the old photographs of the Manhattan skyline, or more like the old movies in which you catch a glimpse of the Twin Towers. Up to that point, the movie is nothing but an old movie, but suddenly it gives you a glimpse of the future.

That was how I looked at the photograph of my wife — and what happened then was what I had been afraid would happen all along; the irreparable happened, without my being able to stop it.

Once, her eyes had spoken of nothing but the future — it had been there, somewhere between the sequoias and the earthquake, that we had decided to have a baby together — but from here on out it would be a different future from the one I had always counted on.

21

The next afternoon I collared Alderman Van Hoogstraten in the corridor outside the council chambers; it was half an hour before the start of the windmill debate.

"Something else," I said. "I mean, it's your territory, after all. The bottle banks. The sorted waste disposal system."

"Hmm?" The alderman turned his head, bringing his face closer to mine at the same time, as though he was hard of hearing. I looked straight into his blue eyes and tried with all my might not to think about this same face bending toward my wife with puckered lips.

"I was wondering about something. The old bottle banks used to have three holes. One for transparent glass, one for brown, and one for green. But as far as I know, the beds of the trucks, the ones they used to use to empty the bottle banks, didn't have three separate compartments. Am I right about that? What I mean to say is: If all that glass was thrown together in the back of the truck, why did we ask people to divide their bottles over three different holes?"

Was I imagining things, or did I see something like a flicker of relief in his eyes? Had he been expecting a different question? Different questions? Recently — no, not at all recently, ever since the Christmas recess in fact, he had stopped shaving. Like so many men his age, he probably thought a beard would make him look like a movie star or soccer player, that it would make him younger and therefore automatically more attractive to young people — to younger voters. The beard was largely gray, and translucent at the cheeks, like a newly mown field where you can see the soil amid the stubble. Like so many men his age, he didn't realize that a beard only made him look older. If you were asked to name this man's profession, your first guess would probably be: a high-school German teacher.

"Yes, that's correct," he said. "I've heard how that went. They set aside a budget for the separated collection of glass. About ten years ago it was, I think. The bottle banks were manufactured in Poland. With three holes in them. But by the time the bottle banks were delivered, the money was finished. It was more expensive than they'd thought. The city had no more budget to outfit the trucks with three separate compartments. 'That will come later,' that's what we must have figured back then. Or what my predecessor must have figured back then, actually, because I wasn't here yet. But it never came later."

There was something about his voice. I'd noticed it before. Not exactly a lisp, but too much air came out of his mouth, he made a quiet hissing sound with every *f* and *s,* like someone opening the valve on a bicycle tire.

"But people actually thought it mattered, which hole they threw their bottles into," I said. In my mind I caught a flash of the woman on the carrier bike, the eco type who had upbraided my neighbor for not putting his glass in the right opening. "That's peculiar, isn't it?"

Alderman Van Hoogstraten narrowed his eyes; maybe it was body language, maybe he was going to try to deny it. But there really wasn't anything to deny, he had already more or less admitted to the whole thing.

"The idea was important, though," he said. "It was a good thing that people back then started to get used to the idea that everything would soon be collected separately. And with today's bottle banks, you don't have to separate the colors anymore. So, looking back on it, trucks with separate compartments weren't really necessary anyway."

I stared at him. I was suddenly reminded of the fountain. The fountain in my old neighborhood. The unveiling of it, when I had given a short speech. Everyone was pleased with the fountain, but what I remembered most was the folder the people in the neighborhood had received in their mailboxes and that landed on my desk, too, a few days before the unveiling. The construction itself: that was what the folder talked about. About the material that had been used — granite — and about the Chinese laborers in Fujian province who had cut and rounded the granite blocks. About the working conditions in the granite quarry, the inadequate safety measures, the long working days, the months on end that the workers had to spend away from home.

The alderwoman at the time had gone to China, along with other city officials, to view the situation with her own eyes. Despite the starvation wages and slave labor, they came to the conclusion that the laborers had worked on the project "with dedication and pleasure." The most remarkable thing about the folder was that it described everything in such detail, that it didn't try to hide anything. An alderman found to have frequented a pickup spot in order to lay his hands on two-bit hookers had been forced to resign; an alderwoman who had a fountain built by slaves, just like the ancient Egyptians, received applause from the neighborhood at the unveiling.

I could have gone on questioning Alderman Van Hoogstraten. About the torn garbage bags and shards of glass beside the containers, for example. Why was there enough money to pay public overseers to cut garbage bags open and uncover an offender's identity, but no money to empty the containers more than twice a week? How did one go about explaining that to one's friends and family, that one cut open garbage bags for a living?

I could have come back at him with something about the fraudulence of having people drop different colors of glass through different holes in the bottle bank; about how peculiar it was, to say the very least, that everyone in town could see with their own eyes that they were being bamboozled. But no, I realized the next moment: only those who lived higher than the bed of the truck itself, who could look down on it from the second, third, or fourth floors, had been able to see that with their own eyes. And even then, you could wonder whether it had sunk in right away — the way it had with my neighbor across the canal.

And then again: What was I whining about? The ordinance concerning the separated collection of glass had been axed years ago.

"Is everything okay, Robert?"

I had thought I was still looking the alderman in the eye, but it was probably in a way that no longer conveyed anything like attention. Maybe I had wandered off into my own musings too far and for too long; in any case, I realized that I was blinking my eyes, as though Van Hoogstraten had awakened me from an afternoon nap.

"I'm sorry," I said. "I was thinking about something else for a moment there."

Maarten van Hoogstraten raised his eyebrows. "Are you feeling all right?"

"Excuse me?"

"I asked whether you're feeling all right, Robert. You look . . . You look tired. And not just tired . . . I mean, are you ill? Do you have a fever? That's what it looks like, like you're running a fever."

"No, I don't have a fever. Tired, yes, probably. I didn't get quite enough sleep last night."

That morning, Sylvia had found me beside our bed. On the wooden floor. It was around six in the morning when I'd finally gone back to our bedroom. An hour before the alarm would go off. I suspected that I'd tried my old getting-to-sleep trick, but that I'd been too exhausted to get back into bed on time.

"And you said something . . ."

"We were talking about the bottle banks."

"No, I mean after that. You whispered something, I couldn't hear you very well, as though you were talking to yourself, Robert. So I wondered —"

"Rabbits," I interrupted him. "I wanted to ask you something about rabbits."

What had I been mumbling, for God's sake? I had to be careful about that, it had happened with Diana once, too, that I started thinking out loud without realizing it. Like the faithless husband who moans the name of his mistress in bed, at home, rather than that of his wife. And was Van Hoogstraten really telling the truth when he said he couldn't hear me well? Maybe he had heard something that absolutely was not intended for his ears.

"Rabbits," I said. "I said something about

rabbits."

This was not going according to plan, not at all. I'd meant to ask the alderman about the rabbits, but casually, parenthetically — now, though, there was no going back.

"We're thinking about getting a pet," I said. "For Diana's sake, mostly. And we were thinking about a rabbit. Maybe even more than one."

Did that sound implausible? Being honest with myself, I could only say it did. The alderman opened his mouth, he seemed about to say something, but I beat him to it.

"Diana, our daughter," I said quickly. I couldn't automatically assume that he knew our daughter's name. And if I was lucky, he didn't know her age either. Rabbits for a daughter who was almost twenty, how plausible was that? "Someone told me, I don't remember who, that you have rabbits at home. I was wondering, how do you like that? I mean, do you think it's a good idea to have rabbits, or do they actually belong in the wild?"

I looked into his eyes. Did I see perplexity there, or was Maarten van Hoogstraten starting to suspect which direction this implausible rabbit story was taking? I had a sudden flash of intuition, maybe the wrong kind of intuition, but that would become clear enough soon.

Once I'd dealt with the rabbit issue, I would be done with the whole thing. The way you might wake up in the middle of the night, you've been having strange dreams, your forehead is covered in a cold sweat — the realization that you have to throw up comes only then. For a few minutes you try as hard as you can to keep it back, and then you remember: the shawarma pizza you had earlier in the evening. Maybe it was the sauce, maybe it was the meat itself; in a few steps you reach the toilet.

When it's over, there is relief. You're filthy, you stink, you have chunks of shawarma in your throat and in your sinuses, but you're done with it.

"I remember now," I said, keeping my eyes fixed on the alderman. "I remember who told me. My wife. Sylvia. According to Sylvia, you told her something about rabbits once."

"Could I talk to the two of you for a moment?" Alderman Hawinkels suddenly appeared at my side and seized me by the upper arm. He did the same to Alderman Van Hoogstraten. "I'm sorry if I'm intruding, but I really need to talk to both of you. Before we get started on the wind turbines,

I mean."

"Of course," Van Hoogstraten said. "Robert and I were just discussing . . . Well, it doesn't really matter, it wasn't that important."

Right then, my cell phone beeped. *Diana,* I read on the screen after pulling it out of my pocket. There are people — names — who can always wait. As a rule, I almost never answer my phone right away, I use it more as a sort of mobile voice mail. Or maybe not even that; the old habit of actually leaving a message has pretty much died out: it's enough to see that they called. After that, the ball is in your court, it's your turn to knock it back.

Diana, though, is the exception to that rule. Even when I see my wife's name on the display, I don't always answer right away. Sometimes I'm on my way home on the bike and she asks me to pop by the drugstore to buy honey licorice, or toothpaste. Much better, then, not to respond, to say when you get home that you didn't hear the phone because you were on the bike.

I remember the time Diana called from the airport in Budapest because she'd lost her passport and all her bank cards; or that other time, when I was trying on a pair of trousers in a fitting room in Milan and Diana called to say that she'd left her keys that night in the front door of our house in Amsterdam. You always have to answer. Always. Preferably within five seconds.

"Excuse me," I said to both aldermen. "I really have to take this."

I turned my back on them, then stepped aside and opened the WhatsApp message; my heart was already pounding.

Daddy

That's the way my daughter always started off: first that one word, to get my attention, then the actual message itself, often sent in three or four separate blocks of text.

typing . . . , I read at the top of the screen.

Did you see Emmy this morning?

Emmy. I thought quickly. We let our cat out into the garden fairly regularly, but only when she stood meowing at the door. A few years ago we had bolted closed the cat flap in the kitchen door, because we were kept awake at night by other cats who came in and started fighting for Emmy's territory; to mark their claims, they also pissed all over the couches, chairs, and rugs.

From that time on, Emmy had taken to meowing at the garden or kitchen door until someone let her out.

Because I got up at ten, and she wasn't there.

The cat usually came back after a couple of hours, often sooner than that. The evening before, when I came back from my conversation at the containers, it had been around eleven. Diana was already upstairs. Sylvia was lying on the couch, reading *Anna Karenina.*

And the cat? Had the cat been lying on her lap, or beside her on the couch? I closed my eyes, but I had the feeling I was receiving only *old* images. Images in which Emmy was somewhere in the living room, as always. On the couch, or lying on one corner of the rug. As close to us as she could get, in any case. Never in a room that was deserted at that moment.

And now it's two and she's still not here.

Last night, after looking at the pictures in the box of photos, I had gone into the garden. It was too cold for just a T-shirt and underpants, in fact, but I felt like having a cigarette. It turned out to be three, which I smoked leaning back and looking up at the night sky and the moon that was almost full — before going up the stairs again, teeth chattering and shivering all over. Apparently, though, I hadn't had my fill of the cold, because at seven this morning Sylvia had found me on the floor beside our bed.

Had I seen our cat then, in the living

room, or in the kitchen, where I lit my first cigarette off the gas burner? I couldn't remember, and the fact that I didn't remember could only mean that I hadn't seen Emmy at all.

Suddenly, though, I remembered something else. When I opened the sliding doors and stepped into the garden, a bird had flown up in front of me. Right in front of my feet — almost as though it had been waiting for me there. A thrush, or a blackbird, I know nothing about birds. It was a little brown bird, in any case, with a yellow beak, I saw later, after my eyes grew accustomed to the dark and the bird had perched on the back of a chair, across from where I was sitting. The sudden movement at my feet, the flapping when the thrush or blackbird flew up and landed on the table, had startled me badly. From there it hopped twice and landed on the chair.

The bird's presence also meant something else, I realized now, as I also had the previous night, after I lit my second cigarette off the first and was looking at the bird. And the bird at me: yes, I couldn't rid myself of the feeling that it was observing me, its head tilted a little to one side, the way birds do when they've caught sight of a worm or some other edible thing wriggling around on the ground.

That a thrush or a blackbird was sitting calmly on the garden chair could only mean that our cat was not in the garden at that moment; not in the living room either — I hadn't closed the sliding doors behind me. Looking back on it, there was no way she could have been there. If Emmy had spotted me leaning back and having a cigarette, sitting in one of the garden chairs (I had my legs up, so I could rest my feet on the wooden table frame), she would never have missed such a golden opportunity. She would have come after me and settled down purring on my lap.

The only other possibilities, that the cat was somewhere else in the house or prowling around in the neighboring gardens the whole time, seemed improbable.

Where's Mama? I messaged back, trying to win time.

No, Emmy would definitely have heard me come down the stairs; while I was sitting on the couch with the box of photos on my lap, she would have been nuzzling up against my ankles.

For the first time, I thought about a third possibility: that our cat had slipped outside earlier that evening, on the canal side, when I opened the door to take out the empty bottles, the garbage bag, and the pile of old newspapers. Or later, after I had already come back. I could hardly imagine it; in all the years we had lived there, Emmy had snuck out onto the street in an unguarded moment only four or five times at most. Usually she ran straight to the waterside. There she would stand for a few seconds, petrified, between the parked cars, her back arched and her tail puffy with fright, before shooting right back inside.

And what about when I came back in? After my phone call with Bernhard. No, that's not the way it went, I was still talking to Bernhard when I put the key in the lock. Leaning against the door, with one foot outside and the other on the doormat in our hallway, we had gone on talking for ten minutes or so.

I don't know where Mama is

. . . typing . . .

She was gone when I came down

. . . typing . . .

Where are you?

While I was reading these lines I noticed that, at the top left-hand corner of the display, under the heading *Chats,* there was a "1" in a circle: an unread message.

I clicked on *Chats.* The unread message was in between Diana and Sylvia, in fact

301

under Diana and above Sylvia. Not from a known sender on my list of contacts; it was a number I didn't recognize. There was no profile photo either.

Dear Robert, I read in the notification bar. *Dear Robert, we're going to do it tomorrow. Wait for 24*

Yesterday, it said at the top right-hand side.

I tapped the screen to open the entire message.

Dear Robert, we're going to do it tomorrow. Wait for 24 hours. Try not to see it as a sad thing. Our lives have been more than rewarding. All the best to you, Sylvia, and Diana. Your parents.

Below the message, to the right, there now stood — instead of *Yesterday* — the exact time when it was sent: *21:45.*

I tried a reconstruction. Where had I been right then? I hadn't looked at my watch the previous night, but in all probability I was still outside at the containers, talking to the neighbor, or else on my way back to the house, talking to Bernhard on the phone.

That was the most logical explanation for why I hadn't heard the beep or felt the vibration in my pocket.

Or had I . . .

I saw Alderman Hawinkels gesturing to

me, acting as though he was looking at his watch. Yes, it was time, time for the windmill debate.

I wasn't going to be there.

"Listen," I said, stepping up to the aldermen — there was something humiliating about having to say what I was about to say now in front of Maarten van Hoogstraten. I was going to have to choose my words carefully. *I'm sorry, but I can't take part in the debate. My parents, you see, have just committed suicide.* That was out of the question. For a brief moment I considered saying it was something with my daughter, but that wasn't good either. They would be bound to remember something like that and ask me about it tomorrow.

"Something's happened," I said. "I have to go right now."

Both aldermen looked at me. "Something bad?" Hawinkels asked.

"My wife," I said, looking only at Alderman Van Hoogstraten — let him worry about it all through the windmill debate, I thought. "Sylvia. I really have to go."

22

Most days I covered the short distance from the mayor's residence to city hall on foot, but that morning I had taken the bike; the first item on my agenda had been a lunch with Pijbes, the director of the Rijksmuseum. It was a lively lunch; the museum director spent the first half hour giving me a crash course in art history, from the first rock drawings all the way to Jackson Pollock and Jeff Koons. Then he got down to brass tacks, to the real reason why he had invited me to lunch.

Might it be an idea, he started in enthusiastically — we were seated in the museum garden and had opened a second bottle of red — to use Barack Obama's visit as a way to promote Amsterdam? In the form of merchandising? He was thinking, more specifically, in terms of coffee mugs, cookie tins, T-shirts, beer coasters, shot glasses, the whole kit and caboodle that already bore the likenesses of *The Night Watch* and *The Milkmaid.*

By then the second bottle was half finished; when the director tried to refill my glass, I held my hand above it. It was okay to be a bit tipsy during the windmill debate, but not flushed or otherwise visibly under the influence. Just the right, relaxed demeanor, that was the ticket; if I was 100 percent sober, I wouldn't be able to sit through the debate anyway.

"The pictures of President Obama in front of *The Night Watch* were seen all around the world," the museum director was saying. "Fantastic free advertising for the product Amsterdam. Why not make use of that? A cookie tin and a T-shirt with Obama and *The Night Watch* as background. Who wouldn't want to have one of those? That way the picture would go all over the world again, but this time the museum would make a little money on it too."

The look on my face gave me away, I suspect. I told him I needed to think about it for a bit. That I wasn't sure whether you could just do that, without permission from the president himself.

"Of course, that's why I came to you first," Pijbes said. "I saw how the two of you clicked, I saw the chemistry. The way

305

you winked at him during the prime minister's speech. Maybe what we need is the direct approach. From mayor to president." And, with a malicious smile, he added: "I would never dream of asking our prime minister to do something like that. No," he said, shaking his head. "Perish the thought."

On my way back, I cycled along the Amstel. In front of the Carré theater, I pulled my phone out of my pocket and looked at my father's message again. *All the best to you, Sylvia, and Diana. Your parents.* I'd never known that my father (or my mother) used WhatsApp. They had kept up with the times in every other way, though. E-readers, iPads, cell phones held no secrets for them. My mother had had her own Facebook account for the last five years or so. Not me. But my daughter was one of her friends. Sometimes I would hear Diana laughing on the couch beside me, and when I asked what was so funny she would say: "It's Grandma again. She's so hilarious!" But there was one area in which they had remained "old-fashioned": neither of their cells were smartphones; they were old Nokias, fit only for text messaging at best.

Just past the Amstel Hotel, halfway through the tunnel under the side canal, I stopped and looked again at the message, which was easier to see there in the shadows. I didn't know my father's cell number by heart, but this one seemed different to me in any case.

Again, I checked the time — *21:45* — when the message was sent. And suddenly I knew . . . A little beep during a phone call.

The kind of beep that lets you know someone else is trying to reach you — or that a new message has come in.

Knowing that, what had I done? Nothing, apparently. Last night I had listened to Bernhard and told myself that, as soon as our conversation was over, I would find out who had tried to call or text me.

In the end, though, I'd forgotten all about it. I got to the house, remained standing in the doorway for a while, went on talking, and then went upstairs to where my wife was reading *Anna Karenina* on the couch.

And after that? After that, I'd gone to my study for a bit. To prepare for the debate, I consulted a couple of American websites about wind turbines. Admittedly, I looked mostly for the disadvantages of wind turbines, but, admittedly as well, I didn't find them. A few minor disadvantages at most. Besides the well-known visual pollution, both sites emphasized the large number of birds that, unable to judge the speed of the rotating vanes, were chopped to pieces. I went in search of reference material. Exactly how many birds were killed by planes, trains, or cars? But I couldn't find those figures either.

From my trip with Bernhard through the western United States, I remembered a wind park in California, not far from the town of Mojave. In an otherwise empty landscape, without a single building, there were thousands of turbines scattered across a dozen low hills on the horizon. It was an impressive, perhaps even a lovely sight, insofar as you might think of thousands of spinning vanes as "lovely." At least it didn't hurt your eyes: the emptiness there could accommodate it. During the debate, without using the word "lovely," I would emphasize that emptiness. In Holland, emptiness had been banished at least half a millennium ago.

Then I would switch to the sea. Where, in these surroundings, did one find real, endless emptiness? At sea. A few thousand wind turbines in the sea, far enough from the coast that you couldn't see them. Anyone who didn't actually go to sea would never be confronted with the presence of those wind turbines. Who knows, for the crews of passing ships it might even be a lovely sight.

I had forgotten about the beep. It was that simple; what's more, it wasn't the first time either. To leave a message unanswered was not uncommon for me. One of the disadvantages of WhatsApp was that it beeped only once; after that, you had to figure it out for yourself.

Later last night as well, in the garden, I hadn't looked at my cell phone. In fact, I had actually left my cell beside the bed when I went downstairs to look for the photograph of my wife in the redwood forest.

Yesterday afternoon was when my father had come by city hall to tell me that they were going to carry out their plan a bit earlier. Sometime in the next couple of weeks, he'd said. And then? Yes, now I remembered: when I told him that I wanted to talk to my mother before then, he acted casual and said I could call her that evening.

Tonight, he'd said. Literally "tonight."

Call her tonight.

And the next moment I knew it with such certainty that it felt like a sudden change in temperature running down my spine; not a shiver, more like someone had dropped a popsicle down the back of my shirt

He had known already, that afternoon . . . He had come to me at the last possible moment, so that I couldn't interfere anymore, so that I couldn't try to make them change their minds.

Or at least try to make my mother change her mind. *Call her tonight.* In the end, though, I hadn't. I had taken the garbage out to the containers, intending to call her when I got back.

But then Bernhard's phone call came in and interrupted things. *21:45.* Back at the house, I hadn't thought about the beep anymore, and not about my mother either. Yes, later on I did, I remembered now, too late: I had thought of her while I was brushing my teeth, it must have been around eleven thirty. There was still plenty of time, I thought, I would call her the next day.

I looked at the display again. For the first time I turned my attention to the ciphers at the top of the message, which showed when someone had most recently been online. Sylvia and I always checked those when Diana was out late. Sometimes she would send a message at four thirty in the morning, saying she was sleeping over at a girlfriend's (never at the new boyfriend's, his house was too crowded for that, she claimed, but we figured it was more likely that his parents wouldn't allow it, because of their cultural background), but sometimes she forgot. It was always reassuring then, the next day, to at least see that she had been online at 07:02 that morning.

last seen today at 06:41, said the little timestamp under the number I didn't recognize, above the only, and most probably the last, WhatsApp message my father had ever sent me.

Today. I checked the time at the top of my display: *14:35.* I've said it before, I'm no good at math. I first had to convert the ciphers in my mind to "around six thirty" and "a little past two thirty" After that, it took me at least fifteen seconds to realize that about eight hours lay between the two.

Eight hours ago, my father had used WhatsApp. Eight hours ago, he was still alive — they were still alive.

I brought my weight down on the pedal, got the bike moving, and cycled out of the tunnel. Eight hours. I saw people sitting on the patio outside De Ysbreeker. In blissful ignorance. From that moment, and maybe even from the moment I first read the message and ran out of city hall, a parallel world had been set in motion.

On the one hand there was the normal, visible world, the world of people blissfully drinking their coffee or walking the dog; on the other there was the real world in which things happened. Real things. Life and death. A plane exploding in midair, a ship full of refugees capsizing and sinking a few miles off the coast, two old people giving each other a final kiss, a final hug, and then dying.

At first I cycled at top speed, but on Weesperzijde, across from the rowing club, I let the bike freewheel and gradually slowed down.

Why was I hurrying? Twenty-four hours, that's what my father had said. *Then you have to wait twenty-four hours and then come and take a look.* I automatically put my hand in my right pocket, I knew I had it with me, I almost never forgot my key ring. "Key ring" was actually a pretty grand word for the two keys I needed to open our front door, and the other two for my parents'.

Eight hours ago. No, there was no sense in hurrying, I would get there too late anyway. Sometime this morning, before or after their final breakfast in bed or at the little table in the kitchen, my parents had taken what they had to take to put an end to their lives. How fast did that work? I realized that I had never asked him about it, about whether they were planning to use pills or something else (a potion?). Or how they had come up with the idea; no, that was another subject I felt I could never bring up myself.

Twenty-four hours. *We're going to do it tomorrow.* Was I supposed to start counting off those twenty-four hours from 21:45, or from 06:41? Strictly speaking, wouldn't it be better to just turn around and wait until tomorrow morning?

But there was another factor in play. Maybe there was no reason to hope that I would still find them alive, but now, as I turned left past Café Hesp and the Portuguese restaurant, I thought for the first time about the possibility that maybe they hadn't completely succeeded.

Maybe they had taken the wrong dose, too much or too little; maybe they had vomited up half of it but were too weak to call — to ask someone (their only son) for help.

I crossed Wibautstraat and raced down the incline, along the Ringdijk and into the deeper-lying polder of Watergraafsmeer. Four meters. The polder there is four meters under sea level. If the dikes broke, the ground floors of the houses in Watergraafsmeer would be completely underwater. At the bottom, though, at the deepest point, I stopped pedaling. I went slowly, in a way visible to all. More than on other days, I was conscious of my visibility as a famous face. *Look, there goes the mayor.* For the first time since leaving city hall, I asked myself how I would go about it: how I was going to bike down the street where my parents lived, lock my bike, and then open the front door of their house.

It's a street where privacy is less of an issue than in other neighborhoods in Amsterdam, that's one way of putting it. There are benches in the front gardens, on sunny days everyone sits out on the street side. Maybe not yet, not now, most people were still at work. Sometimes the neighbors barbecued in front of their houses. Children scribbled with colored chalk all over the sidewalks. When the weather was nice, to the outside world it looked almost idyllic. "Fantastic, the way people live out on the street like that, isn't it?"

No, we haven't seen your parents since last night. The curtains are closed, you're right, we noticed that too. Let's wait until five, we were saying to each other, then we'll call the police.

The neighbors didn't just sit on the benches and drink beer, no, they literally occupied the whole street, they appropriated the sidewalks. The public space no longer belonged to everyone, the paving stones served as chalkboards for their children.

What are you doing here, stranger? That's not only the way they looked at people from outside the neighborhood, no, that's the way they acted too — they even dressed like that, in shorts and unwashed T-shirts, or with nothing covering their upper bodies at all. As though you'd walked into their bedroom. With their scantily clothed bodies, their white, hairy bellies, they encouraged you to move on as fast as you could, because you had no business being here anyway.

Before my parents moved into the house, before I was appointed mayor, the two of us had lived in it for almost fifteen years. I, too, dressed in a way that bordered on the decent, used to sit on the bench in front of that house, a bench we bought at the Intratuin garden store on Nobelweg that very first summer. Diana was only eighteen months old. We had a sandbox in our 1,400-square-foot garden, but from the very first day she played only on the street. She made friends easily there, learned to ride a bike, it was there on a warm Saturday afternoon, shortly after her fourth birthday, that I took the training wheels off her bicycle. I no longer sat in the back garden to read my newspaper, but on the bench by the front

315

door. To keep an eye on our daughter as she was playing, I told myself. And that was true, of course, but only partly so. I was also sitting there to keep an eye on the street, the sidewalk, my sidewalk. From behind my newspaper I greeted my fellow sentries, my neighbors — and neglected to greet the people who weren't from around here.

At the end of the Ringdijk I turned right onto Middenweg, then left at the lights onto Hogeweg. I was cycling a little more hunched over than on the first stretch along the Amstel, bent down a bit more over the handlebars, so that not everyone would recognize my face right away.

So that they wouldn't say, later on: *Yeah, the day those two old people were found dead in their house, we saw the mayor there too. Close to there. Those were his parents, weren't they? Didn't he go inside? Didn't he come out the front door?*

I cycled past the fountain at the corner of Hogeweg and Linnaeusparkweg, chiseled from granite by Chinese slave laborers, and one block later I turned right, down Pythagorasstraat.

So far, there was no one out on the street. Still, I remained bent as low as I could, like a bicycle racer; I breathed in and out deeply.

I tried to breathe as normally as possible, I didn't want to sound out of breath, not if I had to say hello to one of the neighbors, an old acquaintance, and be forced to exchange a few words with them. No exchange at all would be seen later, in hindsight, as abnormal.

But I was in luck. By the time I placed my bike in the rack in front of the house and locked it, I still hadn't seen anyone. In theory, though, there could always be someone sitting at a window, half hidden behind the drapes, the lace curtains or venetian blinds, but I had to keep going. If I hesitated too much, if I looked left and right too often, the neighbor behind the lace curtains might describe that later as strange behavior.

After a bit of fiddling with the key, I stepped inside.

"Hello?" I shouted — not too loudly, not too quietly: normally.

In fact, I knew right away. It was the silence. The kind of silence.

The bedroom door was closed.

"Hello?"

I pushed the handle, opened the door a crack.

My parents were lying beside each other in their double bed. On their backs, their heads on the pillows.

317

My mother's mouth was open slightly, but it took no practiced eye to see that there was no breath passing through that mouth.

I don't know what it was that alerted me, when I turned my gaze to my father. Maybe the color in his face. It also reminded me of all those times I had climbed out of bed in the middle of the night and gone to Diana's crib. From the day she was born until her first birthday, maybe once each night. I listened and I looked. I tried to pick up the sound of her breathing, to tell from the slightest movement of her little blanket that she was still alive.

Now I was standing here, in my parents' bedroom, the same bedroom that once, long ago, had been our bedroom — Diana's crib stood at the foot of the bed for the first few months — and stared at the duvet on my father's side.

For the space of maybe five seconds — it could also have been three — I thought I was imagining it. The way you sometimes think that the train you're in has started pulling away, but it's a different train, the one on the track beside yours, that is in motion.

No, I wasn't imagining it.

There was movement beneath the duvet.

The movement of respiration that was weak, perhaps, but undeniably regular.

■ ■ ■ ■

PART III

■ ■ ■ ■

23

What form would fascism take these days, were it to present itself to us anew? Wind, I have often thought. The new fascism will tolerate no back talk, and who would be foolish enough to talk back to the wind? To *wind energy,* to be more precise. Indeed, who would have the gall to protest against clean energy sources? Water and wind, nature in all its purity, vast forests, unaffected by the blight of acid rain — those have always been the natural allies of fascism. Dark, eternally green forests where you can walk with your dog for hours without seeing another person, where you can set your thoughts free. Thoughts about a massacre, for example — no animals being slaughtered, of course, only humans.

The new fascism will, above all, adopt a human face. It will laugh more readily than the old fascism. Look less grim. Above all, it will act as though it understands us, as though it can easily understand our doubts. "Take your time and think about it," it will say. "Here are a few folders, read them when you get the chance. Many of the problems we're struggling against are your problems too."

Fascism with a human countenance creeps beneath the skin of the environmental activist, burrows its snout like a tick into the calves of those fighting for equal animal rights, it nods to us understandingly, pretends to be listening, but meanwhile launches into a monologue about global warming, the melting ice caps, the cruelty of the battery cage. The new fascism puts on its friendliest smile, helps old people across the street and carries their heavy shopping bags up the stairs. It feels at home in minds that are a blank slate, minds like an unfurnished house, without too many thoughts of their own: it provides you with advice about what colors to paint the walls, about the best lighting, it tags along with you to IKEA. "Just hang in there, we're almost to the cash register," it says as you load a box containing a chest of drawers onto your cart, a chest of drawers you didn't want in the first place.

It's not enough to just pull the tick out of your skin. The head will still be in there.

Tomorrow that head will grow a new body, which will once again suck itself full of blood. No, more drastic measures are needed. We have to go deeper than that. A few centimeters of our own flesh will have to be cut away, around the spot where the tick has burrowed in. If it's not already too late, if it hasn't already infected us with its fascistic ideas.

"Look what a lovely windmill," says the tick. "Do you know how many households one windmill can provide with electricity?"

The new fascism comes up with figures. About the pollution caused by coal-fired power plants, about CO_2 emissions, about the greenhouse effect. You try to come back with something about the windmill. You wish you could say that you don't think it's lovely at all. That it ruins the view. That a windmill on the horizon makes our country even smaller than it already is.

After "wind," "meatless" comes in a solid second. Do I need to present here a list of all the dictators, psychopaths, and mass murderers who were vegetarians? There are those who take it even further: no fish either, no eggs, no leather shoes. Veganism. Am I the only one who thinks of something very different when he hears the word "vegan"? One look at a vegan's face and you know enough. It's not just the absence of color — a bloodless absence, like recycled cardboard — it's a colorlessness that tolerates no back talk. They refuse to walk in shoes made from animal hide, but feel no shame at displaying their pallid feet, their ghostly white toes, in ecological sandals made from some vague artificial fiber. What do they call those things again? Birkenstocks! Am I, once again, the only one who thinks of something very different when he hears the word "Birkenstock"? Of an obscure spot in the Polish hinterland, its precise location unknown to anyone; of a T-shirt reading I SURVIVED BIRKENSTOCK?

That's the way it will go. That's the way it already is. A hidden camera will record how we fail to properly dispose of our waste. How, out of recalcitrance — a final act of resistance — we purposely toss the white bottles in the hole meant for the green ones. Our garbage bags will be cut open — what am I saying, our garbage bags are already being cut open! Amid the rotting apple cores, teabags, and moldy leftovers, the municipal inspectors will have no trouble finding evidence of resistance: a battery that should actually have been brought to the chemical waste car (am I the only one who thinks of something very different when he hears the term "chemical waste car"?), a glass jar that the label says once contained pickles, a plastic bottle with a film of detergent at the bottom. Perhaps the garbage bag has simply been placed beside the tree (or beside the perpetually overflowing container — emptied as it is only twice a week) too early in the evening. Amid all that forbidden garbage the inspectors find something else too: a torn love letter, an envelope bearing an address. There is, in any case, evidence enough to impose a fine. We receive a payment slip in the post. Let that be a lesson to us. From now on we will put the garbage out only after nightfall, or let the bags stink up the house until the containers are finally emptied.

Film clips of the worst offenders will be put online. So that everyone can see how that inconspicuous man from the fourth floor (first name, surname, and house number appear at the bottom of the screen) glances to the left and right, forty-five minutes before sundown, and then drops a bag full of plaster chips and drywall into the paper bin.

"Amsterdam to Build Two Hundred Wind Turbines," the headline in *Het Parool* said, the day after the windmill debate. The debate I had missed because at that very moment I was standing at the foot of my parents' bed, my mother dead and my father still breathing faintly. Two hundred! I had always thought they meant only a couple of dozen. Out by the Schellingwouder Bridge and the Zeeburger Tunnel, along the Amstel in the direction of Ouderkerk, and the rest spread out around the western harbors. Even a couple of dozen wind turbines would ruin the looks of Amsterdam for good. I had seen the drawings — the misleading drawings, because they were nothing but charts showing only the possible locations. Some of the turbines being announced now were of the very newest kind, the tallest models. Two hundred meters high, if I remembered correctly. From any number of spots downtown you would be able to see the spinning rotors over the rooftops. A crime.

I had missed the debate. The Dutch democratic system stipulates that the mayor has no vote. Don't ask me why. It's as big a mystery as how anyone actually gets to be mayor in this country. By election, you would think. In 99 percent of all democracies, a mayor is appointed by means of free and open elections. But not in Holland. In fact, the appointment of a mayor here is as nontransparent as in North Korea, Cuba, or South Ossetia. No, I'm putting that the wrong way; it's not *just as* nontransparent, it's many times less transparent. In North Korea, the only candidate is elected by 99 percent of the vote; that, at least, is a great deal more transparent than the way it goes with us.

So I wasn't there, and my vote — my non-vote, rather — could never have tipped the scales; but I probably could have steered the debate. Pushed the various parties in the council, by means of a briefly conclusive and businesslike speech, in the direction I wanted. And maybe a speech wouldn't even have been necessary. I could have made do with body language. Shaking my head in fatigue during the plea held by Alderman Van Hoogstraten, the great advocate of wind turbines. A roar of laughter when the number "two hundred" was mentioned. *Two hundred! Did you hear that?! Did you hear what he said?!* I would make the council members see the other side of things. The absurd side. *Amsterdam is already fairly small,* I would say. *Our city is renowned throughout the world for its human scale. No overwhelming, intimidating buildings here, not like in London and Paris. In Amsterdam a person can still feel like a person. In most of the world's metropolitan areas, a person feels like nothing. Puny. And that was precisely what all those kings and emperors were after, too, to make the citizens of those capitals bow their heads in submission. The greater the power, the bigger the buildings and the smaller the people. We need think only of Albert Speer's plans for Berlin, about Nicolae Ceauşescu, Kim Il-Sung. We should be thankful that we have never had such despots here. Not in our country. Not in our city. The merchants and the small businessmen run things here. The more accessible the city, the more hospitable, the more tolerant as far as I'm concerned, the more profit can be made there.*

I would not have used the word "rustic." I would have gone on emphasizing the human scale. A wind turbine in New York (a whole wind park in the Mojave Desert) is not the same as a wind turbine in Amsterdam, I would have said. That scale is exactly right, at this moment. We shouldn't do anything to ruin it. We have to be careful not to make the city itself puny.

Powerful despots, kings, presidents, dictators, and mayors have left their own personal marks on their capitals. Working on behalf of Napoleon III, Georges-Eugène Haussmann razed the crowded medieval neighborhoods of Paris and replaced them with long, broad boulevards. The same boulevards we now think of first when we think of Paris. None of that had anything to do with democracy, let alone with popular resistance. It simply happened in the same way that, in our own century, an entire working neighborhood in Beijing could be bulldozed to the ground in a single day and turned into a construction pit dozens of meters deep. Five months later, standing at the same spot, you had twelve residential towers more than sixty stories high. I've already mentioned North Korea. Hitler's plans for Berlin. François Mitterrand took a slightly more modest approach: he had a pyramid of glass built at the main entrance to the Louvre. Whether you like that pyramid or despise it doesn't really matter: *it's there,* that's the message it is meant to convey; and the Louvre will never be the same again.

In a free and open democracy, things go differently. Especially when you involve the local people in your decision-making. If the citizens of nineteenth-century France had been allowed to vote, Paris today would still be a stinking, medieval city. The ugliest building in Amsterdam — and perhaps in the entire country — is, by a long shot, the city hall. The same city hall I go into through the main entrance every day, but that in all types of weather — rain, sun, snow — is a pain to behold. This ugliest building in town (in the whole country!), which shares a roof with the opera house, was created in a democratic fashion. By means of consultation — "opportunities for public comment" — with the locals. Wherever people are given an opportunity for public comment, you get ugliness. Not just ugly buildings, but also ugly, nondescript politicians. The Obamas and Kennedys of this world, those are the exceptions. All you have to do is think back on our own prime ministers during the last seventy years. A rogues' gallery of the nondescript. The majority always picks the ugliest wallpaper. WOULD YOU BUY A USED CAR FROM THIS MAN? was the caption once on a poster showing the face of presidential candidate Richard Nixon. The poster was meant to show the candidate's unreliable character, but unreliability is still less stultifying than blandness. WITH WHICH OF THESE MEN WOULD YOU CARE TO DRINK A BEER? should be the caption under the faces of our prime ministers.

No, the truly charismatic leaders rarely come to power by democratic means. From Julius Caesar to Fidel Castro, from Alexander the Great to Mao Tse-tung, from

Jesus Christ, Robin Hood, and Che Guevara to Osama Bin Laden: each and every one of them owed their charismatic magic not to free and open elections, nor to opportunities for public comment from the entire neighborhood.

Dutch prime ministers who have stirred the imagination can be counted on the fingers of one hand, or no fingers at all, but mayors are a very different thing. Dutch mayors, who are not elected in democratic fashion, by a majority of the popular vote, but are appointed from on high. The current mayor of Rotterdam possesses more statesmanship than all our prime ministers put together. What's more, our country is teeming with mayors who have been involved in scandals. Who have sometimes had to resign in the face of said scandals. What prime minister can say the same thing? Behind the empty faces, there is only true emptiness. A face with only the facade still standing, the building behind it has been razed, there isn't even any rubble left, that too was carted off long ago.

It would be odd, at this point, to say nothing about myself. Hypocritical. Perhaps even vain. *He's not mentioning himself on purpose. We're supposed to fill it in for ourselves, that he considers himself on a par with his colleague in Rotterdam.* But it really is true. There are lists going around that include the two of us when it comes to the most suitable candidates for the prime ministership. On those lists, we are always numbers one and two. Sometimes he's number one and I am second. Sometimes it's the other way around.

The original plans for the opera house showed a building made of white concrete. Too big, the neighbors reckoned. Too white. A vote was taken. Everything had to be downsized a bit. Red bricks were substituted for the white concrete. Democracy in a nutshell. Wherever a vote is taken, the people go for something more picayune, made from the same material as our own, cutesy little houses.

Then someone came up with the brilliant idea of combining the two projects. The new city hall and the opera house. That would save money too. The definitive triumph of democracy.

It was, above all, a missed opportunity. Amsterdam may have its canals, but it has no landmark. No Eiffel Tower, Statue of Liberty, or Big Ben. The opera house in Sydney is a landmark. You used to have picture postcards, these days you've got selfies. The Amsterdam city hall, the city hall—

334

cum–opera house, is not featured on a single postcard. No self-respecting tourist would take a selfie with the Stopera in the background.

If I were allowed to choose my own landmark, to choose what I as mayor would leave behind for the city, the way Mitterrand did with that glass pyramid in front of the Louvre, I would go for the tearing-down of the Stopera. A new building at the same place. At that lovely spot, one of the loveliest spots on the Amstel, where the river disappears into nothingness. Something that could be put on a postcard without embarrassing the hell out of you.

But a new city hall is, of course, a castle in the air. It's like abolishing the monarchy. Not open to discussion. Not a single political party is willing to stick its neck out for that. Yet another fund-guzzling project — beside all the other money-guzzling projects that still need completing — is precisely one project too many.

No, a new city hall, a city hall that would immediately become the city's landmark, too, was not on. But in that case, I wanted to leave Amsterdam with something else: a windmill-free horizon.

I was the only speaker at my mother's

funeral. It was what they call a "direct burial." A plain coffin, Édith Piaf's "La Vie en Rose," and her favorite flowers: white roses. My father sat in the front, Sylvia and I at either end of the row. Diana was on his right and Bernhard, who had come over from Boston for a couple of days, was beside her. Christine wasn't there: she was already five months pregnant and didn't want to fly anymore.

I kept it short. My happy youth. My parents' love for each other. Our biweekly lunch at Oriental City. We had decided to invite only family and friends. So there would be less explaining to do. About the actual cause of death, for example. For friends and acquaintances, we stuck to "she died in her sleep." My mother's two elder sisters had died fifteen and twenty years ago. My father had only one brother, eight years his junior, who lived in Portugal and with whom he hadn't been on speaking terms since he was forty.

"I don't get it," my father told me, almost twenty-four hours after I'd called their family doctor and then the ambulance from the house on Pythagorasstraat. "I gave us both the same dose. No, that's not true. I gave myself a slightly higher dose, just to be sure." He looked at me, his eyes still sleepy and his eyelids drooping with fatigue. Every now and again they fell shut, like the eyes of an animal sunning itself in the grass. "To make sure it worked," he added after a brief silence. "I'm sure I did it right."

I hadn't been there when he woke from his stupor about three hours earlier. We had taken turns watching at bedside, Sylvia, Diana, and I. He had a private room on the seventh floor of the Academic Medical Centre. Diana had just taken over from my wife when my father started blinking his eyes for the first time.

"What did he say?" I asked my daughter in the hospital corridor, after hurrying out of another council meeting. "What did he say, exactly?"

"He blinked his eyes," she said. "He looked around a bit, then he saw me. 'What a lovely day,' is what he said. 'And how are you doing? When do your finals start?' "

After three days, he was released from the hospital. We insisted that he stay with us for the first few weeks, but he was having none of it. "I'm tired," he said. "And I want to go home."

We didn't ask him the most important question of all, not then, and not after the funeral either. The five of us were standing around my car. Sylvia, Diana, Bernhard, my father, and I. The sun was sparkling on the water of the Amstel, a swan paddled by along the bank, with a ribbon of cygnets trailing behind.

Now what? What are you going to do now?

First we dropped Bernhard at his hotel.

"Lunch tomorrow?" he said; I had climbed out of the car, we hugged, and he patted me on the shoulder. "Dauphine?"

There was no place to park along Pythagorasstraat; I stopped the car in front of the house.

"Are you sure about this?" Sylvia asked my father. "Don't you want us to come in with you?"

He shook his head. "No, let me go. I have to let this sink in first. I'll call you tomorrow. Or in a couple of days."

Now what? What are you going to do now? It wasn't the kind of question you ask someone every day, not something you could ask by the bye. That's why we didn't. Not in the hospital, and not so soon after the funeral either.

"Maybe we should leave it for the time being," Sylvia said. "Maybe we should just wait and see if he starts talking about it himself."

And I, as I so often did, agreed with her.

24

"The steak tartare was for . . . ?"

We hadn't gone for an appetizer; with a smile, the girl placed my order on the table in front of me, then the rib eye with Béarnaise for Bernhard. Dauphine was one of the restaurants in Amsterdam where I felt most comfortable. Not only because of the relatively simple menu, but because of everything: the roominess — a former Renault garage, hence the name — without the frills or humbug, the prompt and always-friendly waiting staff, and the relative anonymity: precisely because there are so many tables, but also because other famous faces tended to come here; the customers at most looked up only briefly when yet another famous face entered, then went back to their meals in feigned boredom.

"Could we also get two beers?"

"Two beers, coming up."

The boys and girls on the waitstaff did

not feign boredom when they showed a famous face to his or her table, but having the mayor in their restaurant didn't make them needlessly nervous either. Not like the panic on the faces in one of the city's hipper eateries the time I showed up unannounced, without a reservation. When I came in and asked cautiously whether "there might be a chance" of them having a table for my wife and me, we were given the nicest table at the window, and the cooks hurried out of the kitchen to shake my hand — after that one time, I never went back there again.

"I hope you're still willing to do this for me," Bernhard said, picking a French fry off his plate, swishing it through his cup of mayonnaise, and putting it in his mouth. "If you're not, I'll understand, we'll just drop the whole thing. But we can make history, Robert, really. Normally speaking, I don't like sweeping phrases like that, but this is a unique opportunity. We can make history together."

"No, sure," I said. "I'll do it, I already promised you I would, you can count on me."

"Great," he said, and he glanced at the tables to the left and to the right of us — a mother and daughter, and two men with laptops, iPads, and phones beside their plates of salad — before leaning across to me: "Listen up. Here's the idea."

And he started in. First he gave me a brief recap of what he'd told me in our garden a few months earlier. The incomprehensibility of the beginning and end of the universe, and then the equally incomprehensible mystery of death. What if these two major mysteries were closely connected, he'd said. Our brain, ingenious as it may be, is a limited instrument. Our powers of imagination are limited. Remember the deaf people who are incapable of hearing. With our limited understanding, we can't grasp the two great mysteries of life. Not only of life, but also of nonlife, because of course the entire cosmos has no need of us. The universe got along without us for billions of years, and for more billions of years, after we're gone, it won't miss us for a moment either.

"My theory's quite simple, really," he had told me in the garden that night. I wasn't able to see his face, I listened to his voice and saw only the glowing tip of his cigarette. "The way all major theories are always simple. Archimedes, Newton, Einstein. I could put on the false modesty now and say that of course I don't mean to compare

341

myself to those bigwigs, but I'm not going to do that. If my theory isn't correct, it can go right in the trash. I can go right in the trash. Maybe no one will ever know about it, I leave that completely up to you, Robert. As far as I'm concerned, you're free to use it as an anecdote to tell your friends and family, and you can all have a big laugh about it. 'You remember Bernhard Langer? Do you remember what he thought?' But" — and here he paused to pull another cigarette out of the pack — "if I'm right, if what I'm thinking is right, it's going to be bigger than Einstein. It will be no less than the explanation of how the world works. I'll get the Nobel Prize. Posthumously, but in the context of completely explaining life and death, that makes absolutely no difference anymore. You know what I'm like, Robert. I don't give a fuck about Nobel Prizes. About recognition. Even without prizes, my life is interesting enough. But will you promise me one thing? If I get it, will you go to Stockholm to pick it up for me? Whatever the case, it will belong to both of us. You can give a nice speech, you're good at that. Tell them about our friendship. Friendship that extends beyond the grave."

During our lunch at Dauphine, though, the Nobel Prize didn't come up again. Bernhard emphasized how he had kept his distance from wishy-washy stuff his whole life. After our joint teenage experiments with Ouija boards and tarot cards, and devouring books that were popular back when we were about seventeen, books with titles like *Chariots of the Gods?* and *The Morning of the Magicians,* his career in the natural sciences and astronomy had kept him down to earth for years. He had become convinced that the palpable world contained mysteries enough, and that there was no need to go rummaging around in what he called the "immaterial" world.

"Still, you never shake it off completely," he said now, dipping a piece of rib eye into the bowl of Béarnaise sauce. "Once you've believed in life being brought to Earth by alien cosmonauts, you can never completely go back. Of course, it's all a load of rubbish, that's what you tell yourself, but then all the great discoveries were considered rubbish at first, too, by most people. That the earth is not the center of the universe, that it's not flat, that there may be a western passage to India — all truths we now accept as self-evident, but they brought only ridicule to their first proponents, and led quite a few of them to the stake as well. I've immersed myself in black holes, concentrations of matter that exert such a powerful attraction that even light disappears into them. Why, I kept on asking myself? Why are there black holes? Isn't the cosmos puzzling enough as it is? Stephen Hawking once said to me: 'You know, Bernhard, sometimes I think about a future in which all the research we're doing now will be seen as child's play. As the preparation for something much bigger. As though we're proud of having invented the safety match, and then they show us an atomic explosion.' I've never forgotten that. We discover something — the roundness of the earth, the theory of relativity, the cell phone — but it doesn't amount to a hill of beans. It's only the beginning. Not even one half of one percent of the discoveries that are still coming."

He paused for a moment, signaled to the waitress, and pointed to our empty beer glasses. "Getting back to how it all started," he went on. "With *The Morning of the Magicians* and *Chariots of the Gods?* Like I said, you never completely get over something like that. Do you remember how we read that book by Thor Heyerdahl, about the voyage of the *Kon-Tiki?* How he tried to prove that the ancient Egyptians, long before the start of our calendar, must have crossed the Atlantic, that they must have helped the Aztecs, the Mayans, and the Incas to build their pyramids? It's not about whether it's true or not, it's that you don't start laughing at a theory like that right away, that you're provisionally prepared to accept it at face value. They've got a fashionable term for it these days: 'thinking out of the box.' People always laugh, and most of the time rightly so, at quasi-scientific experiments with thought waves, near-death experiences, and reincarnation. You can dismiss it all as nonsense, that's usually safe, because no conclusive proof has ever been offered for those phenomena. When you're a scientist, you have to watch your step. One dubious, wishy-washy experiment and you're on the sidelines for years, maybe forever. You remember Rupert Sheldrake? He showed that the sparrows of Northern England had discovered a trick to remove the caps from milk bottles. The milk bottles delivered by the milkman and left on the stoop for a while, unattended. Less than six months later, the sparrows in the south of England knew the same trick. Without a single sparrow having flown down from the Far North to teach them: he actually had sound scientific evidence for that. His theory was that when intelligence increased within a small group, intelligence throughout the group as a whole increased too. And where is Rupert Sheldrake these days? Is he still alive? Do you have any idea? Do I have a clue?"

The waitress came to ask if we were finished. She didn't ask whether we had enjoyed our meals, not the way they did in some places after you'd only had a cheese sandwich. She simply asked whether everything had been okay, and whether we wanted to see the dessert menu.

Bernhard and I didn't even have to look at each other before I ordered two espressos and two grappas. "The clear one," I added. "The normal one."

"It's sort of like having believed in Communism," Bernhard went on. "We used to believe in that, didn't we? The Che Guevara posters on the wall, the Viet Cong, who we didn't call the 'Viet Cong' the way the supporters of American imperialism did, but the 'National Liberation Front of Vietnam.' As time goes by you gradually lose that belief, but it never goes away completely. Who was it who said: 'If you're not a Communist at the age of eighteen, you have no heart; if you are still a Communist at the age of twenty, you have no brain'?"

"George Bernard Shaw?"

"No, he went on believing till the bitter

end, didn't he? Anyway, it doesn't matter, what I'm trying to say is that your sympathies remain with the bearded revolutionaries for the rest of your life, even if you've come to know better. You never swing all the way to the other side. You don't suddenly become enamored of generals with stupid hats and dozens of medals pinned to their chests."

The table next to ours was empty. Not so very long ago, my bodyguards would have been sitting there. Back when there were still four of them, one always stood close to the door, the second one sat at the bar and scanned the customers in the restaurant from behind his sunglasses, a measured sweep, never any faster or any slower, like a radar scoop or a lighthouse. Numbers three and four sat at the table beside mine and acted like they weren't listening to the conversation between me and my guest or guests. But it was always striking to see how little they had to say to each other. A few tables farther along I'd once had lunch with Bill Clinton, who hadn't been president for very long by then. It was one of the rare occasions on which I felt the presence of a personality stronger than my own. Or at least a personality that seemed to gobble up other personalities. A sort of turbo-version of myself. Bill Clinton makes you feel as though you're the only one who matters, that nothing exists outside the conversation he's having with you at that moment; the outside world literally falls into nothingness. I'm not the only one who's experienced a meeting with the former American president in that same way. Everyone who has ever been around him describes the experience in those same words. My two bodyguards were seated at the table to the right of us; to the left of us was a table with four Secret Service agents. They looked exactly the way they do on TV or in movies: white shirts, black suits, sunglasses, earpieces. Somehow, in a way I can't really describe, they looked more plausible than my own bodyguards. Bill Clinton, too, seemed realer than most of the Dutch politicians I'd had lunch with at Dauphine. "Larger than life," they call that. Maybe it was a matter of the TV footage racing out ahead of the former president himself, but he literally towered over the little table, his upper body was out of proportion to the tabletop, he grasped the edges of it firmly with his big hands, as though he might pick it up at any moment and hurl it across the restaurant.

I remember quite clearly what we talked

about. I can't repeat it all here, not without getting myself into serious trouble. That morning, in The Hague, he'd had a meeting with our then prime minister. "Could I ask you something?" he'd asked me. "And I expect an honest answer." His question had to do with the prime minister, I regret not being able to reproduce it here, but it was a private conversation and I can't quote from it without permission from the former president himself, I can imagine he might not like that. Suffice it to say that Bill Clinton's eyes grew wide when I tried to answer him as honestly as possible. Then he made a disgusted face. "Really?" he said. He shook his head and burst out laughing. "Unbelievable! I suspected something like that, but this is really unbelievable, Bob." That's right, he called me Bob, after he had said that I should call him Bill and I had said that he should call me Robert. It was hilarious, the former president of the United States took it for granted that here in Holland we shortened Robert to "Bob" too. Then Bill said something about Queen Beatrix, in whose company he'd had dinner the night before. He said it very quietly, almost at a whisper, I thought for a moment that I'd heard him wrong, but when he saw my expression he said it again.

At that moment, I remember quite well, I glanced off to one side, at the table where my bodyguards were seated. They stirred their coffee in silence, there was nothing to indicate that they'd heard anything of our conversation. I could only admit that Clinton was right. Kings and queens. You'll rarely find a personality among them. They never have to do their best. Unlike John F. Kennedy or Barack Obama (or Clinton himself), they don't have to barnstorm around the country, trying to win votes. They get it all handed to them on a silver platter. You can tell by their faces. With every successive generation, the faces grow emptier. Stupider. Queen Juliana was already hard enough to take seriously: in her grandson's face there's almost nothing going on anymore. There's no more hiding it: from generation to generation, the quality of the bloodline plummets. The only ones with anything that looks a bit like a personality are the princes- and princesses-by-marriage. They're smarter. More ambitious. Marrying a future king or queen will open every door. They enter into matrimony with a man or woman no one would hook up with voluntarily. The princesses-by-marriage shine beside the empty faces of their husbands. From the steps of the royal palace they wave to the cheering crowds. The princes-by-marriage are now in uniform. The grins on their faces are 100 percent authentic. On their wedding night and a couple of times after that, they perform their duty. The lineage. A successor to the throne. New princes and princesses. Faces increasingly pappy and nondescript. Shortly after the honeymoon, the prince consort goes elephant hunting, flips a speedboat on the Mediterranean close to Cannes, crashes three or four sports cars, and hops from cocktail party to cocktail party aboard the yachts at anchor around the bay. There he hits on everything that isn't already nailed to the deck: movie stars, duchesses, millionaires' daughters. The queen knows about all this. She doesn't need to know all the ins and outs, to hear all the juicy details. She knows that there's no getting around it, that this is the tacit agreement. At home, in a room of the palace lit only by a single floor lamp, she watches the last edition of the evening news at midnight. She dabs at her eyes with a white lace handkerchief. A valet pokes his head in through the door to ask if she'd like another glass of young gin.

"Two parallel lines intersect in infinity," Bernhard was saying. "Do you still remember that, Robert? Second-year physics at the

Spinoza Lyceum? Mr. Karstens?"

I wondered whether I might have missed something; my senses told me that my thoughts had been elsewhere for quite some time now.

"Yes, I remember that," I said. "Parallel lines never intersect."

"Because it's unimaginable."

"That's right." I was sure about it now, something was missing, a piece was gone for good, the way you sometimes doze off during a movie and then can't figure out how the main character suddenly got from the casino to the desert somewhere outside Las Vegas.

"That's what we're going to do: we're going to make the unimaginable imaginable," Bernhard said. "Make the parallel lines intersect. Mark off the beginning and the end of the universe. Or not, of course. The chance that nothing at all can be made imaginable is infinitely greater. But if you don't try, you'll never know. As far as that goes, I feel a bit like Columbus. You have to dare to go to sea without knowing where you'll end up."

"When are you . . . When are you going to do it?" I had caught myself on the point of saying, *When are you planning to leave?*

"The babies are due in four months. So

before then anyway. It's bad enough for Christine as it is. Having to raise twins on her own. It would be unthinkable, having to care for a dying man alongside that."

I looked at our empty espresso cups and glasses of grappa, then flagged down the waitress. It seemed much longer than a week ago that Bernhard had called to tell me about his impending death. A routine examination at the university, the mandatory annual checkup, had revealed anomalies in his blood sugar levels. *How long have I got?* Bernhard asked them. *I wish I could give you a more hopeful prognosis, Mr. Langer, but at this stage it's more like a matter of months.*

"I'm flying back to Boston tomorrow," Bernhard told me. "I want to be with her for as long as possible."

Our second round of espressos and grappas came, a brief silence during which we didn't look at each other and I nodded courteously at the waitress. I still had a couple of questions for Bernhard, but he himself seemed to have nothing more to say.

"And how about you?" he asked. "Anything new? Any juicy gossip?"

We had already talked briefly, at the start of the lunch, about my parents, about my mother's funeral. About my father, and how

353

painful it was to ask him about his plans for the immediate future. Bernhard agreed with me that it was better to wait until he started talking about it himself.

"You were very close with your mother, weren't you?" he asked me at one point. "I mean, more so than with your father, right?"

"Yeah, I think so. In fact, I'm sure so. My mother was always calm, such a good listener too. My father was, is, more the hyperactive type. You remember that; I always got tired when I was around him, even when I was a kid. We would rent a house in the Dordogne and then, early in the morning, I would see him unfolding a map on the table, out on the patio, and flipping madly through all these guidebooks. I would hope, pray, that we wouldn't have to go off to some church or ruin somewhere, that we could just spend the whole day sitting on the patio."

Bernhard laughed. "Yeah, I remember that, he was always that way. And have you noticed anything yet, with your mother?"

"What do you mean?"

"Whether you're already feeling her absence. Or not. I mean, it hasn't been that long. Maybe you wake up in the morning and for a couple of seconds or more you have the feeling that she's still around. I had that with my father when he died. It lasted a pretty long time, for months, maybe a year. Every day, all over again, I had to get used to the fact that he wasn't there anymore. And I saw things the way he would have seen them. In everything I did, I asked myself whether he would have approved."

"But you were a lot younger then. Seventeen, right?"

"Eighteen. A week after my eighteenth birthday."

"That's exactly the age when kids start to rebel against their parents' authority. Or when they're just getting over doing that. So it's only logical that you thought his approval was important. But with my mother . . . I don't know, this morning it did occur to me that, normally speaking, I would be having lunch with her today, instead of with you."

"All I'm saying is that you should pay close attention. You two had a strong bond. The same way we have a strong bond, but with a mother that's even stronger, by definition. It's all still very fresh, you're still open to it. To little changes. Things you couldn't explain unless, of course, your mother had something to do with it."

That had been the moment when they

brought our food, and we'd segued seamlessly into Bernhard's theory about the possible connection between the finiteness of the universe and the finiteness of human life.

During the second grappa I felt the alcohol kicking in for the first time. Afraid that, in a fit of false alcoholic candor I would surely regret later, I might start in about Sylvia and Alderman Van Hoogstraten, I gave Bernhard a brief rundown on the windmill debate.

"The most frustrating thing about it is that I wasn't there," I ended my account. "Because I . . . . Well, because it just happened to be the day that it happened with my parents."

Bernhard knocked back his grappa in a single go; his gaze may have been a bit more watery than at the start of our lunch, but he had always been able to hold his alcohol better than I could.

After the grappa, he raised the espresso cup to his lips and knocked that back too.

"You know what it is?" he said. "This whole climate discussion has been carried out all wrong, ever since the very beginning. Carried out misleadingly. They emphasize all the wrong things. Wind turbines, solar panels, that's fine, they don't do much damage. But in fact, we don't need them at all. Did you know that if everyone in Holland would turn down the heat by one degree Celsius in the winter, we could save the energy produced by ten thousand wind turbines? Ten thousand! One degree, don't get me wrong, I'm not out to get people to sit around in a cold house. It's about a change in mentality. We turn the thermostat up to twenty-two degrees and lie around on the couch in our pajamas. In shorts and a T-shirt. Because that's the way we want to live. Because that's what we're used to. But no government, no political party is going to try to get people to wear a sweater around the house. In fact, it would be much better if we didn't put on a sweater at all. Turn down the heating two degrees and the fat metabolism kicks in automatically. The best diet there is. You can eat as much as you want, as long as you always keep the heating down to twenty."

"But then what is it?" I asked. "Why does it seem as though the windmill advocates are always right?"

"Do you have any idea how much money is involved there? Have you ever taken a good look at the calculation models? It's all been in the newspapers. The whole setup is incredibly expensive, in comparison to what it yields. But everyone's earning a lot of money on it. The turbine manufacturers, but also the farmers who let them put one of those things on their land, get huge amounts of money from the government. And those turbines don't last that long. Not as long as the average nuclear power plant. There was an article about it in the newspaper not so long ago. About the companies that are going to make a fortune on that later on, when they have to tear down all those turbines. And we're not even talking about the foreign market. We've got the technology, the know-how — we're working on it already — to shove wind turbines down the throat of the entire Third World. Even after expenses, it still adds up to a lot more than all the natural gas reserves we've still got in the ground.

"You know, Robert," he went on, after raising the empty grappa glass to his lips and trying to flag down the waitress. "The worst of it is that none of it makes any difference. And that the people who dare to say anything else are called 'climate skeptics.' We live in a democracy, but dissent is not really appreciated. It doesn't matter who's right. Maybe it's going to get colder in the next five hundred years. But there could also be a scorching global heat wave. Those couple of degrees of man-made warming really aren't going to make the difference. In the Middle Ages, there were icebergs drifting off the coast of Majorca; a century before that, there were vineyards in the north of England. None of it under the influence of greenhouse gases. The fluctuations on Earth have always taken place on a scale much larger than the human one. On a scale like that, ten thousand or a hundred thousand wind turbines are only a drop in the bucket. Literally a drop in the bucket: one drop makes no difference, but if you pour the whole thing full of ice water it's the bucket itself that cools down. We may be heading for a future in which we'll have to produce as much greenhouse gas and CO_2 as we can, just to stay a bit warm. One volcanic explosion and it will be two degrees cooler here for the next century. I'm talking about a real volcano, a bruiser, like the Krakatoa. For the first eight years after it erupted, people here in Holland could go skating from September to the middle of May. You see that in the paintings from back then: all those winter landscapes. Or what about the Ice Age? There was no environmental movement back then, only the environment. And that environment did whatever it pleased. Later, when our country is covered in a mile-thick layer of ice, what environmental movement is going to organize a protest march against the new ice age? Earth is an indifferent planet, Robert. When it comes right down to it, she couldn't care less whether she's inhabited by humans or not. Sea level rise? A tsunami? So what? Who told those people to build their houses so close to the coast? Earth is feeling hemmed in, something's too tight. Something pinches somewhere. She stretches a little, and two tectonic plates slide over each other with a crash. That's better, now she can breathe again, that hemmed-in feeling is over. But no one's told her that she's inhabited by people. That their houses collapse when she stretches. The earth shivers like a horse trying to shoo flies off its flanks. She waves her tail, but can't shake more than a few tens of thousands, at most a couple hundred thousand humans, off her back. Sometimes I ask myself whether this is how it was supposed to be, this human life. We've gone in search of voices from space, but just imagine that we are really alone. A hugely empty cosmos with somewhere, almost indiscernible in our galaxy, one tiny little planet where things have spun out of control. A mistake. A chain reaction. We talk about pollution all the time these days, but what if we ourselves just happen to be the pollutant? Not only us: life itself. A fungus on the face of a planet that never asked for that life in the first place. I've tried to imagine that sometimes. Our earth with no life on it. No trees, no grass, nothing at all. You've got places like that in Iceland. Or the Grand Canyon. It's not sad at all, it's actually very beautiful."

I walked Bernhard across the street to Amstel Station, where he was going to take the train to Schiphol. I consulted my public transport app.

"The best thing would be to change trains at Duivendrecht," I said. "That's faster than going by way of Central Station."

On the platform, we hugged.

"This isn't goodbye," he said. "Let's not overdramatize it. We can call, write, text . . . If I get the chance, I'll warn you in time, in the next couple of weeks."

"Weeks?" I took off my glasses and rubbed my eyes.

"At the end of the month there's a conference in Las Vegas that I have to go to. I think I'll take the opportunity to visit the Grand Canyon. The North Rim, I've never been there before."

I put my glasses back on, but the lenses

were fogged over. The train was pulling in.

"You know, Robert," Bernhard said, patting me on the shoulder, "deep in my heart I believe that, in the end, there's nothing. If human life is a mistake, then life after death would be an even bigger mistake. If you hear nothing from me later on, that will be the ultimate proof that there's really nothing at all."

25

And then? Then my wife's behavior really did change — there was no mistaking it this time.

You've been picnicking in the park. Sun, and the occasional cloud. But then suddenly the wind comes up. The branches start to sway, a cold shiver blows through the grass. You have just enough time to fold the blanket and stuff the half-empty bottles and the remains of your meal back in the basket. Then, too close for comfort, you hear the first thunderclap. Fat drops of rain are held back by the leaves at first, but out in the open there's no stopping it. Soaked to the skin, you make it to the parking lot where you left the car.

"I texted you!" she said and heaved a deep sigh. We were standing, facing off, in the kitchen. "Didn't you get my message? Toothpaste and honey-licorice drops. How hard can that be?"

I sputtered something, for form's sake: that I never hear my phone when I'm on the bike. But meanwhile, all my senses were tingling. It was the third time that week that she had yelled at me, the second time in the last two days. Normally speaking, when that happens I ask her whether something's wrong. Whether this irritation is perhaps only a surface thing, whether the cause doesn't actually lie deeper.

But I didn't do that. Or no, let me put that differently: We never asked each other whether there was "something wrong." Never. We waited patiently until the other person took the initiative. Not out of a lack of interest, but out of respect. Sometimes the other person was just in a bad mood that day, how irritating then to be asked if maybe there was something wrong. The next day it would probably be over anyway.

"Is something wrong?" I asked now, and with that I violated our unspoken agreement. "I don't know, but you've been so irritable the last few days. I mean, toothpaste: how important can that be?"

Sylvia looked away quickly and pretended to be studying the best-before date on a can of tuna fish. "Don't worry about me, Robert. I think I'm just a little tired. But it also annoys me so much that I can't even count on you to go to the store for me."

So that time I dropped the subject. But the next day it happened again. The two of us were on the couch, watching the news. Something about a paralyzed woman in Texas who was demanding her right to euthanasia.

"Isn't it about time you called your father?" she asked, in a tone that made it clear she was itching for a fight. "Postponing it for a little while, okay, but that was already a couple of weeks ago."

At that moment, I could have said something conciliatory. Or come up with some hackneyed cliché. *Don't you think we should actually have a talk, the two of us? Because I think this is about something very different.*

But I didn't do either of those things. I felt more like forcing the issue.

"So be glad," I said. "You thought it was so spoiled and childish of my parents to want to put an end to it all, didn't you? So very Dutch of them? Well, maybe he's more attached to living than he realized. Maybe he's actually rediscovered life."

At the moment I said it I realized that, until then, I had never considered that possibility myself. I had called my father a couple of times in the last few weeks and went by to see him once. He seemed more downhearted to me than anything else, almost as though he was ashamed of still being around. I never asked him about it directly, but the last time I called he had started talking about it himself.

"I've been thinking . . . ," he said. "What if I were to do something, one last time. I mean, something major. A real farewell. It's so strange, buddy. Life is horrible without your mother around, but still, I notice that I've started becoming attached to the little things. The sun coming up, the birds in the garden, that kind of thing. I was lying in bed a few days ago, I didn't feel like getting up yet, and at a certain point I realized that I'd been staring at a branch outside for at least half an hour. The leaves on that tree. That's life, too, I thought. You see, those are the kinds of banal thoughts your father has these days. But I did ask myself right away whether it wasn't maybe all one big mistake."

A few days later, I dropped by to see him. You couldn't really say the house was a mess, there were no piles of dirty dishes in the sink, and he himself looked fairly tidy. No, it was something in the details, the things that weren't there anymore: a vase of fresh-cut flowers, a bowl of fruit, the bed — which was made, it's true, but not as neatly as my mother used to. My father was wearing a pair of gray sweatpants and his favorite brown sweater; maybe he hadn't shaved that morning, but he had yesterday or the day before. There was a white spot of toothpaste at the left-hand corner of his lips. That meant he was still brushing his teeth, but he'd apparently stopped looking in the mirror afterward.

"You said something on the phone a few days ago, about doing something major," I said. "About doing something big, one last time."

"That's right."

We were sitting in the kitchen, both with a glass of young gin in front of us.

I sipped at mine. "Your birthday is coming up soon. Might that be something? We could go somewhere. Out of town. To the beach, for example. Have a nice dinner someplace. Just with Sylvia, Diana, and me. Or something here at the house? Sylvia could make something nice. You could invite a couple of people."

"Are you nuts, Robert? Throwing a party after something like this? I can just see the looks on their faces. Maybe they wouldn't dare to ask directly, but you can bet they'd all be thinking the same thing. No, pal, that's the last thing I need."

He glanced at his phone, which was on the table beside his glass of gin. A brand-new iPhone. "It was time for me to get a new phone," he had told me soon after my mother's funeral. "But your mother . . . You know how your mother is. Was. She thought that was all nonsense, a waste of money. *What's wrong with your old phone?* You can just hear her say it, can't you? Then I saw an ad for a special offer. You had to take a new number, that was the thing. But I figured: Who am I going to give that new number to anyway? To the three of you. But nobody else."

At home, and when my mother was around, he had gone on using his old Nokia, he told me. He hadn't felt like defending his purchase. "Maybe that's childish," he said. "I could also have just come out and told your mother about it. But you know her, she could look so disapproving sometimes. And I felt I had a right to something for myself, without having to justify everything all the time." He topped up our half-empty glasses, all the way to the brim. "Sometimes that got really tiring, it was as though she didn't grant me my little pleasures anymore. There was this one time — stop me right away if I've told you this before — but in any case, there was this time on Queen's Day, or maybe by then they were already calling it King's Day, don't ask me. At my age, I figure I have the right to go on calling it Queen's Day. We went out to walk around the neighborhood, and so we finally got to that café, to Elsa's."

He leaned down, lowered his lips to his glass, and slurped off the top layer of gin. "Anyway, at one point your mother went off to the ladies' room, she was gone for a pretty long time; who knows, maybe there was a long line. I started talking to these two girls outside, on the patio. Cute girls. I mean: I'd had a few myself, but those two were knocking back their white wine twice as fast as I could drink my beer. There was one of them, she was really pretty, and that other girl was more usual, but also just cute, if you know what I mean. Anyway, to make a long story short: At a certain point, I noticed something. I noticed that the pretty one kept narrowing her eyes whenever she looked at me. I was telling some silly story, I don't even remember what it was about, but so that girl kept kind of shutting her eyes, and when she laughed she threw her head back, and then she would shake her hair in a way . . . you know, that can mean only one thing. That girl was flirting with me, right out in the open. With me, some ninety-four-year-old guy! What have I done to deserve this, I thought. But at the same time, I thought something else too. I thought: It's not really all that weird. I'm just a nice guy, I tell stories that make nineteen-year-old girls laugh, not every man can say that. And maybe they just looked right past this old face of mine. I know exactly how old I am, but that doesn't necessarily mean I have to think too lowly of myself; if you do that, you start off with the hand brake on, and you never experience anything again."

I looked at him, at his old face, and I had to admit he was probably right. He looked good for his age. And I could imagine it clearly: how, with his easy patter, he had charmed the socks off of two nineteen-year-old girls — I was just glad I hadn't been around to see it.

"It was exciting as hell. I loved it. I acted as though I liked the plainer one the most, I paid more attention to her. That's what I always used to do, too, when there were two girls at the same time. Any other man would go right for the prettiest one. Not me. I let the flirty one play her little game, with her laughing and throwing her head back and shaking her hair. But I could see the way she was glowing. You know what I mean,

Robert, when the girls start to glow? That's the greatest thing there is, as a man, that's what you do it for. Both of them, actually, were standing there glowing. That other girl too. Sometimes they literally start glowing, then they get those red blushes on their cheeks; other times it's more a kind of sultriness, then the glowing takes place mostly in and around the eyes. But anyway, I lost track of time. I got to the point where I would let the plainer one go and turn all my attention to the pretty girl. So I kind of turned to one side, I don't completely turn my back on her, but my body language tells her that from here on out she doesn't really count. And while I'm doing that, I suddenly see your mother standing there. She was standing at one of those high tables all covered in empty plastic glasses, all alone, and the way she was looking at me, buddy, I don't think I have to tell you that. She was too far away, but I could almost see her turning up her nose. The same way she would have turned up her nose at this thing" — he tapped the iPhone with his index finger — *"Toys!* Can't you hear her saying that? *Let him go and play with his toys, in his heart he's never really grown up."*

He raised the glass of gin to his lips and knocked it right back. Then he wiped the drops off his lips with the back of his hand — but not the spot of toothpaste beside them, that was still there. If it had been my mother sitting across from me, I would have wiped the spot away with my thumb, the way I plucked the little pieces of crab out of her hair at Oriental City, but I would never have dreamed of doing that with my father: that's just the way it was, that's the way it had always been and always would be.

"It was time for me to say goodbye. Looking back on it, probably a good thing, too, because what are you supposed to do after that? I mean: I'm perfectly aware that that's all it's going to be, a little flirting and glowing cheeks, I'm not an idiot. But I got such a kick out of it, I don't know how else to put it; a good mood that's just indestructible. But your mother is, your mother was, really good at that, at destroying my good moods. *What exactly did you think you were doing back there? How old are you anyway?* No, she couldn't see the humor in it. All the way home she just kept going on about how immature I was. At a certain point, I couldn't take it anymore. I knew I'd be able to subsist for days on my success with those girls, but then she was going to have to stop nagging. Sorry, son, but that's the way I felt right then. So what did I do? I'd had a bit to drink, of course. And back at Elsa's maybe a couple of beers too many. And too fast. I was a little rocky already, but I could still more or less walk straight, and then I came up with this priceless flash of intuition. 'I'm not feeling too well,' I said, and right away I let myself fall down between two parked cars. That put an end to your mother's nagging. From then on I was a patient, a sorry patient, an old man in his cups. I let her help me up, I tried not to lay it on too thick. Like I said, I'd had too much to drink, but I couldn't go on playing the drunk all the way home, at some point I was sure to blow it. But it went well, I had awakened the nurse in your mother. When we got home she helped me onto the couch and took off my shoes. And she made two toasted cheese sandwiches for me. 'Everything's spinning,' I said, but then I realized I shouldn't overdo it."

He shook his head, rubbed his eyes, and raised the glass to his lips again, but seemed not to notice that it was empty.

"After that I did something I'm not proud of," he went on. "The next day, at breakfast, your mother started in again. About those girls and how drunk I was. But I'd had enough. I wanted to keep those girls for myself. So I acted as though I couldn't remember any of it. 'I must have been completely smashed,' I said. 'I don't remember any of that. What age did you say those girls were?' I asked her. And then I did what she was probably hoping I would do. I acted as though I was dying of shame. 'Oh, sweetheart, that's terrible!' I said. 'That must have been so embarrassing. Can you forgive me?' And I bowed my head, I made myself look like the husband caught red-handed, the contrite husband. But when I closed my eyes the very next moment, I saw those girls again. That pretty girl, the one who looked at me for such a long time with that look that left no room for misinterpretation. Ah, I thought, now they're all mine again."

"My brother's coming next week," Sylvia said.

After a few more cutting remarks about my father, our conversation entered smoother waters and a real fight seemed to have been averted. We talked a bit about Emmy; it had been a couple weeks since she'd gone missing. "It's time to hang up some new posters," she said. "Diana said something about it yesterday. The old ones have almost all faded or been blown away. I printed a new photo from my phone, it's a little clearer and it's in color too. But Diana's going to be starting exams soon, I'd really rather not have her cell number on the posters. It's a distraction, and it wouldn't be good for her right now."

I didn't reply; I waited for my wife to say that she'd put her own number under the picture of our cat. But that's not what she said. "Maybe you could do it this time, Robert? Normally I don't mind dealing with callers, you know that. But could you maybe do it this time?"

She didn't look at me when she asked it, her hands were folded in her lap and she was rubbing her thumbs together. The way she said it — "dealing with callers" — made it sound as though tomorrow, or the day after, scores of people would start calling about the whereabouts of our cat.

At first, I didn't reply. I observed her, her folded hands and the rubbing of her thumbs, I waited for a sign, a moment of weakness — it wouldn't have surprised me if she had broken into tears. *He dumped me, Robert! How dare he! He said I'd become too much of a burden, that he could never explain it to his wife.*

I caught myself in the midst of a sudden swell of rage against Alderman Van Hoogstraten. Indeed, how dare he? How dare he suddenly dump my wife, without a word of warning? But the next moment I had myself under control again.

"That's fine," I said. "Don't worry about it, I'll see to the cat. But can you make those posters? And just put my cell number on them?"

I don't know exactly what I was hoping for. Gratitude, for having given in so quickly? A warm smile, a hand on my forearm, fingers softly squeezing my wrist? *Thanks, you're such a dear.* Or was it something very different, a little tear running down her cheek, a blurted-out confession. *I don't know what got into me! Oh, please, can you ever forgive me, darling?*

For the first time, I thought about the alternative scenario. A scenario in which it was not the alderman but my wife who put an end to the relationship. A desperate Van Hoogstraten who went on blowing up her inbox with text messages, who waited for my wife in a doorway farther down our street, who stalked her — a hysterically weeping alderman who threatened to make the whole affair public if she wouldn't have him back.

Forgive her? Yes, I could do that. Were she to confess everything right now, my first reaction would be to explode in a rage. No, not explode, more like descend into an enraged silence. That had always been more my style: the pursed lips, the head in hands, the occasional deep sigh. I would pace the room with my hands in my pockets, pause at the window, stare outside motionlessly while, behind my back, her sobs and pleas grew ever louder. But I would forgive her. I had already forgiven her, even as I looked at her, at her nervous thumb-rubbing, at the hair fallen over her face. Something would be damaged irreparably, a crack in a vase too dear to you to simply throw away. Vase and crack would remain visible for all time, every day I would see it perched on the table, with a new bouquet each time — but the crack would remain the same. I already knew how I would manage to go on living with the crack. I would be thankful. Thankful that the vase had not shattered and gone out with the trash. That was my usual tack, when people or things conspired against me. Sometimes I would lie awake half the night, after a jealous remark from a fellow party member. A fellow party member who would never, ever become mayor of Amsterdam. No, what am I saying: who wouldn't even become mayor of some whistle-stop of four hundred souls hunched up against the German border. Never, not now, and not in the next life either. Fuming with anger, I would think about how to get back at my fellow party member. How, during some meeting in the future, I would drop some oblique innuendo, oblique but deadly.

And then, suddenly, with no apparent transition, I would switch to thinking about what I already had. About my only real and most cherished possessions. My wife. My daughter. Sylvia. Diana. I listened to my wife's breathing, I heard my daughter rummaging about downstairs in the kitchen, after coming home from some party at six in the morning. That was enough. By comparison, for a few seconds, my fellow party member was only to be pitied, and the next moment he had disappeared from sight altogether.

Yes, that's the way I would do it. I would clutch the vase to my breast, with the crack turned toward me, so no one else could see it.

26

And so it happened, in the early morning hours of the next day, that I found myself walking the canals of Amsterdam with a pile of photocopies, a box of thumbtacks, and a roll of adhesive tape. I started as far from home as possible, at the corner of Utrechtsestraat and Prinsengracht (I had decided to limit myself today to two or three blocks), and I pinned a poster to every other tree.

LOST CAT
[photo]
MY NAME IS "EMMY."
[phone number]

My phone number. I asked myself, and not for the first time that morning, exactly what I was doing. I had put on my sunglasses and my black knitted North Face cap especially for this occasion. It was the same outfit I wore around town sometimes, on days when I didn't feel like saying hello to someone every twenty meters. As a disguise, though, it was not watertight. At the corner of Keizersgracht and Reguliersgracht, I saw a lady of a certain age coming toward me, walking a nondescript little black-and-white dog.

"Good morning, Mr. Mayor!" she said cheerily; the dog sniffed at the tree to which I had just pinned a picture of our cat and lifted its hind leg. "Aw, is that your cat?" she asked, moving her face up closer to the tree. "You know, I live just down the canal here, in the same block you do, and I used to see your cat in our garden all the time. What I mean is: I didn't know at the time that it was your cat, but there's no mistaking it, that black stripe across her head, just like a lock of hair. I'll keep my eyes open. Maybe she's locked up in a shed somewhere. They go into sheds all the time, out of curiosity. Or other houses with cats and a cat flap. Is that your phone number?"

"Yes," I said, a bit too quietly, *reluctantly* even — I suddenly had the fearful premonition that this woman would be calling me soon, cat or no cat.

A few days later, at the end of the afternoon, I was cycling down Hogeweg when a red sports car passed me with the roof down. Passed me so close — as though the driver hadn't seen me at all — that I had to yank on the handlebars to keep his mirror from smacking into me.

"Hey!" I shouted, and before I could reflect on whether it was advisable for a mayor to do so, I had already raised my hand and showed the driver my middle finger. "Look out, would you, grandpa!?"

The man — an old man, I'd noticed that already, whose close-cut, stubbly gray hair reminded me of my father's — apparently hadn't noticed anything unusual in his rearview mirror: taking it easy, he entered the traffic square with the fountain, first a short right, then a left — and it was at those two points that I caught a brief glance of his profile.

I never know exactly whether, at such moments, one's heart beats faster or actually slows down, or whether it just beats louder. Maybe I was wrong, I told myself, even though I knew better. Maybe the driver of the red sports car *was* simply an old man who looked a lot like my father.

But when the car turned right at the next corner, down Pythagorasstraat, and I could see his face from the side again, all my doubts vanished. It was something in the way the old man, in the way *my father,* ground his teeth as he drove, as though he were chewing on something, a piece of gristle. That's what he did whenever he was concentrating deeply: the two of us used to play chess often, and the grinding of his molars was always a sign to me that a decisive move was on its way.

Let me clarify things right now: this was not a Lamborghini or a Ferrari, no, not even a Jaguar or a Porsche, more like something French, I guessed — and that turned out later to be true. I know nothing about cars, but I do like them. When a Bentley or an Aston Martin drives by, I always turn my head and watch it go, the way other men turn their heads when a woman walks by. I look at them, too, of course, but if being mayor had provided me with one sixth sense, then it was the ability to determine the exact moment when no one would see me do that.

I kept enough distance between us, and when I turned down Pythagorasstraat, too, the red sports car was already on the next block, past Copernicusstraat.

Later — a few minutes later, but looking back on it, too, in the days, months, even years afterward — I asked myself whether my father had parked the red, eye-catching sports convertible right in front of his house on purpose; whether he was bound and determined to have everyone see it, above all everyone in this neighborhood, where everyone saw almost everything. It was like the bare windows that the Dutch specialize in, the curtains that are always parted to show that you have nothing to hide.

He could just as easily have parked the car a few blocks away or put it in a garage somewhere. My visit was unannounced. There was no way he could have known that I would see him driving the car past the fountain. A red sports car parked in front of his door didn't necessarily mean anything, it could just as well have belonged to someone else.

Those are the things that went through my mind before I rang the bell, before he opened the door in surprise and invited me in. Had he been acting guilty, I asked myself later, or was he only just surprised? There was, after all, no reason for him to act guilty; the red car parked in front of his house didn't have his name on it. No, there was no reason for him to act that way, not unless he had looked in his mirror and seen me somewhere close to the fountain, or later, when he turned down Pythagorasstraat. That, too, was something I wondered about much later.

Whatever the case, he first pulled the bottle of young gin out of the freezer, poured us both a little tulip-shaped glass full, sat down, leaned over his glass, slurped off the top layer of liquor, and only then looked up at me.

"I want to show you something," he said.

A few seconds later, we were out on the street. It was a bright sunny day, he had simply left the top down. Maybe he was going somewhere later on, I thought later.

He pointed out the various buttons and switches on the steering column and dashboard and gave a brief explanation of how they worked. "This here's the cruise control, and that *S* is the sports mode; it's an automatic, but sports mode makes the car more fun to drive than it is in *D.*" Then he suggested that we go for a ride. When he saw the look on my face, he said: "Just around the block here. I think maybe I know what you're thinking, but there's something I want to tell you."

The prospect of a drive — a "test drive," that was the first term that came to mind — with my father behind the wheel of a sports convertible expressed itself as a heavy sensation in the pit of my stomach. But we were already seated, and he had already started the engine and gunned it a few times before moving the shift to S.

"You should have seen the neighbors' faces the first time I parked this baby in front of the house," he said, braking for the first of many speed bumps on Pythagorasstraat and then turning a little too fast, a little too sportily, down Copernicusstraat. "They didn't say anything, of course not, but I could see them thinking: *Wife barely dead and in her grave, widower goes on a spree.* Well, ever since that first time I always gun it hard before I drive off. Let them think whatever they want, I really don't give a shit anymore."

I kept my mouth shut. I thought about the last time I'd had lunch with my mother at Oriental City, when she'd told me about my father and his dream of buying a new car; a dream she had laughed off at the time as typical of a ninety-four-year-old adolescent who had never grown up.

"I thought you said just a spin around the block," I said as he rounded Galileïplantsoen and pulled out onto Wethouder Frankeweg.

"No use in that, my boy," he said. "With all those fucking speed bumps, you can't tell what this baby is really capable of. If you want a horse to gallop you have to let it run, that's what I always say."

On Middenweg he gave it a little more gas, and I felt my head being pushed back against the headrest as we shot ahead, past Oosterbegraafplaats cemetery and Betondorp, and then up the entrance ramp to the ring road. "He can smell the open road now, buddy," he said, slapping my knee.

It was rush hour: to my considerable relief, traffic in all four lanes was moving at a crawl.

"Goddamn it!" he shouted, smacking the steering wheel with the heel of his hand. With two brusque jerks on the wheel he swung the car out into the middle lane, right in front of a truck that honked and flashed its brights. "We're in Holland, of course, I forgot about that for a moment. Around here the horses are confined to their stalls. Cruelty to animals, that's what it is."

A few hundred meters farther, the neon traffic indicators above the road began to blink: *50*. Within seconds, we came to a complete halt. My father sighed deeply.

"I've been thinking," he said. "I've thought about it. About my birthday, I mean."

"Yeah?"

"I've decided to make one grand, sweeping gesture. To celebrate life one last time, life the way it ought to be lived. Next week I'm going to drive down to France. To the same hotel where your mother and I spent so many happy vacations in the last twenty years. In style. I mean: I'm going to drive there in style, hence this car. Your mother would have disapproved of my buying it anyway. Am I right, or am I right?"

I stared straight ahead, at the motionless sea of cars; above the neon indicators, the sky was turning a dark gray.

"I'm going to do some hiking there, for a week," he went on. "Have some nice meals, a good bottle of wine every day. But I won't tell them. I won't tell anyone there that it's my birthday. Otherwise they may show up with a birthday cake. Or they'll think I'm to be pitied. They'll probably think that anyway. I'm not sure how I'm going to handle it, not yet. They've known us for years. That nice, vivacious old couple. I think I'll just give it to them straight. *I'm on my own this year. My wife died, I'm sorry to say.* To be honest, I'm kind of looking forward to that. To those somber faces. The waiters and the hotel owner, mumbling their condolences in French. Maybe after that they'll leave me alone a bit."

We still weren't going anywhere, this was no normal rush-hour traffic jam; some people had already climbed out of their cars: probably an accident ahead — and indeed, the next moment an ambulance passed us on the shoulder, its lights flashing.

"And after that," my father said, "what I'm going to do after my birthday, I've thought about that too. I know the countryside like the back of my hand. They've got a *gorge* there, that's what the French call it, a narrow ravine with cliffs on both sides and a river down below, sort of the Grand Canyon in miniature. A road runs through it, a narrow road with lots of curves, high above that river. That's what I'm going to do. In fact, it's just death by natural causes. Man with poor eyesight, just turned ninety-five, drives too fast, smashes through the guardrail, and plunges into the ravine. Dead. Maybe I'll have a bottle of wine first, to screw up my courage. Whatever I do, they'll find too much alcohol in my blood. That suits me better than dying quietly in bed. Going out with a bang. What do you think? I mean, I know what you think, what you've been thinking the whole time since your mother died but didn't dare to say out loud. Didn't dare to ask. Well, this is my answer."

27

"Don't stay up there too long, okay?" My wife said. "Dinner will be ready in a bit."

I mumbled something, or at least I made a sound that told Sylvia (and her brother) that I'd heard her. They were sitting at the kitchen table when I got home, a bottle of red wine and two glasses in between them, and they made no bones about the fact that I was interrupting their conversation. The sort of silence with an almost audible static in the background, like when you hit the pause button on the DVD player because you have to go to the toilet.

My wife had picked up her brother at Schiphol Airport that afternoon. His suitcase was still beside his chair, and he was still wearing his brown leather jacket.

When he stood up to hug me, the cheap leather of his jacket made a crackling sound, like when you crush a plastic bottle in your hands. We didn't exchange kisses, but our cheeks — his unshaven — brushed in a fleeting and clumsy greeting.

Upstairs in my study, I opened the balcony doors and stepped outside. The sun had already disappeared behind the houses, but it was still light; a thin, blue column of smoke rose up from a few gardens down.

I looked at the lawn but didn't see the thrush right away, not in the bushes or flowerbeds either, so I leaned out as far as I could to see if he might be sitting on the kitchen windowsill. That's where he had been that morning — that's where he had been every morning, ever since our cat ran away. The way he sat there, with his yellow beak and his head tilted a little to one side, attentively, inquisitively, you almost couldn't help but think that he was looking inside.

I had seen the thrush at other times of day too; a few days ago, as I was carrying a crate of empty beer bottles to the little shed at the back of the garden, the bird had suddenly hopped out of the bushes onto the lawn and followed me all the way to the shed and back — as though he were walking along with me.

Yes, I had even spoken to the thrush — "Hello there, how are things with you?" — in the same way I had wished him a good morning on other occasions. Yesterday at breakfast, as I was standing at the counter waiting for the coffee to drip through and my slice of bread to pop out of the toaster, he had been sitting there too. I leaned forward slowly and brought my face up closer to the window. I was expecting him to fly away at any moment — that he wouldn't understand the glass was enough protection against the big, human face coming toward him from the other side — but he didn't. I came right up close, looked into his one eye that gleamed black as coal without reflecting anything. There was an orange circle around that eye, as though the thrush had applied makeup.

That afternoon, on the ring road with my father, there had been a brief but heavy cloudburst. It could have turned into a scene straight out of a slapstick movie: ninety-four-year-old driver of a red sports car can't find the button that will raise the top of the convertible, beside him sits his sixty-year-old son, the mayor of Amsterdam; within a matter of seconds, they are both soaked to the skin. I had seen quite a few motorists sneaking glances at me in the traffic jam already, and I regretted not having brought along my sunglasses and woolen cap.

But faster than I ever would have expected, my father found the right button. As though he had done it often, that was the first thing that came to my mind. How long had he had this car anyway? Did it matter? He had shown it to me today for the first time, but did that mean anything? Maybe he had bought it a long time ago. Ordered it a long time ago. Unless I was mistaken, you had to order a car like this months in advance.

It was possible that he had ordered the car six months ago already. But a red sports car would have been harder to hide from my mother than an iPhone.

Back at the house he took a new bottle of young gin out of the freezer. "You want to stay for dinner?" he asked. "I don't have a lot, just some leftover mashed potatoes with raw endive. And half a smoked sausage."

I told him that my brother-in-law was arriving later, that I would be heading home after our drink. I looked at him as he nipped at his glass. I tried to imagine him shifting down on a curvy road in France, then punching it and breaking through the guardrail.

"When were you supposed to go in and have your license renewed?" I asked — just to have something to say, or in any case not to have to hear more details about his upcoming vacation. "In June, right?"

"Ach," he said, "that really doesn't matter anymore."

"No, maybe not."

He knocked back his gin and banged his glass down on the table. "It doesn't matter because I lost my license more than a year ago. So now you're all caught up."

I stared at him.

"I went to see our doctor," he continued, screwing the top back on the gin bottle. "I asked him if he knew a friendly ophthalmologist who could help me renew my license, but he wasn't having any of it. That would be unethical, he said. But six months ago, when I went to him for the first time to ask how your mother and I could put a decent end to it all, he was suddenly all generous with brochures and suchlike. He was almost itching to come by and do it himself. That's the way things are in this country these days, son. When you want to die, they can't wait to come by and help. But if you want to enjoy driving for another year, suddenly there are all kinds of ethical objections."

"But . . ." I felt I had to say something, to raise an objection. I thought about our drive along the Amstel in February, to the graveyard in Ouderkerk, about the group of cyclists he had mistaken for a truck.

"If you're going to say that it's completely irresponsible, you're completely right, of course," he said. "I know. The insurance, all that fuss. That's why I didn't tell you before."

He had lowered his eyes; he held the base of his gin glass between his fingers and turned it around slowly on the tabletop. There was a little notepad on the table, beside his car keys. I looked at the logo on it, I didn't recognize it immediately, but then I did. Peugeot. Tomorrow morning, I would call the Peugeot garage. I looked at the notepad. There were things jotted down on it that I couldn't read upside down, probably a shopping list, or other things my father didn't want to forget.

In the upper left-hand corner of the notepad, though, someone had made a drawing. A bird, I saw.

"Could I look at that?" I said, fingering the notepad and starting to turn it toward me. "Or is it private?"

"Huh, what? No, it's something your mother did. I just left it here. I mean, that notepad's been here for weeks."

I brought my face down closer to the drawing. It was, indeed, a bird. My mother had always been good at drawing, but at one point she had stopped doing it much. *Bread, coffee, eggs, Ketel 1,* I read in my father's furious handwriting below the drawing.

"She started drawing again more often, there at the end," he said, as though reading my mind. "Especially things in the garden. Birds, flowers, a spiderweb, that's what I remember. You've got all kinds of things here. Robins, jays, a stork even landed on the shed a while back. That's because the earth is heating up. All kinds of things heading north from down south. Plants you never used to see here. All kinds of animals. Foreigners . . ."

I looked up at him.

"I'm just kidding, pal! Don't put on such a serious face, it doesn't look good on you."

"And this," I said, turning the notepad back so he could see it. "What kind of bird would you say this is?"

He leaned down over the drawing and squinted.

"That's not too hard," he said. "It's done very, very well. In pencil, so you can't see the colors, but there's no doubt about it: it's a thrush. A female. I can tell by the tail, and by the way your mother drew the plumage. In real life, the female thrush is brown and has a yellow beak."

■ ■ ■ ■

After dinner, my wife announced that she was going to take her brother into town. "Just walk around a bit, go to a café or something. He's been inside almost all day."

No one talked much at the table. I asked about my brother-in-law's business — he dealt in used tractors and agricultural machinery — and he in turn asked me a few questions about the city and about my work. When I gave him a quick rundown on the windmills, he looked at me in disbelief and shook his head laughingly.

I may have been mistaken, but I had the impression that he was drinking more wine than usual, or at least emptying his glass more quickly, and Sylvia refilled it each time.

But during dessert, when I tried to give him a refill, he held his hand over his glass.

"No thank you, Robert," he said. "We should be going," he said then to Sylvia.

I waited till I heard the front door slam, then opened the door to the garden. Darkness was falling, a raveled red-and-pink contrail floated above the roofs of the houses across the way. From the garden of a few houses farther along came the sounds of laughter and quiet salsa music, the faint smell of seared meat.

I sat down in one of the garden chairs, put my legs up on the table frame, and lit a cigarette. I had barely taken two drags when the bird, which I now knew to be a female thrush, settled down on the back of a garden chair. She remained there for a few seconds, then spread her wings and landed on the table. I heard the scratching of her claws on the tabletop as she hopped closer to the edge — closer to me.

I looked at the bird, at the thrush — the female thrush! — and the thrush in turn looked at me. In any case, I couldn't shake the feeling that she was looking at me, her body turned to one side, her head tilted a bit, so that she at least had a better view of me with that one eye.

"Hello," I said.

I thought about what Bernhard had asked me during our lunch at Dauphine. *Have you noticed anything yet, with your mother?* I looked at the thrush and thought about the last time I'd had lunch with my mother at Oriental City, about the white wisps of crabmeat on her cheeks and in her hair.

"Daddy?"

I shot half-upright in my chair. The thrush took off and landed one story higher, on the railing of our bedroom balcony.

"Sorry, Dad, I didn't mean to scare you," my daughter said as she walked into the garden, pulled up a garden chair, and sat down across from me. Only at that moment did I realize that I was sitting there with a half-smoked cigarette still in my hand.

"I . . ." I tried to grin as I crushed the cigarette against the bottom of the tabletop. "I suddenly felt this . . . urge. The urge for a cigarette."

My daughter held out her hand.

"Give me one then too," she said. "I could use it. Is there anything to drink? Preferably something strong."

"Your mother and your uncle were just drinking wine. But maybe that's finished already? Look in the freezer otherwise, I always have a bottle of Grasovka in there."

I took the crumpled pack out of my pocket, pulled out two cigarettes, and held one out to Diana.

"How long have you known?" I asked, giving her a light and then lighting my own.

"What? That you've started smoking again? Since Christmas, right? Or am I mistaken?"

She stood up and walked to the kitchen door. "Get a glass for me, too, would you?" I called after her.

When I heard her rummaging about in the freezer, I looked up at our bedroom balcony, but the thrush had vanished.

"How are things with . . . ," I started in, after she sat down and filled our glasses, but realized only too late that I couldn't remember her boyfriend's name.

"We broke up," she said.

I said nothing.

"Last night, at Club NYX," Diana went on. "I went to the ladies' room for a minute. When I came back he was kissing some girl on the dance floor."

I kept my mouth shut again, or rather: I was just about to say something about how much I liked her boyfriend, that I was sure he hadn't meant anything by it, but stopped myself in the nick of time.

Kissing someone else . . . Was that so bad, I asked myself? Was it bad enough to put an end to a relationship?

"He's really sorry now," Diana said. "Outside the club, he got down on his knees. So embarrassing, everyone could see it! And now he keeps sending me messages. Listen, here comes another one . . ."

She looked at the screen of her cell phone.

"Love, my darling love," she read aloud. *"I'll never do it again. I am sooooo sorry! Can you forgive me? I can't live without you!!!!!* Five

exclamation marks! How horrible is that!"

I had a hard time not laughing.

"Yeah, you're laughing, I can tell!" she said. "And that's okay with me."

"So now what? What are you going to do now?"

My daughter topped up our vodkas, then took another cigarette out of my pack.

"First I'm going to let him flounder," she said. "Let him thrash and beg. For starters, I'm not going to message him back. For three days. If he comes crying at the door, I'm not going to let him in. Don't you let him in either, Daddy! You promise?"

I nodded. "I promise. And after that? After three days, what are you going to do then?"

"Then I'll take him back."

I must have looked dumbfounded, because my daughter said: "Don't look at me like that! Of course I'll take him back, he's too nice not to. But then on my own terms."

"And those being . . . ?"

"No more kissing other girls, of course. But also no more looking at other girls. I'm the only one, that's the way I want it to feel, and that's the feeling he has to be able to give me. If he can't, then it's over."

She picked up her glass, held it high in the air.

"Down the hatch?" she said.

I cleared my throat. For a split second I wondered whether I wouldn't be better off keeping my mouth shut. On the one hand I felt admiration for my daughter, for the self-assured way she stood up for herself. On the other, though, I also thought about the boy — about the boy in me, I should really say; about all boys.

"Isn't that sort of one-sided?" I began. "Aren't you coming down on him a little too hard?"

My daughter looked at me questioningly. Or was she looking questioningly at my glass? Was I going to knock it back at one go, or was I an old man who preferred to take little sips?

"You'll take him back," I said, "but then entirely on your own terms. From that moment on, he's one rung lower on the ladder. Forever."

"And what would you suggest I do? Just agree with him that he didn't mean anything by it? That he can go on kissing whoever he likes? That I won't say anything about it? Who'll be a rung lower on the ladder then, as you put it? Him? Or me?"

"You could do the same thing back," I said, before I'd even had time to think what I was going to say. "You could kiss someone else too. Then you'd be even . . . No, that's not a good idea," I added half a second later. "Not a good idea at all. Please, don't listen to your father. Forget I said anything."

"Shall we drink to that, then?"

"Okay. Bottoms up!"

We knocked back our vodkas at the same time. Her phone beeped, twice . . . three times, in rapid succession.

"I'm not going to look at his texts anymore either," my daughter said. "And whatever I do, I'm not going to read them out loud to you, in case you start giving me all kinds of bad advice again."

We both laughed loudly at that.

"Something else," I said, after Diana had refilled our glasses. "Have you been in contact with Grandma lately?"

My daughter stared at me.

"I mean, before she died. Just before she died. Did the two of you talk? Did she send you an e-mail? Anything on Facebook?"

"No, I don't think so. Wait a minute. When did I . . . yeah, I remember now. In that last week, I . . . I biked over to their place once, after school. Grandpa was working in the garden. And Grandma . . . yeah, Grandma was in the garden, too, she was on a lounge chair with a sketchbook on her lap. She was drawing."

"Drawing."

I tried to sound as cool as I could, not to make it sound like a question, but apparently that didn't work too well; my daughter frowned and looked at me questioningly.

"What?" I said. "What is it?"

"I don't know, you look so . . . the way you look all the time lately. As though something . . . as though there's something wrong. Is there something wrong?"

I put my glass down on the garden table.

"I'm feeling the vodka," I said. "I need to be a little more careful with that stuff."

My daughter shook her head, she looked at me almost regretfully, as though she was disappointed in me.

"That's not what I mean," she said. "What I mean is that you . . ."

"What was Grandma drawing?" I interrupted her.

"How should I know? Things in the garden." She screwed up her eyes, pulled her hair back in a ponytail and then shook it loose. "No, I remember now. Birds. Little birds. She showed them to me. They were really good. She could draw really well."

"What kind of birds?" I concentrated on my expression, I tried as hard as I could to look as though nothing was wrong.

"What kind of birds?"

"Yes," I said. "What kind of birds?"

403

■ ■ ■ ■

I lay in bed and looked at the display on my phone: *01:15,* and Sylvia and her brother still weren't back. At midnight I had almost sent her a message, but I stopped myself. I could see it in my mind's eye, the two of them sitting at a table in a café somewhere, my wife looking at her phone. *Robert. Why have we been gone so long . . . He's probably bored without us.*

No, I didn't want to be that kind of spouse. That was the kind of spouse I'd never been. I knew them all too well from our circle of friends: the husbands who couldn't leave their wives alone for half an evening, the wives who resented their husband's only evening out with other men.

Where are you? I texted her at 01:27.

Stay lighthearted, I told myself. I wasn't worried. I was not a control freak. But not contacting her at all wasn't good either. The wrong kind of signal. *It's like he doesn't care at all where I am or how late I stay out.*

I looked at the display. One check mark: the message had been sent but not yet received. Maybe she had turned her phone off, it wouldn't be the first time.

I'm going to call it a day. Sleep well. Have fun! X

I heard footsteps on the stairs, and then in the hall — they stopped at the bedroom door.

"Daddy?" Diana opened the door quietly. "Are you asleep yet?"

She sat down on the edge of my bed and opened the cover of her laptop.

"I just wanted to show you this," she said. "You know, what we were talking about in the garden?"

I clicked on the reading light. My daughter looked at the duvet, folded back only on my side.

"Where's Mama?"

"I don't know," I answered truthfully.

"Look," Diana said. "This is Grandma, it's her Facebook page and it's still active. And this is the picture I took of her, the last time I went by there. You see, she's holding up that sketchbook, like a kid showing off a drawing."

I put a hand on my daughter's shoulder and looked along with her.

"Can you zoom in on that photo?"

"Only a little. But wait a minute, I've got it on my phone."

A few quick swipes of the finger and there it was, on the display. She zoomed in even farther with her thumb and index finger.

"See, they're little birds."

The lines had grown fuzzy, but there were clearly three separate birds on the sketchpad. Three of the same kind of bird, only from different angles.

"And this?" I asked, pointing at the screen of her laptop. "What's this?"

"That's her profile picture. Oh, but this one's new. It wasn't there last time."

She clicked on the photo. It was a photograph of a thrush, taken from a website about birds or from a photo album. *Female Thrush,* read the caption beneath the photo, on which Diana had now zoomed in.

28

It was at 10:35 the next morning that my secretary gave me the news. I remember it so clearly because it was at the exact same time that I glanced at my phone to see if Sylvia had left a message. She should have been landing around then.

There was no message; of course not. Otherwise I would have heard a beep. I checked whether I'd accidentally turned off the sound. Or whether, in a moment of distraction, I had activated airplane mode.

"Do you have a moment?" Mrs. Schreuder was standing in the doorway. I hadn't heard her knock, but from her expression I could tell right away this was news that made knocking unnecessary.

I hadn't slept that night. Hadn't slept a wink. At seven o'clock I'd gotten up. A cup of coffee. A fifteen-minute, piping hot shower. But it didn't really wake me up.

The door to Diana's room was open. Her

bed had not been slept in. It took a few moments for me to realize that this was as it should be, that my daughter had told me last night that she was going to go by her boyfriend's — at that point, in fact, her ex-boyfriend's.

"I don't know, Daddy," she'd said, "he sounds really desperate. I shouldn't push it too far, I think."

She looked at me with her big dark eyes. *What do you think?* her look was asking me.

"You have to be careful not to let him blackmail you," I said. "Emotional blackmail. You have men who start weeping or get down on their knees and beg. If you give in, he knows that he can always get you back by doing that. Then you've overplayed your hand. Then you don't get the result you were after to start with."

"No," Diana had said. "It's not quite that bad. He says he misses me. And to be perfectly honest, I miss him too."

At three in the morning I had sent a message. *Sylvia? Sweetheart* (I used the word for "sweetheart" in her own language), *please get in touch. I'm worried. All I want to know is that everything is okay. X*

At four o'clock, I called her. Within two seconds, her phone switched to voice mail.

I turned on the reading light on her side

of the bed too. I sat up, fished the pack of cigarettes and lighter out of my pants pocket. Smoking in bed! When was the last time I'd done *that*? I took out the three remaining cigarettes and used the pack as an ashtray.

Two cigarettes later, it must have been around four thirty, Sylvia called.

"Robert, were you asleep?"

"No, I was awake, I haven't been able to sleep at all. Where are you?"

"Robert, I'm sorry, I meant to call you earlier. I was hoping you had gone to sleep. But then I saw your messages, that you'd called. I had my phone in my bag, I didn't hear it."

In spite of myself, I breathed a deep sigh that could probably be heard at the other end of the line. "Where are you?" I asked again.

"Listen, sweetheart" (she also used the word for "sweetheart" in her own language, a good sign somehow — or so I thought at the time), "I'm at Schiphol. We're at Schiphol. Robert, are you still there?"

"Yeah."

"Oh, you were so quiet, I thought maybe we'd been cut off. Listen. We heard about it tonight. We were at Schiller. Or actually,

Schiller was just closing. You remember Damian?"

"Sure." About five years ago my brother-in-law got married again, to a woman thirty years younger, and soon after that their only child was born. A boy.

"His wife called, she was in a complete panic," Sylvia went on. "Damian came back from school yesterday, he was running a high fever. She put him to bed, but last night he suddenly broke out in all these brown spots. On his back, his arms, his legs. She drove him to the hospital right away. You remember the hospital, the one that's about sixty kilometers from their house?"

I remembered it. We had taken Diana there one time, during a vacation, when she was stung by a wasp and broke out in a rash all over. She was five at the time.

"My brother wanted to go back home right away. We took a taxi from Rembrandtplein. I'd checked my phone already, there was a late flight. But he just missed it. Another one will be leaving in a little while, at seven forty. He calls his wife every half hour, but they still don't know what it is, and he's not showing any signs of improvement. Oh, Robert, it's so horrible. He's sitting here, crying. That's what I wanted to tell you too. I can't let him go alone like

410

this. I can't let him get on the plane alone, and then drive all that way back home. All the way to that hospital. So I bought a ticket too. He says it's ridiculous, but I know how he is. We're family, Robert. At moments like this, we don't let each other down."

My secretary took a few steps into the office. There were only the two of us, but she still spoke quietly, almost at a whisper.

"It's Maarten," she said. "He had a meeting at nine thirty. At ten, when he still didn't show up, I called him. And because I couldn't reach him, I tried to call his wife, but she wasn't answering either. Ten minutes later, she called back. He . . . Maarten has had an accident, Robert."

My eyelids were heavy from a night of no sleep. All I did was stare at Mrs. Schreuder.

"I don't know all the details, but they found him last night. In a bicycle underpass, not far from his house. With his bike. He probably fell or ran into something; his wife doesn't know yet either. He's at the medical center now, still unconscious. It doesn't look good. There's no reason for you to go to him, Robert, not yet. They're keeping everyone at a distance for the moment. But I just need to talk to you about how we're going to handle the media. Do you want me to wait with a press release? They'll find out soon enough themselves. What do you think?"

29

It took me a couple of weeks to realize that Sylvia wasn't coming back. At first we texted each other a few times a day, but halfway through the third week, when she hadn't reacted to my latest message after three days, I called her.

"I hope you understand that, with things the way they are now, it might be better for me to stay here for a while, Robert," she said. That was probably the longest sentence she spoke.

I said that I understood. I remember thinking, for the first time in my life, or perhaps it would be better to say for the first time since I'd been in office, that a mayor's phone could be tapped too. I wondered whether "with things the way they are now" sounded vague enough, or whether it might lead to more questions from the police commissioner.

In my mind, I could picture him standing

in my office, holding a transcript of our call, his straight-arrow expression. *Are you sure you've told me everything, Robert?*

"Do you know whether Maarten van Hoogstraten has any enemies?" That's what the police commissioner had asked me that first afternoon, after the alderman's accident.

"Enemies?" I asked.

"We're viewing it as an accident, for the time being," he said. "But we can't rule anything out. You've got those bollards at the end of the underpass. Anything's possible, of course, but the doctor in charge says that not all of his injuries can be attributed to falling from a bicycle. He can't remember anything himself, not even whether he fell or whether he ran into something."

Of those first weeks without Sylvia, I remember very little else. A month had gone by since the journalist showed me the photos of someone other than myself beating a policeman with a brick, so I called *De Volkskrant* to ask when the interview would be published. After being redirected a few times, I got someone on the line who asked for my phone number and assured me that they would call back as quickly as possible.

Unexpectedly, the call came within five minutes. A man's voice, introducing itself as the editor in chief.

"It's an extremely sensitive matter, sir," he said. "I'm hoping you'll understand, but first I hope you'll let me explain the situation a bit more."

"Of course," I said. I thought about the pictures, about the immediate consequences they could have for my job. "Go right ahead."

"It's like this: Not so long ago we had to deal with a similar situation," the editor in chief said. "A work student who turned out to have copied most of his articles from other media. In this case, though, it's much worse than that. The journalist in question seems to have simply made up whole sections of her articles. And she's been doing that for years. I won't bore you with an exhaustive account of exactly which articles I'm talking about, but take it from me, these were some very controversial pieces. Situations within the royal family, a bank director in possession of child pornography, an interview with Hillary Clinton, fabricated from start to finish. That's the kind of thing we're talking about."

"All right," I said. I thought about the photos again, but differently now — as

though they were in a box somewhere —
where exactly, even *I* couldn't remember.

"Two scandals like that within such a
short period, that's one too many," he went
on. "We've put the journalist on non-active,
of course, and we've agreed with her to keep
the whole affair quiet for as long as possible. And actually, that's what I'd like to
ask you too."

"But that interview with me," I said.
"That wasn't made up. It actually happened
just that way."

I thought I heard the editor in chief sigh,
but it could also have been the wind in the
background, maybe he was sitting beside an
open window. Looking back on it, I have to
admit that I'd known for a long time that
the interview wasn't going to be published.
That it would never be published. I thought
about my wife. I had been hoping that a
controversial interview, one that would
probably lead to my resignation in the
longer term, might get her to come back.

"That's right," he said. "But I also hope
that you'll understand that we can't take
any risks at this point. The journalist is
'home on sick leave,' that's the explanation
we'll give if anyone asks why none of her
articles or interviews are appearing in the
paper. I could have told you the same thing,

416

but in light of your special position and the nature of the interview, I thought I should make an exception."

"And what about the photos?" I asked. "What are you going to do with the photos?"

"We can use the portrait series made in your office and at your home on some other occasion, of course. At least, if that's all right with you."

"No, that's not what I mean. There were other pictures too." Now it was my turn to sigh. Quite audibly; there could be no mistaking it at the other end. "Photos of hooligans," I went on. "A group of delinquents assaulting a police officer."

I spoke intentionally of "delinquents," a word I would ordinarily never use, to make it clear from the start that I disapproved of the boys with the scarves and crash helmets. But maybe the editor in chief hadn't read the interview at all.

"I don't have that series right here," he said, "but if you like, I can look for them. Delinquents, is that what you said? And what did that have to do with the article?"

"Oh, no, forget it," I said. "It's not really important."

Suddenly, I knew for a certainty that the photo series wouldn't be in there with the portraits. After all, what else could you expect from a journalist who had made up an interview with Hillary Clinton? I was overcome by a deep fatigue, like at the start of a flu. I remembered the editor in chief's words. According to the press release the journalist hadn't been fired or put on non-active, no, she was "home on sick leave." Maybe that would be the best thing for me, too, to call in sick and stay at home. Sylvia, unlike most women who start sighing whenever their husbands show signs of a flu and in fact believe that their "whiny men" are pretty much acting like babies, was a natural-born nurse. Whenever I coughed a little or simply sniffed loudly, she would start insisting that I stay home from work. And when I had a real flu, she would spend all day trundling back and forth with bouillon, antipyretics, and hot milk with brandy. She would bring me the newspaper to read in bed and place her cool hand on my feverish brow.

Might that work? I wondered. If I got on the phone and faked a sore throat and a sickly voice, might that get her to come home?

I assured the editor in chief of my discretion and hung up.

About ten days after the incident in the

bicycle underpass, Maarten van Hoog-straten was released from the hospital.

"It's so strange, Robert," he said when I went to see him at his home a few days later. "It's like a section of your life has dis-appeared. Have you ever had that?"

He was lying prostrate on a light-blue sofa in the living room, his head propped up by two white pillows. That white and that light blue probably threw his face into darker contrast than a more neutral background would have. It lit up a whole host of variega-tions and patterning — an oil painting, that was my first association, a Vincent van Gogh. Deep yellow ochre just below his left eye, dark-blue streaks on his left cheek, a black blotch on his forehead, above his right eyebrow. There were brown crusts on his upper lip.

Sections missing from your life — the final hours of a party at our house, my sixtieth birthday. The next day my wife told me what had gone on during those deleted hours. "You should be ashamed of yourself, Robert," she'd said, and I was — and then, right away, she burst out laughing. "On the other hand, though, it was awfully funny," she said. "As far as I'm concerned, you should do it more often."

"I can't even remember where I was coming from, or where I was going," the alderman continued. "Only a few snatches of that afternoon, a cup of coffee in the canteen, a map being unfolded on my desk. The map of a square. Something about refurbishing that square, I think that's what it was. But which square . . . It's all been knocked into kingdom come."

It was perhaps typical of Maarten van Hoogstraten's straight-arrow ways that he didn't catch the irony in his own words. *Knocked into kingdom come.* Yes, it could have ended that way too. They could also have knocked him into kingdom come.

They. Was this the first time I'd thought about it in the third-person plural? I wasn't sure. During the rare moments in the last week when I had tried to form an image of how it must have gone — or rather, when I had allowed that image to enter my mind for a few seconds — it was always my wife's brother who had acted alone. They were fuzzy images, badly underexposed black-and-white images, like the reconstruction of a crime in a most-wanted television program. Whatever the case, my wife's brother had been alone as he waited for the alderman at the tunnel exit.

On my way to Maarten van Hoogstraten's, I cycled through that same tunnel. At the exit I hopped off and looked around for a moment. Examined the paving stones in the bike path one by one. I don't know exactly what I was looking for, a clue perhaps, the cap of a bicycle bell, spattered blood soaked into the pinkish paving stones, a coat button. In the old detective shows, the sleuth always finds something. A cigarette butt of a certain brand. An earring. A laundry ticket from a given dry-cleaner's: a newly pressed pair of pinstriped trousers leads him to the culprit.

But I didn't find anything. I tried to recall the police commissioner's words, but I couldn't remember whether he had said "at the end of the tunnel" or "as he was leaving the tunnel." I looked around. If you were lying in wait for someone here, what would be the best place to hide? There were a few trees and some bushes, but no trees big enough to hide behind completely. There was a set of stone steps leading to the viaduct above the tunnel. I took a few steps back and looked up. I tried to imagine my wife up there, waiting, her hands on the railing, then signaling to her brother. *He's coming . . .*

"Would you like some more tea, Maarten? And what about you, Robert? Tea as well, or something else? A glass of wine? A beer?"

421

I hadn't heard the alderman's wife come into the room. When she had opened the front door for me, fifteen minutes earlier, we'd hugged. I couldn't remember us ever doing that before.

After I stepped back from the hug, I had looked her in the eye briefly. I was searching for something, without knowing whether I really wanted to find it. How much did she know, in fact? Did she suspect anything at all? Had she and Maarten van Hoogstraten had a serious talk, a talk full of long silences and the occasional bout of weeping, during which they had decided to separate as soon as he recovered? Which one of them would get the children during the week, and which one at the weekend?

In her eyes, though, I read only the emotions you would expect under these circumstances. Relief, because it could have turned out so much worse. No more, perhaps, than a certain resigned awareness that her husband pretty much had only himself to blame. *How could you be dumb enough to fall off your bike?* In any event, no reproach for my not having come to see him in the hospital. I could have done that. It was only normal for a mayor to visit one of his aldermen in the hospital, after he'd had a bad accident. But what had been normal about the last few weeks? What could I have said to his wife if she *had* reproached me? *I had other things on my mind?*

And now, too, as she went to the couch to fluff up his pillows and run her hand tenderly through his hair, everything seemed peachy-keen. But maybe they were putting on an act, a cold truce during which the Van Hoogstratens simply kept up appearances to the outside world. As soon as the guests were gone, only icy glances would be exchanged. A marriage like a winter landscape, a stubborn silence interrupted only by the howling of a bitter wind. Soon, once the alderman was back on his feet, the dissolution of the marriage could continue full steam ahead, and the glasses and plates would fly through the house.

"A beer for me, thanks," I said.

I watched her as she left the room. When I turned back to the alderman, I saw that he had his eyes closed.

"Maarten," I whispered. "Maarten . . ."

His wife was standing at the kitchen counter, her back half turned to me. Not to startle her, I knocked quietly on the frosted glass window in the kitchen door.

"Marianne," I said, thankful now that I had asked my secretary to look up Mrs. Van

Hoogstraten's first name in the black note-book. She smiled, picked up the can of Jupiler that was ready on the counter, and handed it to me.

"Would you like a glass?"

I shook my head.

"Marianne," I said. "I wanted to ask you something. Has he said anything yet? I mean, did he say anything after the accident? About . . . how it happened? I mean, I just cycled through that same tunnel. There are these bollards at the end of it. Did he run into one of those?"

"He really doesn't remember a thing," she said, taking the kettle off the stove and pouring boiling water into a mug. "Not even about the first three days in the hospital. All gone. I don't know how that works. I asked the doctors about it. They say his memory may come back, but that for the same money it may never come back at all."

From a little tin on the counter she produced a teabag and hung it in the mug. It was then, at that moment, that I saw the bag on the kitchen windowsill. A brown and yellow bag, I recognized it right away because I myself had bought so many of them at the pet store, the store called Animal Palace or Animal Paradise, I couldn't remember which.

I automatically stepped to one side, to get a better look at the garden through the glass doors. But that wasn't even necessary. From where I was standing, I could already see the hutch. It was about five meters from the door, on a patio of paving stones, up against a green wooden fence.

From that point on, my memory has lost its grip on chronology. I no longer know for sure which came first: the long telephone conversation with Sylvia in which we discussed the immediate future, not only our future together, the length of her stay in her native region, but also the future of our daughter, Diana.

"She's coming down this summer for a few weeks' vacation," my wife said. "With her boyfriend. I've talked to her about it already."

I remember, during those first weeks, that I asked my daughter regularly whether she'd heard anything from Mama. And that I always received an affirmative, albeit brief, reply. I never asked any further. I tried to let life go on as normally as possible. My daughter was in the middle of her finals. Her mother was tired. Overtired. I avoided the word "overstrung." She missed her family. Her country. Why she couldn't have postponed her bout of homesickness until her daughter was finished with her exams was a question I didn't raise. As long as Diana didn't raise it herself, there was no need to come up with an answer. Nor did I ask Sylvia about that.

"This summer?" I said, instead of asking the question I perhaps should have been asking. "But how long is this going to last, Sylvia? How long are you planning to keep this up?"

No, I didn't call her by name. I said "sweetheart," in her own language. Since my discovery of the rabbit hutch, I had started listening to her voice in another way. To all her intonations, and to what might be behind those intonations. Insofar as possible, I tried to run back through all the conversations we'd had in the last few months, starting with that evening at Café Schiller, after the New Year's reception, when she told me that "funny story" about the rabbits chewing their way through the TV cables. I listened differently to her, the way you can never listen to a piece of music in the same way once it's been played at the funeral of a friend or loved one. Her story in Paris about her betrayed Japanese girl-friend. Sadako! A name you would never forget — and that name, too, somehow sounded different than it had back then.

"You have to give me time, Robert," my wife said. "Right now, it just feels better to me this way."

And that's what I did. I gave her time. I waited. I didn't know exactly what for, only that it wasn't what I'd been waiting for back before I discovered the rabbit hutch.

Sometime during that waiting I received a message from Bernhard. It was in the middle of the afternoon, I was at Van Dobben's snack bar, having filet américain on a bun with chopped onions. A WhatsApp message with a photo attached. A photo of the Grand Canyon. *What we talked about not so long ago: our planet with no life on it. Beautiful, isn't it?*

On my way back to city hall, I suddenly heard a loud thud. A deep, heavy thud, like a single clap of thunder. But it was a clear day. I wasn't the only one who stopped and peered up at the bright blue sky. And I also wasn't the only one who finally picked out two white spots up there. White spots, occasionally a flash of silver, circling around each other — when I squinted a bit I could pick out the wings of both jet fighters.

At the pedestrian crossing to the Blauwbrug, I had to wait for a tour bus that was pulling out; across the street, a red sports car stopped to let a family with young children and a pram take the crosswalk.

I looked at the driver's checkered cap, his sunglasses, the scarf around his neck — a "choker" was what they called a scarf like that, it was fashionable only among men of a certain age — and at his checkered tweed coat. Then I looked at the woman in the passenger seat. The sunglasses and the floral kerchief on her head made it hard to judge her age, her lipstick was a fiery red, but from this distance I couldn't see whether the skin between her upper lip and nose was already wrinkled.

All in all, it didn't seem completely real; this couple seemed to be reenacting something, a movie from the late fifties, early sixties. A French movie in which Alain Delon, driving a red sports car like this one, slowed on the boulevard to get a better look at the legs of the girls strolling by.

My telephone vibrated in my pocket. As the sports car accelerated and turned onto the Blauwbrug, I answered it.

"Hello?"

"Hello, is that you, Mr. Mayor?" said a somewhat older-sounding female voice. "This is Mrs. Drimmelen. You probably don't remember me, but we ran into each other a while back, along the canal. You

428

were hanging up posters for your missing cat."

"Oh, yes."

"Well, I found your cat. A few doors down. A lawyer and his wife. They haven't lived there very long. But it looks like your cat has moved in with them. I was on my balcony, and I noticed it by accident. They were sitting in the garden, and your cat was lying on one of the lounge chairs. Like she'd been living there for years! I rang their bell this morning, and yes, they confirmed that your cat showed up at their door about a month ago."

I picked up the pace and trotted across the crosswalk. By the time I got to the bridge, I was running. The red sports car was driving past city hall, headed toward Waterlooplein.

"Hello?" said the voice in my ear. "Are you still there?"

"Listen, could I call you back later?" I said and hung up without waiting for her reply.

The sports car slowed at the lights, but when the light turned green it shot ahead — the woman in the passenger seat placed a hand on her head to steady the flapping kerchief, while the car turned right onto Jonas Daniël Meijerplein and disappeared from sight.

This was all a couple of weeks after I'd visited Maarten van Hoogstraten, for I was barely in my office when he knocked quietly on the open door. Maybe it was his first day back at work, or his second — his face still bore vague traces of the accident, a dark stripe on his cheek, a white spot on his upper lip.

"Have you got a moment?" he asked.

I gestured to the chair in front of my desk; he sat down and crossed his legs.

"This is a sensitive matter, Robert," he began. "And I hope you'll treat it that way."

I braced myself. What was this? He wasn't suddenly going to come up with a confession, was he? A confession was the last thing I needed. It would, at a single blow, destroy almost everything I had built up so carefully in the last few weeks — a still-shaky framework to which I had nevertheless attached all my hopes for a future together with my wife.

But there was something else too. What was I going to do? How was I supposed to react to a confession? Was I to burst out in a rage? Rise from my chair and grab the alderman by his lapels?

Yes, I could take all the necessary steps, perform all the actions given and granted to a deceived husband. A fist in his face — *his already battered face* popped into my mind — would be viewed with clemency. "Mayor KOs Alderman." A nice headline. An incomprehensible headline too — until you read the article that followed. I could count on leniency. The media would pounce on the story, the same way they had pounced on other mayors caught up in a scandal.

I thought about my wife's country. We were all familiar with the footage of members of parliament who engaged in fistfights, who tossed water on each other or sprayed tear gas in their opponents' faces. That happened in countries about which we couldn't care less. Countries we could laugh at.

But in those same countries, a cuckolded husband was also cut more slack. The leniency didn't stop at a punch in the face. I thought about the Jericho in my desk drawer. It would be easy enough to lean forward and open the drawer. *I have that dossier in here somewhere . . .* It wouldn't take me more than thirty seconds to load the clip. In my wife's country, I would be let off scot-free. Mitigating circumstances. In Holland, I would go to prison for years. That wouldn't do anyone any good. I thought about my daughter. About Diana. She would go on visiting me faithfully, I was sure of that. But it would also be a burden for her, she had just finished her finals, she was still much too young. I tried to adopt an interested expression and waited for what was to come.

"Before long, they'll be talking about a third term, Robert," the alderman continued. "I know how you feel about that. I know you'd be pleased to go for another six years. And your popularity in the city is unequaled, I know that too. But now something has come up . . . something that . . . I saw it. A journalist showed it to me. And now I'm wondering whether that won't have a disastrous effect on your plans for a third term."

I breathed a sigh of relief, not too loudly, not too visibly relieved, but still: the shaky framework was not going to collapse. At least not today.

"I wondered whether you had seen it too," Van Hoogstraten said, looking at me gravely. "At least that's what that journalist told me, that she was going to show them to you too. I assume you know what I'm talking about."

"Yes, of course, Maarten. I saw that photo series too. And I made my decision a long time ago. I had been meaning to tell you about it, but just then you got . . . you had that accident, and I didn't get around to it."

I kept my eyes fixed on the alderman as I

pronounced the word "accident," but nothing in his eyes or in his expression changed.

"It would be giving the wrong signal," I went on. "A mayor who was a delinquent as a young man — well, we could overlook that. But a policeman crippled for life, that's going too far. I think resigning right now would also be going too far, but — as long as this remains strictly between the two of us — I can tell you here and now that I won't be seeking a third term."

PART IV

30

This morning, by way of the dry ditch at the back of the garden, I climbed the narrow, winding path to the top of the hill. There, in a cleft in the rock, is a big boulder that is almost flat on top. That's where I sat down.

The old, dusty hotel where Bernhard and I took a room thirty years ago is still there. It doesn't get a lot of visitors, that's my impression — this is still a region skipped by mass tourism.

This morning, at the top of the hill — from here I could see only the red tiles on the roof of that hotel — I thought back on the evening when Bernhard had to talk me into going out somewhere for a drink.

Very briefly, for no more than five seconds, I'd guess, I entertained the thought: *What if we had stayed in our room that evening?* We would have traveled on to the capital the next day, as planned, and I would not be sitting on this boulder right now.

Diana would not have been born, would not exist.

For the next five seconds I thought about my daughter's face, her laughing face, her head of long black hair that she had a way of tossing back when she thought I had said something stupid.

Who, then, would have pointed out my stupid comments? A different child, other children, a child of a woman other than Sylvia.

That other life would simply have been lived out, too, albeit at another spot. That other woman would perhaps have asked me, at a certain point, what I was thinking about, at a breakfast table somewhere in Holland. And what would my reply have been? The truth? That I was thinking about a different life, the life I hadn't led because, thirty-three years earlier, I had remained lying in a hotel room with a headache?

The café that Sylvia and her eighteen-month-older sister had come out of was still there, too, even though I couldn't see it from here. The chairs outside were a newer model now, albeit still plastic.

I closed my eyes. Bernhard went into the other café, the café that had closed down about a year ago and then reopened as a

438

sort of kiosk where you can buy nuts, candy, and soda pop — in any case, thirty-three years ago Bernhard went in there to buy a pack of cigarettes.

In that other, parallel life with the Dutch wife and children, he would have had enough cigarettes already and we would have strolled together to that deserted patio on the far side of the dusty square. Of the two of us, Sylvia immediately thought he was the cuter.

Having arrived at that point, I thought no further. I thought about Bernhard's funeral; or rather, about the brief ceremony during which his ashes were scattered to the wind. He had, as it turned out, left detailed instructions about where and how this was to be done, about who was to be invited and who definitely not.

Our little group stood there at the edge of the salt flats at the entrance to Death Valley. The same salt flats that Bernhard and I had driven past eighteen years earlier — where we had seen the mock dogfight between two circling jet fighters. Where we had talked about the existence of God and the right to bear arms. And now, here we were again. A little group of us, as I said. Christine, Bernhard's children from his two earlier marriages, two colleagues from Harvard, and

Stephen Hawking. The way it goes with people you recognize from countless photos and television footage, and recently from a film version of his life as well, it was hard to see the scholar in his specially adapted wheelchair as a person. It was as though he never stepped away from his public persona, not for a moment — I caught myself looking around to see if there was a camera somewhere, and a director who was going to yell "Action!" at any moment.

The sign was still there, announcing that there was no gas to be had for the next hundred and fifty miles. Eighteen years earlier, Bernhard and I had stopped here to look out over the endless white flats, at the two glistening dots of the fighter planes high in the clear blue sky, and today we were scattering his ashes here. *For the last time,* those were the words that came to my mind at that moment, and absurd as it may sound, they were the only true words.

A little over a week before, Bernhard had left his hotel in Las Vegas, where he'd arrived two days earlier to attend a conference about the bending of time. He rented a car and drove to the Grand Canyon. When he didn't return to the hotel that evening, no alarm was raised. Early the next morning, in the parking lot on the North Rim, two rangers noticed that a car was parked there, the only one at that hour. An initial search party found nothing. Only when a helicopter was called in did they find his body. *Slipped and fell:* that, in the absence of a note or anything else pointing to suicide, was the tentative conclusion.

"He wasn't depressed, was he?" I asked Christine — needlessly — once the ashes had been scattered and I took her briefly in my arms.

"Bernhard? Depressive? Are you kidding?"

I thought about the last time we'd talked, at Dauphine, when he asked whether I'd noticed anything special after my mother's death. And about how he had gone on to describe the Grand Canyon as "the best evidence" that a planet without human life, without any life whatsoever, might have been the idea all along, that what we had now was all one big misunderstanding.

Now, when I look back on it, I know for a certainty that my mother was already dead when I went downstairs that night to look for the picture in the box of photos. The thrush was already waiting for me in the garden; that had been my initial impression, too, when I opened the back door — in retrospect, the only true impression.

At 21:45 my father had sent me the text

441

message saying that they were going to do it that day, the next day. But at 06:41 he had sent another message. Or received one. In any case, at that point he had been online.

On his birthday I thought about calling him, but in the end I didn't. I was afraid of hearing something, or rather, of hearing nothing at all. An unnatural silence, the kind of silence that falls when someone has emphatically asked you to be still. A finger held to the lips. In this version of events, I always saw (and see) in my mind the floral kerchief. The same kerchief I saw five years ago, beside my father in the red sports convertible crossing the Blauwbrug. In my thoughts it was draped (and is still draped) casually over the back of a chair in some French hotel room.

Next week my father will turn one hundred. I still remember what he said, the last time I visited him, a couple of months ago. "On my hundredth birthday, we'll have our picture taken together," he said. "Whenever someone turns a hundred, they always have their picture taken with the mayor." I didn't contradict him. I didn't say that I'm not the mayor anymore. But even when I still was the mayor, there was no longer any way to deal with it: every two or three weeks we got a request from the family of a centenarian. Five years ago, those requests were already being deflected politely.

His comment about the mayor was made during one of his moments of clarity. It's not as though my father doesn't recognize me anymore. It's just that he loses track of things every now and again.

The last time I visited, we had dinner together downstairs, in the restaurant of the nursing home. A meatball, mashed potatoes, and applesauce, vanilla pudding for dessert. The kind of meal that disgusts people in my circles, that they shake their heads and act sarcastic about. But I remember how it went with me. With every bite I took, I sank further and further into a time that I had thought was gone forever. When was the last time, in the last fifty years, that I'd eaten a meatball like this? Mashed potatoes? Applesauce? I looked at my father, at how he spooned up the last bits of his vanilla pudding in deep concentration. I was, at one and the same time, there and somewhere else.

"Well," I said, once our bowls were completely empty and I had slid my chair back. "Shall I walk you to your room?"

"My room?" he said. "Do I have a room here?"

I explained to him that his room was on

the first floor, that an hour ago we had taken the elevator down from there to eat in the restaurant.

"The restaurant," he said, looking deep in thought. "You mean *this* restaurant. But what I can't figure out is, where *is* this restaurant then?"

That's what I mean when I say he has clear and less-clear moments. Another moment — but I still can't decide whether it was a clear or a less-clear one — came along, as a sort of curtain call, as I was releasing the hand brake on his chair and turning it toward the elevator.

"Your mother and I are going to climb the mountain tomorrow," he said. "You were always too lazy for that."

Five years ago he had driven back from France to Holland. Whenever I imagined that journey home, one time I would see him all alone in the red sports car, the next time I would see the woman in the floral kerchief beside him. Whatever the case, he had not driven off the road, not crashed through the guardrail and plummeted into the ravine.

"I don't know, buddy," he'd said to me a few days later, when I invited him to have lunch with me at Dauphine. "It just felt weird, I don't know how else to put it. I

444

hiked all over the place there, through dry riverbeds, past waterfalls . . . I climbed the mountain to the eleventh-century castle your mother and I went to last year. It's so beautiful there, you can see around you for a hundred kilometers in all directions. Not a sound, nothing, only the wind blowing past those old walls. And while I was standing there, I thought: Did we do the right thing? Wasn't it stupid of us to want to take things into our own hands? Maybe even arrogant? To try to beat God, even though I don't believe in God, at his own game? While I was standing there, I thought about all that. I could have been standing there with your mother too; I thought about that also. On top of that mountain, I asked her forgiveness. Just in case we, I, had done things wrong. But something else occurred to me too. Could it be? I thought. Could it be that, here in France, on top of this mountain, I've started to feel like living again? And should I feel guilty about that for the next few years?"

This morning I looked out over the town, first off in the distance at the fields where the buildings stopped, and at the hazy, grayish-blue silhouettes of the mountains on the horizon; and after that I looked at the parts that were closer by, at the red roofs, at our own house. The garden where we'd celebrated our wedding, thirty-four years ago. I'm going to raise a corner of the veil here. The animal, the entire animal rotating slowly on the spit back then, was a pig. The sausages and hams hanging in the shed, and that are still hanging there today, come from pigs. I remember the fat dripping into the flames, a tuft of bristles crackling as it caught fire, the men with their long knives. There was music, children were playing hide-and-seek behind the trees and in the bushes.

Four years ago, right after I moved here, I found myself sitting with Sylvia's brother at the bottom of this hill, in the dry ditch. It's become the spot we go to whenever we have something to discuss. We sit there and smoke a couple of cigarettes — in the meantime I have really started smoking again, I no longer have to sneak off somewhere to light one up, everyone here smokes — and talk about the affairs of the day. Simple things, how business is going, the new supermarket in the provincial capital sixty kilometers away, a shop in the village that's closing down, the Champions League matches that are coming up.

Four years ago, her brother — I still feel bad about not being able to mention his name, it would explain a lot, maybe even everything, and that's why I won't do it — had placed his hand on the back of my neck again, just as he had on the afternoon of the wedding.

"Robert," he said; he didn't knead my shoulders this time, just laid his hand there. "Of course, things have happened. We don't have to go into the whole thing, and after today we don't have to talk about it anymore either."

I said nothing, I had promised myself to say as little as possible, not to Sylvia and not to anyone else either — the less said, the less that would have happened in the long run, that's the way I saw it back then, already.

"Here, with us . . . ," her brother went on slowly, "no one would blame you if you . . . if you were to do something."

I kept my mouth shut, I felt the weight of his hand on my neck, but I didn't dare to move.

"Don't get me wrong," he said. "It's my own sister. If you were to . . . to do something, I in turn would feel the need to do something. But I would contain myself, not with my feelings, but with my mind, with my understanding of how things go here. How balance is restored here."

I felt flushed, I wanted to move, what I really wanted was to get up and pretend as though this conversation had never taken place. One afternoon, I can't remember whether it was just before or just after the wedding, in any case, one afternoon Sylvia had told me what had happened in this ditch, years ago, at a time — and I have to be careful here, an all-too-specific allusion would be a grave misstep, the story about the pig is enough for the time being — when this country, my wife's native country, the region where she was born, had gone through a period of unrest. Sylvia's parents were very young at the time, not even in their twenties. They lived in the house that belonged to her father's parents. They had left for the market in the provincial capital very early that morning. It was midsummer, and they got back only very late in the afternoon.

They saw the smoke from a long way off. A column of smoke was rising from their house; it had not burned to the ground, but everything inside was covered in ash, the outside walls were black with smoke above the windows.

They didn't have to look for very long. Sylvia's grandparents were lying beside each other in the dry ditch, peaceful and still, as though they had just lain down for a nap. But there were already flies buzzing around, not a lot, just a little more than normal on a hot summer evening.

Later, Sylvia told me, when the situation had changed, they had done something in response, something similar, in another village — or in the same village, I can no longer remember.

After that talk with my brother-in-law, there had been perhaps one single moment. It was on an evening when the hot wind off the flats to the south was roaring around the house, rattling at the shutters. The warm wind they have a name for around these parts; freely translated, it's called "the Sigher." People become more irritable when the Sigher is blowing, I've experienced it a few times myself; it starts with a slight pressure behind the eyes and ends with a piercing headache. In court cases, the Sigher is often advanced as a mitigating circumstance: perhaps the defendant would not have reached for the axe if no wind had been blowing that day.

Sylvia was busy hanging the framed photographs of the American freight train. Except for about thirty pictures of our daughter, those were the only photos I had brought with me from Amsterdam. It had taken a few months, but one day Sylvia came home with the picture frames. She distributed the boxcars across twenty frames or so, about three cars to a frame, and hung them up at regular intervals, five centimeters apart. From the kitchen wall, across one wall of the living room, to our bedroom.

I was standing in the doorway, my hands in my pockets. First she asked me whether the final frame was hanging straight. Then she turned to me.

"Do you remember the noise that train made?" she asked. "The way it blew its whistle? Three times. The engineer was saying hello to us, and we waved back."

The shutters rattled. Somewhere out in the yard, a bucket or some other metal object had been caught by the wind; it blew across the gravel and then came to a halt against the outside wall.

"What is it?" Sylvia whispered; her eyes got big, she raised her hands to her face. "Robert, please, what is it?"

I said nothing. If there had been anything, it was over. My wife no longer looked at me in shock, but coolly, challengingly. She shook her head. She was married to a Dutchman. *Dutchmen get ideas, too,* she said with that cool, challenging look, with that shake of her head. *But in the end, they don't actually do anything.*

That was the moment. The only moment. Later, we stood close together at the kitchen sink. Sylvia rinsed off our two plates, two glasses, two forks, and two knives under the tap. I dried it all. That has become our regular ritual. We have talked about buying a dishwasher once or twice, but the idea always fades as quickly as it came. I think we are both afraid of the same thing — afraid of disturbing something.

We don't say much, more often we say nothing at all. We don't talk as much as we used to. But we are together. We stand close together.

This morning I sat on the boulder at the top of the hill and saw Sylvia come out of the house. She walked into the garden and looked around. Then she looked up. I waved; she waved back.

There she is, I thought. *My wife.*

I stood up; I went down the hill.

ABOUT THE AUTHOR

Herman Koch is the author of seven novels and three collections of short stories. *The Dinner,* his sixth novel, has been published in twenty-five countries and was the winner of the Publieksprijs in 2009. He currently lives in Amsterdam.

The employees of Thorndike Press hope you have enjoyed this Large Print book. All our Thorndike, Wheeler, and Kennebec Large Print titles are designed for easy reading, and all our books are made to last. Other Thorndike Press Large Print books are available at your library, through selected bookstores, or directly from us.

For information about titles, please call:
(800) 223-1244

or visit our website at:
gale.com/thorndike

To share your comments, please write:

Publisher
Thorndike Press
10 Water St., Suite 310
Waterville, ME 04901